Also by Barbara Cleverly

Joe Sandilands Series:

Laetitia Talbot Series:

And stories:

The Corn Maiden

A romantic historical mystery

Barbara Cleverly

ISBN: 1517585414
ISBN 13: 9781517585419

1

Park Lane, London. 1814.

"*I* would rather marry one of the baboons at the Tower than Jemmie Fanshawe! No, Stepmama! I will not have him! And I beg you will not mention his name to me again!"

Nell Somersham's face was bright with anger as she rounded on her stepmother—an anger she had for months been struggling to conceal. Even Cecilia, Lady Hartismere—hardly the most sensitive of step-parents—was taken by surprise and flinched away from the unexpected outburst. Nell stood resolutely at the foot of her stepmother's ornate bed and watched as Lady Hartismere chose to ignore her, feigning a deep interest in the morning's post. From the pile of letters and invitation cards littering the coverlet, her Ladyship selected one by which she affected to be completely absorbed, holding it lightly between elegant fingers.

Nell was used to these games. She sighed and remained silent, waiting for the next piece of sly manipulation. She breathed deeply and used the moment to prepare herself to make a stand and fight to the last ounce of her strength against her stepmother's marriage plans for her.

The older woman rallied and favoured her with a haughty stare, but after a moment her eyes slid guiltily away and back to the letters. Nell glanced at the pile with misgiving. This was likely to be her morning's task—hours of sorting, discussing, and answering. She foresaw the messages on the cards leading to a series of overcrowded rooms in which she would be offered not-quite-cold champagne, a procession of dinner parties seated between men she hadn't seen before and wouldn't want to see again, drawing rooms where string quartets sawed their way through the works of Haydn and Mozart with not enough chairs and certainly no chair for anyone under twenty. Boring, tedious evenings, but fraught with danger.

Worst of all her fears, she foresaw the seemingly unavoidable Sir James Fanshawe, her so assiduous suitor, at her elbow wherever she went.

"Nell, my dear..." said Lady Hartismere in an attempt to be at once placatory and repressive, "do be seated." She put down her letter and waved a mannered hand at a chair by her bedside. "You make me feel nervous, towering and lowering over me like that, looking every inch the Queen of the Amazons. I hope quite fervently that you are not about to make a habit of bursting into my room during breakfast. Why, it is not yet ten o'clock, my girl!"

Nell remained standing, hand on hip. She was hanging onto all the advantages she could muster, and if appearing at this early hour fully dressed in her dark blue riding habit, booted and hatted, gave her a moral advantage over her indolent slugabed of a stepmother—well and good! She was not prepared to give that advantage away. Nell's glower intensified. She looked down at the remains of her stepmother's familiar morning routine, at the disordered piles of lace-trimmed pillows framing the petulant face, at the breakfast tray with its cargo of chocolate pot, cup and saucer, and rack of toast. She wrinkled her nose with distaste as a furry white face stirred in Lady Hartismere's arms and snuffled its way onto the tray to steal a buttered crust.

"Webster!" Nell called, greatly daring, to her stepmother's maid who was standing nearby—ready to retrieve the scattered correspondence, pour out more chocolate, or butter another piece of toast. "Her Ladyship has finished breakfast. Kindly remove her tray and take Suzette downstairs. It is time for her morning toilette."

The maid stared in surprise and alarm, paralysed by indecision. Then, after a quick exchange of confirmatory glances with her mistress, she obeyed Nell's orders and dragged the unwilling poodle away by its pink velvet collar. Nell turned and walked to the window, trying to hide her disgust. The air in the room was thick with her stepmother's scent and the smell of the poodle. She hated the dog, and it hated her. Fluffy, beribboned, curled, overfed, and perfumed, it symbolised for her the hated artificiality of London life and made her long for her own dogs at home in the country, in the county of Suffolk. They lived outdoors and worked for their living—farm dogs and gun dogs, sometimes flea-infested and often muddy—Nell knew and loved them all and had, for the first eighteen years of her life, grown up surrounded by them. They knew their place and none had ever ventured above stairs.

Nell pushed up the bottom sash, eager for fresh air. She knelt on the window seat, rested her elbows on the sill, and gazed out through the yellowing leaves of the crowding plane trees into the cool green distance of Hyde Park. The crisp morning air of early September was welcome on her flushed cheeks. She lingered there for a while, gaining the strength and resilience to go on with her struggle to be heard, determined to make her stepmother pay attention to her wishes...preparing, through desperation, as a last resort to play her trump card.

A crocodile of schoolgirls hand in hand in bonnet and shawl, small ones at the front, large ones at the back, a grim-faced maid on either side, and two pretty young teachers bringing up the rear, chirruped their way along Park Lane on their way to take their daily walk around the Achilles statue behind Apsley House and back to their select boarding establishment in the newly built houses beginning to line the Bayswater Road. A smart butcher's trap rattled noisily to a halt below. A carriage, the necks of its two ponderously trotting horses strained to an arch by the cruel but fashionable bearing rein, clattered by, eliciting an exclamation of dismay from Nell and an exaggerated shudder from Lady Hartismere.

"Do close the window, Nell," she commanded, the ribbons of her lace cap aquiver with a pretended shiver. "You know I take a chill so easily these autumn mornings, and my nerves cannot bear the street noises."

"Then perhaps we should return home to Suffolk, Stepmama," said Nell quickly. "It is very calm and peaceful there in September, you'd find. The harvest will be in by now, and the apple picking will have begun. Cook will have put away the jams and jellies, and she will be boiling up the puddings for Christmas. And Kenton—he will be needing me to go over the estate books with him. This is a busy time of year for the steward, and I should like to..."

For a moment, her face came to life at the thought of her home, where she could be useful and happy. The bright eyes, the luminous alabaster skin and sweetly curving mouth, the strongly boned face framed by a shock of dark blond hair should have melted the hardest of hearts, but Lady Hartismere remained immune to and even irritated by Nell's unconscious ability to charm. Nell broke off. She knew exactly what the response would be and had been every time she had made the suggestion of returning to Somersham since her father's death a year before.

"Kenton! Huh!" her stepmother exploded. "I declare, child, you spend too much of your time with your steward! What your papa was thinking of, allowing you to become so embroiled with the management of the estates, I cannot imagine! I know of no other girl who thinks it *clever* to know the price of a ram or a bushel of wheat! And the damage it does to your complexion, hacking about the farms and the fields in the summer! I was mortified to present you to the Duchess of Irchester at the start of the Season! She must have thought I was trailing a gypsy girl around behind me! And she was not at all pleased to see how you monopolised her husband, the *Duke's,* attention with your inane chatter! The whole table heard you prattling on: 'A diet suitable for ewes—to encourage them to give birth to twins.' Indeed! Did you suppose the *procreation of sheep* to be an acceptable topic of conversation between a well-bred young girl and the nephew of the monarch?"

Nell bit back a truculent comment that the Duke of Irchester had been a more than willing partner in the conversation. A countryman himself, he had been delighted to share his interests with a young woman. But logic and information were never welcomed by her stepmother. Speculation and prejudice were meat and drink to her. Nell did not reply. Cecilia knew perfectly well that her husband, Lord Hartismere, had been failing in health for a year before his death and had, with much relief, discovered that Nell already knew a great deal about the running of a large estate since she had spent most of her lonely childhood hours trailing around behind the steward, the cook, the housekeeper, in and out of the stables and kitchen, listening and learning. He had gradually handed the reins of management to Nell, aided by the elderly but efficient Kenton.

Lady Hartismere, once started on one of her favourite topics, was flowing on, "And you know I cannot bear the country! What? Live again at Somersham Hall? That horrid, musty pile crumbling into its moat! How many times I begged Hartismere to fill in that vile sewer I don't care to remember! 'It can't be healthy,' I said. 'Night vapours rising round a dwelling house,' and Doctor Brewster quite agreed with me: 'I can think of nothing more injurious to your ladyship's constitution,' he said. No, for the last time, Elinor, it would be death in life for me to immolate myself there!"

"I think you mean *immure*, Stepmama," muttered Nell, thinking that either fate would be an acceptable solution to her problems. She closed the window with a bang.

Paying no attention, Lady Hartismere rattled on. "But there are matters much more important than my own comfort to be considered, I will allow, my dear, and I must have a thought for your future. I must abide, at whatever cost to myself, by your dear father's wishes and see you settled, and only when I have seen you suitably married will I be at liberty to give any consideration to my own pitiable circumstances.' Her eyes narrowed, and she added slyly, "And, of course, until you *do* marry, you remain my ward and must live in *my* household under *my* protection."

Nell had no answer.

Cecilia's gloating tone was replaced, to Nell's surprise, by a genuinely thoughtful look as she ventured further: "I must avow, Nell, it has always been a puzzle to me too...why Hartismere, who listened to you, flattered and indulged you beyond reason in everything, should have—and almost with his last gasp—cheated you of what you most desired. That *I* should be one of your guardians is self-evident, but to choose as your second guardian a remote Scottish cousin of his, unknown both to him and to you, when he could have appointed any of a hundred friends or relations here in London? It is unaccountable...perhaps, at the last, his faculties?"

"His faculties—as you choose to label my father's fine brain and powers of reason—remained undimmed to the end!" Nell said sharply. "Or was Papa perhaps out of his mind to leave you your very generous jointure and this house?" She bit her lip, knowing that she had gone too far.

Strangely, Lady Hartismere seemed gratified by the spurt of bad temper she had elicited from her ward and continued to torment her. "And as long as you are in my house, Miss," she reminded her, "you will please mind your manners! If, as you never cease to tell me, you wish to achieve a state of independence from me and set up your own establishment, you know quite well what you have to do. When you are married, well, that will be a different matter—you may persuade your husband to live wherever you choose. With the wealth that will come to you on marriage, you will be able to settle anywhere in the kingdom. I'm sure Jemmie would indulge your odd whim to live in the country...for a while at any rate."

Nell almost laughed out loud at the picture of pale-faced, dissolute Sir James Fanshawe, who spent half his days in bed and half his nights in the candle-lit reek of gaming clubs, transplanted to the spacious cornfields and water meadows and the wide skies of Suffolk. One lungful of the fresh air off the North Sea risked felling him on the spot.

"But, Stepmama, I am not yet one and twenty. There is no need to hurry into matrimony with the first man who offers for me!"

"Lady Elinor!" snapped her stepmother. "You do not deceive by playing the innocent! You are not just out of the schoolroom! You are in your third season. You know perfectly well that Sir James is not the first man to offer for you. Your father in his last months rejected several suitors—and rejected them at your insistence, I do believe, Miss! And, of course, an heiress of your importance is able to take her pick of any of a score of eligible men. When I think of the titles and the fortunes that have been dangled before you! But—oh, no! None of them will take the fancy of Lady Elinor Somersham, spoilt daughter of Lord Hartismere!

If your poor brother Rupert were still alive, you could not have afforded to be so *nice* about your choice, I can tell you!" And, choked by her spite, she burst into a fit of coughing.

"Stepmama, I will not marry any man who values my fortune more than he values me," began Nell with determination. The remark triggered a further scorching look from Lady Cecilia.

"Fairy tales, my girl! This is the reasoning of fairy tales!" she screeched. "Silly chit! You'll be going about barefoot and ragged in the street next to find a husband who loves you for your face and not for your fortune!"

"My fortune makes it all the more imperative that I choose with care..." Nell began wearily to repeat a well-worn formula. "I will not take a husband who gambles away my father's fortune! I watched him build it by safe husbandry and clever dealing over the years—the money you are now enjoying, Stepmama, was hard-earned, and not by you. I will not let it fall into the careless hands of the likes of Jemmie Fanshawe. I would rather remain unmarried and run the estate myself with the aid of Kenton. You know I have proved myself perfectly competent to do that, and indeed, that is what I should be doing now, not frittering away my time in idle pursuits in London."

But, of a sudden, at the sight of the closed, impassive face before her, it came to her that she would never be free from the determination, on the part of her stepmother, that she should accept the despised James Fanshawe. Never, that is, unless she gathered the courage to reveal her knowledge of a very dark secret and make a ruthless end to this charade.

"You may trust me to choose with care, my girl! I have a much wider understanding of society after all, and the ways of the world. Sir James is simply the most suitable husband for you. He is a good few years older than you, which is an advantage. He has sown his wild oats and is ready to settle. He is a man of the world—you are a headstrong girl, as all will allow, and it is my belief that you will benefit from his direction. He is of a good family and will, in the fullness of time, inherit when his grandfather dies; and you will become a Viscountess. The *on dit* is that old Blakenham is breaking up fast on the rocks and is not reckoned to live out the season. What better prospects could a girl have? Well, Miss? Well? Jemmie won't wait forever, you know!"

She took the letter she had selected from the pile before her on the bed and waved it at Nell. "See here! He is to call on us at eleven o'clock this morning and positively seeks my permission to address himself to you. May I have your assurance that you will at least hear him and respond sensibly?"

Nell tugged nervously at a lock of hair hanging heavily onto her shoulders and replied in a tone of weary control, "Jemmie Fanshawe is old enough to be my father..."

"Nonsense! Why, I happen to know that he is the same age as myself—in the prime of life!"

"Forty-two...and I am twenty. That is a great difference, Stepmama. And I do not love him. I do not even like him. I find him repellent, and I have no wish to share my life and my fortune with him. I suspect—no, I am certain—that he wishes to marry me for the money and the estates that will be mine on my marriage, and that I cannot bear."

"You impudent hussy!" Her stepmother's voice rose almost to a scream. "'I do not love him...'" she mimicked cruelly. "'I find him repellent...' What do you expect of marriage? A woman would be fortunate indeed to be able to—" She cut herself short abruptly, realising that she had gone further than she ought.

At the last, Nell hesitated. To go forward or to turn back? What she had to say to her stepmother would bring to an end the shallow pretence that had kept the peace between them. Was she ready for that? A glance at the angry and duplicitous face before her gave her the courage she needed. She drew a deep breath, and her reply when it came was quiet, calm, and delivered with the assured finality of a *coup de grâce*.

"Yes, I know, Stepmama. You need no longer attempt to dissimulate. I know you did not love my father. I know that you are not unhappy that he is dead. I can only be thankful that he did not discover for himself what your true feelings for him were."

She paused, looking pitilessly down at the staring eyes and at a face beginning to mottle with rage and wondered briefly what were the qualities that had attracted her father to this woman. The strong features were still handsome, the chestnut curls escaping from her cap were untouched by grey, and when it was to her advantage to charm, Nell had seen her smile and flirt and flatter. And yet, perhaps her father had been more aware of his second wife's character than Nell had realised, since, although he had left Cecilia generously provided for in her lifetime, his great fortune was to pass eventually to his only surviving child, his daughter—to Nell herself.

Her stepmother had not foreseen the assault. She gaped speechlessly. Nell seized the silence and pressed on. Time to fire the second barrel.

"And pray do not try to deceive me any longer in the matter of Jemmie Fanshawe. I know full well, as does the whole of society, that he is gravely in debt and has, indeed, taken out loans on the security of his grandfather's demise. Should Viscount Blakenham discover this, Jemmie would be in a pretty stew! Even in the circles frequented by Jemmie and his cronies, raising money on postobits is looked at askance! Moreover..."

She paused briefly, teetering on the brink of destroying forever the fragile relationship that existed between her and her stepmother, and then plunged, "Moreover, I am aware of his relationship with _you_. I am aware that he is your lover and may well have been your lover for some years, for all I know!"

At a dreadful gasp of astonishment and rage from Lady Hartismere, Nell held out her hand to cut off any protest and continued firmly, her bridges burned now, "Do not attempt to deny it—you will embarrass both of us. Just accept that I know. You have been growing increasingly indiscreet in your assignations. I am a light sleeper, and I rise early. Let us say no more. And if I am aware at last of what is going on under this roof, then certainly the servants are aware also and so must be the whole of London. And you attempt to foist this...this..." her voice choked with rage for a moment, "this ageing paramour of yours onto me in a wicked attempt to secure my family's money for yourselves! Madam, I refuse Sir James Fanshawe, and that is my last word on the subject! This is 1814, not 1614, and you have not the power to compel me to marry against my wishes. I bid you good morning. I am going out for my ride, and I shall not be at home to Sir James when he calls."

Flicking aside the trailing skirt of her riding dress, Nell turned and walked calmly to the door and left without another word, closing the door quietly behind her.

"Oh, Webster," she said to the maid approaching along the corridor with a freshly coiffed Suzette under her arm, "go to your mistress. Fetch her salts and laudanum. Lady Hartismere would seem, I fear, to be on the verge of a seizure."

She hurried down the stairs, trembling and sick with anxiety yet buoyed up by a thrill of excitement at her own boldness. She was eager now to escape from the house, which she guessed would soon be ringing with the sounds of a raging tantrum, with shrieks and yells and slaps. She strode out into the sunlit courtyard behind the house, where her groom was patiently waiting with the two fine horses he had just walked over from the mews. His wrinkled face lit up with pleasure when he caught sight of Nell.

"I saddled up Rowan today, your ladyship," he said, touching his top hat. "He's bursting to go."

"Good, Turvey, good. His mood chimes with mine. You'll have to work old Snowberry hard to keep up with us!" she said with an affectionate nod to the noble but elderly grey he had made ready for himself. Disdaining the mounting block, Nell placed her booted foot in Turvey's hand and was swung into the saddle. She clattered off over the cobbles, followed at a respectful distance by the grey.

Many curious and admiring glances were thrown towards the supple figure as she trotted across Park Lane and into the park, heading for Rotten Row. The dark blue wool of her riding coat outlined a neat waist; strong square shoulders and firm arms skilfully controlled the spirited chestnut she rode; and her hair gleamed with gold to rival the brilliance of the turning leaves, shining in the slanting autumn sunshine and bobbing with the horse's stride under a jaunty black three-cornered hat.

Turvey enjoyed these rides. It was the culmination of his efforts in the stables to present the horses in the peak of Park condition and to ride behind his young mistress, delighting in the interest and admiration she attracted from the other riders. He was delighted, too, that she rode seriously and never used these occasions as a sociable amble and an opportunity to gossip with the other fashionable members of the ton, loafing by the railings or titupping carelessly along in chattering groups.

Amongst these, Nell spied the one figure in London that she most wished to avoid: Jemmie Fanshawe, dawdling his way to Park Lane and his eleven o'clock tryst with, Nell remembered angrily, his mistress and his innocent bride-elect—herself!

His hand went up to sweep the hat from his head in an elegant bow. "La! Lady Elinor! What radiance! Dammee! I was persuaded the sun had risen a second time today!" And turning to a vacuous companion who stood by sucking the knob of his cane, "Did I not say? It is the dawn—dammee—and Elinor Somersham is the sun!"

Elinor, stony-faced, looked him up and down. "I had supposed that the declining sun at evening was more to your taste," she said. "Save your compliments for Lady Hartismere," she added, and, turning away, she said brusquely, "Follow me closely Turvey!" She clapped spur to Rowan's flank—very much to his surprise but with the desired and immediate effect. He leapt from his steady trot into a hand-canter and, under Nell's urging, into a full gallop.

As graceful in her habit as the wing of a bird and as solid as a rock in the saddle, Nell, with a firm hand, bent the now-racing Rowan in and out of the crowd of carriages and riders, clods of tan flying from his drumming hooves. After a startled moment, the faithful Turvey dropped his hands and, cursing, spurred in pursuit. "Don't gallop, Miss Nell!" he shouted. "Park Rangers will get 'ee up before the Magistrate! Do 'ee slow down now!" But Nell took no heed.

This, she thought, *is just what I needed! I'll show 'em!* And, laughing, she raced on. "Ware hounds!" she yelled in warning to a portly, pink-faced gentleman who was ambling along on a gleaming hunter at the head of a loitering group. By a touch of instinctive horsemanship, he controlled his mount and narrowly avoided the onrush of Nell who was now going at a full and illegal gallop. Spluttering, he shook an ineffectual whip at her retreating back. His pack of followers bayed well-bred abuse after her, and Nell raised her crop, twirling it above her head in mocking riposte.

Leaving the fashionable crowd behind, they drew into the less frequented northern side of the park. "Come on, Turvey!" she shouted. "Race you to Tyburn Tree!" and when, finally, they drew up, Snowberry lathered and panting but full of fight, Nell asked, "Who was that stout gentleman I so nearly overset a quarter of a mile back? I seemed to know his face."

Turvey was unable to suppress a broad grin. "Why, 'twas the Prince Regent, my lady," he said. "You'll be under lock and key in the Tower by next Tuesday, shouldn't wonder! Up on a charge of attempted regicide, like as not. Best flee the country!"

An exhausting hour later, Nell was being helped out of her riding clothes by her personal maid. The daughter of a tenant farmer, pretty, brown-eyed Lucy had arrived as a between maid at Somersham Hall five years before and, liking the girl's cheerful efficiency and speed in learning new tasks, Nell had persuaded her father to allow Lucy to change her position to train on as her lady's maid. All in all it had been a successful arrangement. Nell repaid Lucy's devotion with confidence and friendship, and Lucy had become her small but faithful ally. Her Suffolk voice was a constant solace and reminder of home to Nell, and her clever parody of the gratingly refined tones of an upper-class London lady's maid a source of amusement. Unlike her mistress, Lucy revelled in London life and was a good source of gossip and information. And more than that, in a situation where Nell was feeling herself increasingly cut off from the world and watched over by her stepmother, Lucy was a friend and a confidante, a discreet listener who knew how to keep secrets.

"That was the last straw, Lucy!" Nell stormed as she washed away the morning's exertions. "That monster is even tracking me down in the Park to force his unwanted attentions on me! Everywhere I turn it seems there is Jemmie Fanshawe looming at me with his ingratiating leer! And always there is Stepmama—'Take Sir James to the wilderness, Nell, I'm sure he would adore to see the roses...Ah, here comes Jemmie! Nell, will you not sing for him that sweet song you were just practising?'" Her imitation of her stepmother's fashionable drawl never failed to make Lucy giggle guiltily.

She shrugged into the blue silk peignoir Lucy handed her and began to pace about the room deep in thought.

"That'll be all his lordship's fault, I suppose—that old will of his..." Lucy swung into the tired chorus, repeating a well worn but always pertinent sentiment.

"I'll never be able to understand what possessed Father to do that," said Nell sadly. "I may understand one day just what he was about, but at this moment I confess I am baffled by it. His design becomes no clearer to me, Lucy. He's made me the target for every fortune hunter in the country! I am to inherit all his money and his estate in Suffolk and, if that were not enough, a castle and half Scotland, it seems, that come to me from my Scottish great-grandfather. And what do I have to do to enjoy all this? I have to wait until I am five and twenty! Five and twenty, Lucy! Five more years of living with Stepmama!"

Nell's eyes narrowed with calculation as she went on, confident that her audience never tired of hearing her repeat the terms, striving always, with her mistress, to understand and interpret. "But there is an alternative. Father stipulated that I could have my inheritance earlier on condition that I marry with the permission and blessing of a nominated guardian."

"And that's 'er Ladyship, o' course," said Lucy, making the ritual, dismal response. "Can't see any way around that. I do see as how you've got your problems, Miss Nell, meaning no offence."

"Yes, that's her Ladyship, I'm afraid, but it's someone else as well. I've never spoken of it because it seemed immaterial...too...too ludicrous and far-fetched to be of consideration...an aberration of Father's...I had dismissed it as an abstruse legal requirement he was fulfilling. Or a family pledge of some sort." Nell frowned in an effort to recall the terms of the long will wrapped in lawyer's terms. "Father named *two* trustees, and either one may give consent. Stepmama is one, and the other is his cousin, his Scottish cousin, who, I suppose, must therefore be *my* cousin once removed. A distant enough connection as to be disregarded, one might have thought. But not so. As my guardian and trustee, he is responsible for the management of my estates in Scotland for me now and until such time as I inherit."

"What kind of a man will he be, then, Miss Nell, your father's cousin?"

"I've really no idea, Lucy. I've never met him. There was a severance between the two halves of the family many years ago, and it's very odd, but I'm not certain that my father even knew his cousin Roderick. And yet he places me in his power...I cannot account for my father's eccentric stipulation. I am unable to marry without his cousin's consent, and the man has sole charge of my Scottish estates for the next five years if I do not. Clearly, this crusty old Scotsman will be only too content to deny me consent so that he may take his time to profit from my inheritance. After all, the longer he can hold me off, the longer he has to make use of it. Father, what on earth were you thinking of?"

But today, the customary question and answer did not end in the usual hopeless hand-wringing. The acrid smell of burning bridges was urging her to action. She could no longer simply stand still and exchange sighs and laments with Lucy.

Nell stopped pacing, her chin went up, her eyes narrowed with determination, and she went on. "Well, at least this morning's encounter with Fanshawe has made up my mind for me. I will not be herded into a corner, bullied and cajoled, and worn down! I will not spend the next five years of my life fending off the likes of him! I see that I shall have to battle to take control of what is mine, and I shall start tonight. I have decided what I must do! Lucy, get out my best evening dresses, the new ones from Madame Lenoir's!"

"Your evening dresses, Miss Nell?"

"Yes. I want to try them on. You must help me select a confection that will dazzle the world this evening, Lucy! Stepmama and I are bidden to the Duchess of York's ball tonight at St. James's Palace, and I intend to come back from the ball with a husband!"

2

"Lucy you may announce to her Ladyship that I am ready."

Nell stood smiling confidently at her image in the cheval glass in her bedroom. Lucy had worked busily for hours crimping the honey-coloured curls and arranging them artfully twined about with pearls and piled high on top of Nell's head, emphasising her graceful neck. Her face looked eager, the clarity of her eyes enhanced by the arch of her brows, which were of a darker shade than her fair hair. Her straight nose and the tilt of her chin, however, gave her an aura of cool distance, which those who had been rebuffed by her were quick to dismiss as haughty pride.

Her white dress of finest silk was cut daringly low, revealing far more of her breasts than she secretly thought decent but, after all, she reminded herself, she was playing for high stakes tonight. The dress was caught up under her bosom by a wide sash of blue and green silk, and a heavy necklace of sapphires set in silver, a gift from her mother, flashed a fire as bright as her eyes. Neat white kid dancing shoes with the tiniest of heels, white silk stockings, and long white gloves completed a picture of beauty, purity, and swan-like simplicity.

"There! I've set my trap! Now to catch my rabbit! Lucy, pass me my Kashmir shawl, will you? Stepmama chooses to go in the open carriage—to give London the chance to admire her, I suppose. But if her constitution is as weak as she constantly tells us that it is—I think we may have a price to pay!"

With increasing excitement, she floated downstairs to greet her stepmother, who was waiting below and tapping her foot in a marked manner. Cecilia sniffed loudly with disapproval at her stepdaughter's appearance.

"Your mother's sapphires, I see? Much too old for you, Elinor! Let me look at you. What a sketch! That dress is far too revealing! Completely unsuitable! But no time to change—as no doubt you had calculated! We really must engage a proper lady's maid who understands fashion and can guide your taste. I will lend you Purdey until we can replace that silly young bumpkin of yours. I declare we shall be the target of all eyes! What my friend the Duchess of York will say, I shudder..."

Nell closed her ears to this speech, which continued as they took their seats in the carriage and proceeded to bowl down Park Lane and to take the awkward turn in Hamilton Place. Cold it was, but Nell was glad to be in the open and to watch the passing scene. Link boys, their flaming torches held aloft, plied for customers to light through London's dark side streets. The press of carriages was such that at each crossing, swept clear at intervals by sweeper boys of the ordure accumulated in a day in horse-drawn London, a queue of pedestrians had formed. Naphtha flares illuminated the stalls lining Green Park, and as the carriage swung into St. James's, Nell marked the absence of the usual gathering of vacuous members staring from the clubs' bay windows. "Bored they may be, mock the Prince and the Royal Family they may, but I notice they've all gone to the ball! Well, that's good! There should be a good field for me to choose from. Everybody who thinks he's anybody will be there tonight!"

As soon as the carriage turned into St. James's, Nell saw the brilliantly illuminated façade of the Palace. She saw also the dense press of spectators on either side of the canopied red carpet leading from the road's edge to the wide entrance. Side by side, they swept up the steps, Nell much amused by the broad and appreciative comments that followed them and smiling back at the crowd.

"Give us a kiss then, Pretty!" shouted one. "Never kiss a maid when you can kiss a missus!" shouted another, leering through the cordon of protective footmen at the mortified face of Lady Hartismere.

Nell noticed that her stepmother's tirade had been switched off abruptly the moment they had arrived at Carlton House and had been replaced by a charming smile and sweet tone. Entering the ballroom in her stepmother's wake, Nell was determined that she too was going to charm this evening. Instead of attempting to avoid the lineup of hopeful young men paraded before her at these balls, she was going to take fate into her own hands. "Choose, don't be chosen," had been the advice of her French governess on launching Nell into society three years before. *Well, Thérèse,* Nell thought as she accepted a glass of ice cold champagne from a footman, *I shall take your advice tonight, but I do not think you would approve of my motives!*

Looking around the brightly lit ballroom, Nell was suddenly daunted by the task she had set herself. She was instantly surrounded by a group of chattering, smiling friends and, though she went through the motions of laughing and exchanging gossip with them, her eyes were darting around the room in search of someone suitable to complete her schemes. There were hardly any new faces. Most of the gentlemen were wearing dark colours this year, evening coats of blue and black or buff with cutaway tails to reveal faultlessly tight pantaloons, fitting without a wrinkle down to short silk stockings and buckled pumps. Here and there, a pretty waistcoat relieved the gloom. Their hair was dressed uniformly *au naturel,* sweeping attractively forward in curls over the forehead.

They formed a sombre background for the rest, the military men wearing their bright uniforms. The scarlet coats and gold epaulettes of the infantry were the colours that caught her eye. A soldier? A good thought! An inspired thought! A wicked thought! Many of them were younger sons with their way to make in life, pushy young men who would count themselves fortunate indeed to attract the attention of an heiress such as Lady Elinor. There were wars aplenty raging all over Europe, were there not? Her adored brother Rupert had indeed lost his life four years before in the ill-starred retreat to Corunna. Soldiers were apt to be sent away from home for long periods to remote and dangerous places like the Peninsula, places from which they quite often did not return. Why, poor Nell Somersham might well find herself a very young, very rich, and very independent widow in no time at all if she married one!

Fighting down a spurt of shame at the way her thoughts were running, Nell, grimly determined, sipped some more champagne and let her eyes run speculatively along the lines of uniformed men. Soon the first dance would be over, the couples would break up, and she would find herself besieged by hopeful acquaintances asking to book dances in her *carnet de bal*, which, for the moment, was empty.

As she looked about her, her attention was suddenly taken by a tall figure in a Hussar uniform. She looked more closely, feeling that the man was strangely familiar. The frogged grey and silver tunic with its dolman jacket worn dashingly over one shoulder, the long slender trousers, grey with silver embroidery emphasising the length of the leg, the immaculately shiny black boots—the uniform of the Hussar, she thought with a sigh, was by far the most attractive uniform of all.

And only Henry Collingwood, she reflected crossly, was capable of failing to make such a uniform look romantic!

Henry Collingwood, her friend Sarah's older brother, whom she had known since they were children. Henry Collingwood—weak, lazy, overweight schoolboy—was now grown, it seemed, into a weak, lazy, overweight soldier. Although four years older than Nell, he had, when they were young, been her devoted slave, and she remembered with embarrassment the appalling way she had treated him, though she remembered also, with a guilty smile, that he had at least had the sense—or was it the lack of courage?—to disobey her in the matter of crossing the paddock with the bull in it.

"Sarah!" she exclaimed, moving over to stand by her friend's side. "The tall Hussar over there, helping himself to an iced cream, looks uncommonly like your brother Henry! I thought he was away at the war?"

"Oh, Nell! You are not mistaken. It is indeed Henry. He is just returned from Lisbon. He is injured—do you see his dolman disguises a sling? His regiment have sent him back to recover, but also on a recruiting mission until he shall be well again."

"Poor Henry! How was he wounded?"

"Ah...he was not exactly wounded, Nell." Sarah's eye sparkled with complicity. "Henry was riding through Lisbon, and he fell off his horse when the creature shied; he broke his shoulder."

"Poor Henry!" Nell exclaimed again with rather less sympathy. "He never had much luck, especially with horses," she said, eliciting a gurgle and a flash of amusement from Sarah. "But perhaps he has had better luck with women? Is he now married? I had not heard it announced..."

"No indeed, Nell! Were you not aware? He has always held the unreasonable hope of making a match with you!"

Nell smiled with satisfaction. "Sarah, I wish you would present your brother to me. I should like to meet him again after all these years. I am sure we shall have much to talk about."

A few minutes later, Nell found herself circling the floor in the arms of a blushing Henry Collingwood. "Gad, Lady E.," he said breathlessly, "it's prime to see you again. I vow I often thought of you in Spain. But all the fellows said, 'Nell Somersham! Forget it! With all her tin! Lor!—you'll find she's long hitched when you get back!' But, Lor! Here you are, as free as your humble servant."

Nell couldn't help remembering an unkind story told to her by a cousin in the Dragoons and of which Henry Collingwood was supposed to be the hero—"Once there was a Hussar officer who was so stupid all the other officers noticed it!" But she favoured him with a dazzling smile as she said, "Yes indeed, dear Henry, I remain unhitched. I'm as free as a bird!"

"Dammee!" said Henry ecstatically, aware for the first time that he was the subject of envious male attention. "Dammee—as free as a bird, and, er, as, er, as pretty as a bird, 'pon my soul!"

So overcome was he with this bold sally that he could only gaze and swallow till Nell rescued him from his embarrassment by saying, "But as hungry as a horse—would you escort me to the supper room, Henry?"

"Yes, yes!" said Henry excitedly. "We might perhaps occupy one of those little booths, eh, what? Have more of that capital iced cream?"

Lucy was waiting eagerly for news of the ball when Nell returned after midnight. Nell danced into her room, pink and triumphant, kicking off her shoes.

"Lucy, bring me pen and paper! At once!" she called out.

"Pen and paper, Miss Nell? But 'tis after midnight, madam."

"I have a very important letter to write, Lucy, and you must take it off as soon as you can in the morning and put it in the mail. The express mail!"

She pirouetted happily around her room until Lucy scurried back with her writing case and then announced triumphantly, "I've done it, Lucy! I have found a husband! I am—unofficially, of course—engaged to be married to—oh!—the most wonderfully, perfectly, incredibly, utterly dull man in the world! It just remains for me to secure my Scottish guardian's consent to marry him, and I am free of my stepmother forever. I shall be, at last, in charge of my own life!"

She settled down at her desk and wrote to Roderick Lindsay, Esq., of Callander, Scotland.

> *Dear Cousin Roderick,*
>
> *You will be aware that, under the terms of my father's will, if I marry under the age of twenty-five, I must seek your approbation. I am writing, accordingly, to solicit your written consent to my contracting such an alliance with the Honourable Mr. Henry Collingwood. Mr. Collingwood, who is of good family, being the second son of Baron Dunsford of Dunsford Hall, Great Missenden, a family well respected in Buckinghamshire, is currently in England recovering from injuries sustained whilst in service with his regiment in the Peninsula.*
>
> *I will not deceive you, Sir, but will openly declare that Mr. Collingwood is without means of support beyond his army pay, but I am persuaded that, due to circumstances with which you will be familiar, I need not be seeking the support and fortune of another.*
>
> *Your most obedient,*
>
> *Elinor Somersham*

"There now," she said, sanding the letter carefully, "the die is cast! All I have to do is wait in patience for my reply. Surely my cousin cannot refuse me?"

Twelve days later, Lucy heard with dismay a shriek of distress coming from her mistress's room. She hurried anxiously along, expecting at the very least that Suzette had at long last sunk her tiny teeth into Nell's leg, to find Nell shaking with rage and exclaiming in very unladylike language learned from her country childhood—one solid advantage of having been brought up in the company of farm boys and stable men. She was stamping about the room brandishing a letter.

"How dare he treat me in this way? What an uncivilised, crusty old Scots curmudgeon I have to deal with! And he does not even deign to reply to me in his own hand! See here, Lucy.' She waved the letter in front of Lucy's nose. "He has had his Man of Law write on his behalf! How unfeeling! What a lapse of manners!"

She read again the distressing letter, hoping against hope that she had misconstrued its meaning, looking carefully at the precise, old-fashioned clerkly handwriting and narrowing her eyes with distaste at the dry, formal phrasing. "Listen, Lucy!"

And she read out with heavy emphasis, and with her best essay at a Scottish accent:

Mr. Adam Renfrew of Glasgow writes:

I am required by my client, Mr. Roderick Lindsay, to present his compliments to Lady Elinor Somersham and to respond to her letter to him of the 2nd of September. Mr. Lindsay has, of course, given the closest attention to her request. Knowing something of the gentleman to whom Lady Elinor refers, he is, however, unable to accede.

In the alternative, he is able to put forward a proposal that, he is persuaded, will be to their common advantage.

The proposal—and the word, Lady Elinor will appreciate, is used advisedly—is a simple matter of business, namely that, abandoning her

intention to marry the Honourable Henry Collingwood, she should con-
tract a matrimonial alliance—and, again, the word is used advisedly—with
Mr. Roderick Lindsay.

In proposing this, Mr. Lindsay is influenced by the apprehension that
her intended betrothal to the Honourable Henry Collingwood was unat-
tended by any mawkish sentiment of romance. She will be merely changing
one business proposition for another. She would achieve what Mr. Lindsay
conceives to be her principal end—namely, the release of her fortune—with
the consent of her guardian. In exchange, Mr. Lindsay would expect that, as
an aspect of the marriage settlement, the Scottish estates should be settled
on the House of Lindsay absolutely and in perpetuity.

So confident is Mr. Lindsay that this proposal will commend itself to
the good sense of Lady Elinor that he has embarked on exploratory dis-
cussions on the matter with his man of business (your servant, ma'am) in
Glasgow, following which, he will write to her further.

"What kind of man must he be to write to his ward in such terms? What can he possibly mean by 'knowing something' of Henry? What is he hinting at? This is very mysterious! How can he be acquainted with Henry? And 'a mawkish sentiment of romance,' if you please! What a phrase! There is a sly irony there that makes me think that my dear Cousin Roderick is surely teasing me. At all events—what I have from my estimable cousin is a flat rejection of my request to marry Henry and, instead, he proposes marriage—a marriage of convenience—with himself! This is the outside of enough! I suspected that he had designs on my Scottish estates, and here is the clear proof! He does not even attempt to disguise it! I fear, Lucy, that he is going to refuse any request I might make to marry. Why, if the Prince Regent himself were to propose, I wager Roderick Lindsay would withhold his permission! And my stepmother is going to refuse her consent for me to marry anyone other than her own nominee, odious Fanshawe!"

She crumpled up the letter and hurled it with all her force at the wall. "I'm a puppet, Lucy! And people pull my strings to make me dance to their tune! All I have to look forward to is five years of being held almost a prisoner in my own house. And now Stepmama speaks of sending you back to Suffolk and putting some condescending London maid in your place. The next thing I shall hear is that Turvey too is being dismissed at the end of the month, and then there will be no one near me in whom I may trust or confide! She means to wear me down until I accept Fanshawe! Oh, Papa, what were you about? What on earth could have persuaded you that this Lindsay would be a suitable guardian for me? I wish I could understand!"

Pale and distressed, she sank into a chair, head in hands, while Lucy fluttered round her, tidying and straightening the already tidy room. Finally, Lucy plucked up the courage to ask, "Begging your pardon, Miss Nell, and please tell me if I am speaking out of turn...but...but...' She took a deep breath and went on resolutely, "Have you ever been to Scotland, madam?"

"Certainly not, Lucy," said Nell, raising a tear-stained, impatient face. "And I should not wish to go! I loved my Scottish grandmother. Her name was Alice, and I remember her well from my childhood. Indeed, she taught me many Scottish songs and told me stories of her own country, but I believe it to be very remote and cold—a poor country and one that hates the English. The inhabitants eat the stuffed stomachs of sheep, so I understand, and mountains of salty porridge...The women are red-haired and unattractive, and the men even more so. They wear thick skirts and are much given over to sheep stealing and killing each other with broadswords."

She gave a sigh that turned into a shudder.

"Then you would never want to go and live on your Scottish lands, madam? And if it is the poor country you describe, the estate cannot produce much of value? They are nothing to you then?" said Lucy carefully, head tilted on one side.

Nell looked at her maid's flushed and eager face, fished out a kerchief, and blew her nose. "Lucy, what is this, pray? Can I possibly understand you correctly? Are you trying to put it into my head that I should...? I can't believe it! Besides, it would surely be base and scheming, as you must see, to...?"

"Can't see the difference," said Lucy stoutly, "to be honest, madam—
if it comes to base and scheming—between marrying Henry Collingwood
and marrying this Mr. Lindsay, except you'll lose a bit of Scotland and a
draughty old castle that you can't be doing with anyway. And the gentleman does say as how it's a *business* proposition, doesn't he? I mean, Miss
Nell...um..." Lucy coloured and hesitated, wondering whether she was
going too far and finally plunging in with, "You wouldn't have to be...
er...*obliging* him, if you take my meaning?"

She retrieved the letter and smoothed it out. "All you'd have to do
is sign a piece of paper. This old codger writes like a schoolmaster and
talks like a lawyer...He'd have it drawn up in no time. He'd be happy,
and you would certainly be happier. Imagine, Miss Nell, being a married lady! You could tell her Ladyship what to do with herself, you could
take your rightful place in society—we could even go back to Somersham
if you wanted. And all without the bother of a husband trailing about
after you."

"Lucy! You are an inspired plotter and a disgrace! But you forget
something: one day I should like to be married to someone I love, and
when I want to have children I shall be frustrated by a legal tie with a
crabby old Scotsman! Marriage is easy—divorce is impossible."

"Well, look at it this way—if he's your father's cousin, Miss Nell, he
must be quite old, wouldn't you think? Lord Hartismere was no chick-
en—nearer sixty than fifty, if I recall? And if Scotland is as cold and
dangerous a place as you say, then this old bird very likely won't last
much longer, surely? You'll soon be free to marry again—and someone
of your own choosing!"

Nell's astonishment turned to a bubbling laugh. "I do believe you're
right, Lucy! But you can't be...and yet...it would certainly be one way
out of my predicament. Could it possibly work, do you think? Perhaps I
should try...I won't be beaten! I will control my own affairs! I will!" She
paused, and her eyes narrowed; her chin rose in a mutinous expression
that Lucy knew meant trouble. "I'm going to Scotland, Lucy! *We're* going
to Scotland! I'm going to beard this supercilious, decrepit old money-
grabber in his awful Scottish lair! I'll meet him and deal with him face

to face. I'll marry him! After all, as my guardian, he may himself give consent! I'll sign his papers and come straight back home a free and independent woman!"

"We're going to Scotland? What, all the way to Scotland?" asked Lucy, who had been imagining that all the arrangements could be made by post. "But Scotland is a terrible long way off, is it not, Miss Nell? Farther than Norwich, I do believe?"

Sensing her maid's rising panic at the idea of leaving civilised London and risking the dangers inherent in the company of wild, porridge-eating Highlanders armed with broadswords, Nell said, more gently but still firmly, "Yes, about three times more distant, I should guess, so Lucy, the sooner we get started, the better. It's early September now, and it will take at least a week to get there, possibly a week to conclude our business, and a week to travel back. We must return as soon as possible to avoid bad weather on the roads..."

Her mind was racing now, challenged by the idea of doing something greatly daring, something that would require courage and, above all, careful planning.

"Say nothing to Stepmama," she said unnecessarily. "You may start to pack a portmanteau with things we shall require—sufficient for three weeks. And, Lucy, take care to put in warm clothes, as I dare say it will be chilly and wet. We must travel by post chaise! But how would one arrange that? Turvey! He will know how to hire a post chaise! I will engage him to secure one for us for tomorrow morning as early as may be. We will travel in comfort, Lucy! The mail coach would be slower, and we would have to travel crowded in with other passengers. I do not wish to make conversation with strangers for a week, and we would run the risk of being overtaken and brought back if Stepmama or Fanshawe found out what we were about. They would never catch us in a post chaise—why, I believe they go along at ten miles an hour on the good roads!"

"But how will we pay for it, Miss Nell? They do say them post chaises is terrible expensive!"

"I've thought of that too! My father always kept a small store of guineas in a secret drawer of his desk. He showed me how to open it when I was a child, and I have been adding to it a good part of my monthly allowance since he died. It's not a fortune, but it should be adequate for our needs. Go quietly now and get a portmanteau down from the attic. If you're discovered, you must burst into tears and say that Lady Cecilia has dismissed you and you are packing to return to Suffolk. I'll go and find Turvey and have him arrange our journey. Poor Turvey! It would be a kindness to send him straight back to Suffolk lest Stepmama should choose to vent her anger on him when she discovers we are gone.

"Oh, Lucy!" she said, turning to her maid with glowing eyes. "I begin to come to life!"

"Yes, Miss Nell," said Lucy miserably.

3

*A*fter a night of fierce rain, a sparkling Scottish morning greeted Nell and Lucy as they climbed aboard their post chaise for the eighth day on the road and, with the now expert eyes of seasoned travellers, assessed the skill of the new pair of postilions as they whipped up the fresh horses and the carriage clattered out over the cobbles of the Saracen's Head Inn in the centre of Glasgow.

"Thirty miles to Callander. We should be there by the middle of the afternoon, if the post houses along the way are well run. A good way before dark, anyhow," said Nell with satisfaction. "At last, Lucy, journey's end (or very nearly). Shall you be glad to step out of the chaise at last? And bid goodbye, for a while, to post houses? Never shall I forget the bulletproof mutton chops in Newark, shall you?"

"No, Miss Nell, but then there was the beefsteak pie in the Bell at Stilton and that great old double bed in the George at Stamford. I declare, you looked like a tomtit in a haycock!"

Nell listened to Lucy's flood of reminiscence and imagined every turn of the long road, faithfully remembered, being laid out on return for the edification of the staff in Somersham, until Lucy concluded at last, "Madam, will not Mr. Lindsay be surprised to see us? Will he be at home? What shall we do if we are stranded in this wilderness?"

Crags and mountain torrents, castles, lakes, and Gothic ruins—to say nothing of gnarled pine forests—were the very stuff of lending library romance, and Nell, clutching on her knee Sir Walter Scott's newly published *The Lady of the Lake* exclaimed and pointed as she identified scenes from the poem. Unimpressed by their literary pedigree, Lucy looked out with fear and distaste at the rugged, heather-covered hills trooping by on either side of the coach road.

Nell smiled with confidence. "I made good use of our day of rest at the Saracen's Head," she said. "I sent a letter on ahead by the mail coach to Callander. My cousin Lindsay will know by now that I am coming, and he will not have had time to put me off. If he is there, he must receive me. He is my kinsman, after all, however distant."

After a luncheon of venison pie and a mug of ale as they changed horses at a wayside post house, they started out with a fresh team on the last ten-mile haul in the direction of the Trossachs. Nell eyed the postilions critically. "Young local lads," she whispered to Lucy. "I can't understand a word of their language—they must be speaking Gaelic. I'm not impressed by their horsemanship, and they don't seem to be working very well together. You would swear they did not know their wheeler from their leader! We're making very slow progress, I'm afraid. Hairy-heeled horses too—would be more at home behind the plough, I believe. It's not all their fault—these Highland roads are not so smooth, and last night's rain has softened the going. Ah well! Only a few more miles now. However unbearable my old relation is, it will still be a welcome change to be sitting still under his roof for a few days!"

An hour or so later, as the sun was sinking towards a high western ridge of hills, a cry of alarm went up from the postilions. They swung the carriage aside at the last moment in an attempt to avoid a cascade of mud and stones that the recent rains had brought down from the hill. With a lurch and a bone-shaking thump, the nearside wheel slid into the roadside ditch. Lucy squealed, Nell cursed, the postilions broke into a jabbering flood of Gaelic, and the horses' hooves fought and scrabbled for a purchase in the mud.

Anxious and frustrated to be delayed so near her goal, Nell leapt from the carriage to take stock of the situation. The postilions, neither of whom was much older than herself, were quarrelling noisily, each apparently blaming the other for not anticipating that the swollen mountain stream would have burst out and caused this havoc on the road.

"Come on now!" Nell yelled at them, hoping that they understood. "Both of you! Get down here and back the horses—there's no room to turn. Lucy, get out of the coach—we must lighten it! Come over here and help me to push!"

A few minutes of heaving and pushing and coaxing the horses to move backwards produced no result, and Nell called a halt. Turning to escape from the mud and anxious not to ruin her precious London boots, Lucy lost her footing and fell, twisting her ankle and squeaking with pain. With rising frustration, Nell helped her to the safety of a nearby tree stump. She fetched her fur-lined cape from the coach and placed it around the girl's shaking shoulders, saying as patiently as she could manage, "Don't worry, Lucy. It's not broken, it is just a sprain, I think. Stay here and keep warm. We'll soon have the carriage moving again."

She returned to the slippery morass and looked at the two lads, whose activity had ceased the moment Nell had left them. They looked back at her, waiting expectantly for further instructions. "Look, haven't you got a cart jack?" she asked, remembering a lazy Suffolk afternoon when she had watched the farm boys at Somersham dealing with just such a situation when a runaway cart had become lodged on the river bank. In this wild country, events of this kind must be a daily occurrence. Surely they were prepared to deal with them? She mimed the pumping action of one using a jack, and instant comprehension flooded their features, followed by embarrassment at not having thought of it earlier. One of them dashed to the rumble and took out a square-based wooden pyramid and a long handle. They proceeded to assemble the device and position it under the axle.

"Wait a moment!" said Nell. "You!" pointing to the larger of the two. "Go into the woods and pick up some branches. We'll need to have something for the wheels to grip when this thing starts to move again."

She looked up anxiously at the sky. The sun was now touching the rim of the Trossachs, and to the north, black clouds were massing. The woods on either side of the road seemed denser and more threatening. There was no traffic on the road, and Nell was acutely aware that they were too far from the post house behind them and from Lindsay's house that lay ahead to reach either on foot before dark and very likely a heavy rainstorm swept down on them. Moving the coach was their only hope of reaching safety that night. With renewed determination, she rolled up the sleeves of her chestnut wool travelling tunic and kirtled up the soggy hem of her long skirt, tucking the ends into her belt as she had seen the farm girls do when they were about to walk through the mud. Luckily, her brown leather walking boots were giving her a good grip on the slippery road surface. Shouting words of encouragement, she held the horses steady by the head while the boys pumped away at the jack, raising the wheels above the surface of the mud.

"Now put those branches, some stones, anything you can find, under and behind the wheels so they can get a purchase."

The boys scurried about obediently until she called, "That's good! That'll do! Now, take a corner of the coach each—here—and push when I shout, and I'll urge the horses backwards. Ready? Go! Come on! Harder! Push!"

Muscles, equine and human, creaked and strained, and the carriage groaned. Nell yelled like a Fury making full use of her Suffolk farm vocabulary, and five sweating minutes later, the wheels were back on firm ground. The postilions gave a great whoop of delight in unison and the lead horse, which Nell was holding on to, shook its head violently in surprise. Nell's legs shot from under her and she sat down with a smack in the mud in a swirl of petticoats.

At first, the postilions were too shocked by the sight of the fine London lady sitting on her bottom in two inches of mud to react, but finding first Nell and then Lucy prepared to treat it as a joke, they joined in, shyly at first, but with increasing freedom, till all four were laughing heartily together.

Aching but flushed with triumph, Nell, still laughing helplessly, rolled forward with a squelch onto hands and knees to push herself up. But the laughter froze on her lips as she became aware of a still, grey shape lurking in the heather by the side of the road. The grey form moved stealthily forward, and she found herself looking, mesmerised, into a pair of amber eyes.

With a shudder, she had first thought: "Wolf!" but now she identified the stately beast advancing on her as a deer hound. Fear vanished in admiration for the enormous animal, which was fixing her with a feral stare of mixed interest and disdain. Remaining on her knees and judging it a good idea to make no abrupt movements, she found herself on eye level with the creature, which came cautiously forward, pausing a yard away from her, one paw elegantly raised. Nell decided the moment had come to work her charm on the dog. Dogs, all the dogs in the world it seemed, apart from Suzette, accepted her, but she never took this for granted.

Murmuring admiring endearments, she held out a steady hand to the hound. It moved closer, sniffed, and then opened its huge jaws and began to lick her muddy fingers with a long, slathery pink tongue. With her other hand she began to stroke its wiry chest from neck to shoulder, and the dog began to whine its appreciation and friendship.

"Leave the dog alone! He's working!" a cold voice commanded.

Startled, Nell spun round and confronted her second pair of amber eyes that day.

The hunter had moved silently from the fringe of trees and was now standing and looking down at her with eyes the same colour as his dog's but much less friendly. "Lupus! Heel!" he called to the dog and added something unflattering in Gaelic. The dog slunk apologetically behind his master and sat down. She now found herself the target of two pairs of calculating eyes.

What to do now? Nell was acutely embarrassed at being caught by a stranger on her knees in the mud in a slurry of dirty petticoats. Embarrassment swiftly gave way to fear. This man appearing so abruptly by the wayside could be—almost certainly was—a hunter. But he might be a poacher. Perhaps a cut-purse? This was the country that had bred Rob Roy MacGregor, after all. Two English girls, defenceless save for the ineffective pair of grooms, would so easily fall prey to a man of evil intent. She peered at the rough figure through the deepening gloom. With a chill, Nell decided, noting the man's confident bearing, that he was most likely a highwayman. The ruffian stood shaking his head at the scene of chaos before him, his long gun slung across one shoulder.

To Nell's relief, the two postilions at least seemed to know him. They both came eagerly forward with broad smiles, doffed their caps respectfully, nodded, and muttered, "Good day to ye, Moidart." So, not a highwayman then, she reasoned. Postilions did not show such warmth and deference to highwaymen. They certainly would never utter the name of a Gentleman of the Road.

The stranger leaned forward, seized Nell under the elbows, and swung her to her feet. A strong man and tall, she noticed, her nose finding itself on a level with the top button of his waistcoat. Could he be a Highlander? Was this the Highlands? Where did the Highlands start? He was wearing riding breeches of rough tweed with a length of dark red and green tartan cloth slung over his shoulder and fastened with a silver eagle's claw. His jacket was of dark blue duffel, and he wore a floppy blue bonnet with two ribbons trailing down behind.

Nell's eyes opened wide as she took in the details of this, the first wild Scotsman she had met. She found it difficult to meet his gaze. He was staring at her with open curiosity and, for a moment, she was uncertain how to react. She guessed that, at the end of a day's hunting or whatever activity he had been engaged in in the wilderness, the last thing he would want to encounter on his way home to his hearth and his supper was a pair of ladies in distress and a broken-down coach.

Searching his face for some clue as to his intentions, she noticed that he was quite young, a man perhaps in his late twenties, with dark hair and straight black eyebrows. His face was lean and brown, his nose prominent, and his mouth a tight line of irritation. Abruptly, the mouth twitched into a grudging smile, which lit up his face, and he spoke again.

"Well, I'll say this for ye, lassie, ye've a lot of courage and a fine pair of lungs. I heard ye screeching half a mile away!"

Angrily, Nell pulled her arms free from his grasp. "And you were not gentleman enough to come and lend us a hand? If you were rushing to our aid, sir, I did not observe it!" Suspicion slowly dawned as he continued to grin down at her. "Why! You were standing there in the trees watching us struggle, were you not?"

He did not deny it. "Oh, I could see that the whole operation was in capable hands," he said casually. "And besides, I was fair enjoying the sight of a braw, strapping young lass kicking about in her underpinnings. It's rare that I catch a glimpse of a neat pair of ankles on the moor. And it's some while since I encountered a face and a voice sweet enough to charm my dog!" His eyes were alive with mischief, and his mouth took on an unmistakably sensuous slant as he held her a little way from him and looked her over from head to foot with open appreciation.

"Sir! You should look to your manners!" was all Nell was able to gasp. She was blushing at the undisguised warmth in his stare. Not even the despised rake Fanshawe had dared to look at her in this shaming way.

"That's enough of your sauce for now, my girl! We'll have dealings later, I'll promise ye that. But—you're right. I should indeed look to my manners. I should be presenting my compliments to your mistress." He seized her by the shoulders, spun her around, smacked her playfully on the bottom and set off through the mud towards Lucy, who was sitting anxiously on her tree stump, watching the proceedings with increasing alarm.

Outraged by his behaviour, Lucy staggered up from her tree stump, straightened her spine, tilted up her nose, and addressed him in the glacial tones of a London Lady's Maid in high dudgeon. "And what, pray, do you think you are about, sir?"

"My compliments, madam," he offered cheerfully. "Rorie Moidart at your service." He doffed his blue beret with an elegant gesture. "I'm thinking you'll be the house guests Lady Kintoul is expecting. Her cousin, is it not? Kintoul Castle is quite a way distant I'm afraid—near on twelve miles—and you'll never arrive there before dark. If you'll take my advice, you will allow me to turn the coach around, and I'll have the lads take you back to Vennacher to spend the night. Madam? I have the honour of addressing?" He waited for her to give her name.

"I do not give my name to any passing scapegallows," Lucy said repressively. She pointed an imperious finger at Nell. "And I take advice only from my mistress, Lady Elinor."

For a moment, Nell had been puzzled, and then she had realised the man's misunderstanding. There was Lucy sitting comfortably in her mistress's Parisian pelisse watching the activity while she sweated and struggled with hot cheeks and hair flying all over her face like a hoyden, skirts hitched up country-style around her waist and ankles very clearly on display. Delivering oaths too, she remembered guiltily.

"Lor!" Nell exclaimed as he turned and looked from one woman to the other in satisfying astonishment. "This grows more like the third act of a French farce at Drury Lane by the minute! Sir, you are quite mistaken. Entirely excusable in the circumstances, I will allow." She favoured him with her most devastating society smile. "That is my maid, Lucy, and I am Lady Elinor Somersham. I am on my way to visit a kinsman—Roderick Lindsay, who lives near Callander. Indeed, we should even now have been arriving at his house had it not been for this delay. I understand that he lives this side of Callander, and the postilions were going to take us to his very door. But now I suppose, as the road is quite washed away, we will indeed have to take your advice and go back the way we came and overnight at the nearest post house. But may I know your name, sir, and whether you are of the area? Perhaps you know my kinsman? Sir?"

Nell found his expression of surprise and discomfiture entirely rewarding. When finally he found his voice and started to speak, his tone was more civil. He muttered something that might well have been an apology and then stopped, stared at her again, and said slowly, "I am delighted to make your acquaintance, Lady Elinor. As to my name—you have heard it. The lads called me Moidart. That's my surname. My given name is Rorie. Rorie Moidart, and you may call me Rorie if you wish."

"You are very civil, Mr. Moidart," replied Nell with a dignified inclination of the head. She was certainly not going to call this rough character by his Christian name, whatever their own outlandish habits might be.

He smiled sourly at her reprimand and then said, "I am from hereabouts, and yes, I am acquainted with your kinsman. What's more—you have chided me for failing to come to your assistance, perhaps I can now rectify that."

He flung back his head and called loudly into the trees, thickening and darkening in the oncoming twilight, "Coll! Coll! Come here, lad!"

A kilted man came forward out of the trees leading a horse and a pony. Across the saddle of the pony lay a dead stag, its magnificent antlers dipping gently with the movement of the horse.

The red-haired man, who could hardly have been much younger than the man who had summoned him, presented himself with a nod and stared quizzically at the two women for a moment. Clearly trying to suppress a smile, he seemed to have witnessed the exchange and enjoyed it every bit as much as Nell. When he answered, he spoke with what Nell judged to be an affected and playful deference. "Moidart! Will ye be needing any help with the ladies? Or can ye manage the two yourself?"

"It's the horses I want. I'm going to need both of them to rescue these two distressed, benighted Englishwomen. Will you now go away to your home on foot? Oh, and Coll—take the stag and hang it safe in a tree. Mark the spot and come back for it tomorrow, will ye?"

Turning to Nell he asked, "Can ye both ride a horse?"

"Of course," she replied shortly, "but where are you taking us?"

"Well, where do you think, lass? To your kinsman's house. To Lindsay's." He sighed and muttered, "Though I doubt he will be any better pleased to see ye than I am." Seeing her hesitation, he added more kindly, "It's only a wee step from here through the forest ye'll find. The carriage was almost there. You would have seen the Great House had you rounded the next bend. But make up your mind quickly now. Do you go back with the coach or do you go on with me? We'll have to be stepping if you come with me to be there while we still have some light. Folk in these parts don't like to open their doors to callers after dark, I warn you."

Nell made up her mind. "Very well. Thank you, Mr. Moidart," she said with a gracious nod. "And thank you, Mr. Coll. We will be pleased to come with you. Now, could you please help Lucy onto a horse—she has hurt her ankle. And allow me a moment to fetch my reticule from the coach if you please."

With another deep sigh of suppressed irritation and an anxious look at the sky, Moidart strode off and unceremoniously swept a terrified Lucy up into his arms, rapped out a few commands in Gaelic to the two postilions, and returned to the horses. He placed Lucy on the smaller of the horses, a rough-coated, short-legged hill pony, and mounted the other, a large rangy black with a wicked eye.

For a moment, Nell was nonplussed. 'Am I then to walk at your stirrup?" she asked uncertainly.

"Can if you wish, but it's rough going. Give me your hand and put your foot on mine."

She did as she was commanded, and, resting her toe lightly on his leather brogue and springing with the last of her strength as he pulled upwards, she was hoisted into place sitting sideways on his lap. Blushing to find herself so close to a complete stranger, she was relieved to see him smile easily and caught a glimpse of straight white teeth as he grinned down at her and said in his lilting voice, 'And what shall I say when they ask me, 'What did you catch on the moor today, Moidart?'...'Och, I bagged me a brace of rare birds, a pair of braw plump dawties flighting north from England!'"

Nell stirred uneasily in his arms. This was not the mode of address she was used to in London society. Was this how the Scots generally behaved? What did he mean by plump dawties? It did not sound flattering, but she was too proud to ask and too grateful for his help to dash him down. She confined herself to replying politely, "I acknowledge your sacrifice, sir, in displacing your noble-antlered victim (twelve points, I think?) and I am conscious of the nuisance we must represent to you at the end of what I perceive to have been a long and exhausting day."

Innocent eyes of angelic purity looked up into his dirty face, from which the smile was now fading.

A grunt was all she had for reply, but she felt his arms tighten about her as he shortened the reins and urged the horse forward. Nell was acutely disturbed by the contact. Fingertip touches during dancing were the most intimate connections she had ever had with men, and she was finding this close contact with the stranger unsettling. She eyed him covertly in the fading light. He looked completely unconcerned, even rather bored, and was humming a tune softly under his breath as they moved forward at an easy pace down the forest path, with Lucy's pony following dutifully behind and the hound running ahead like a grey ghost through the trees.

Who on earth could he be? Nell's busy mind tried to make sense of the few pieces of information she had gathered on him. It was clear he was not a servant or an estate worker—he had a certain arrogance and air of command about him that argued a position of authority or rank, and, on learning who she was, he had not appeared impressed. Surprised, startled even, but not overawed.

As they plodded on, she shivered slightly in the cooling air. Without a word, he tugged at the plaid around his shoulders, loosened it, and draped a length of the thick cloth about her. The rhythm of the horse and the warmth enveloping her combined with the exhaustion brought on by the last few hours and the week's travelling, and soon Nell was finding it difficult to keep her eyes open. She was drifting into sleep, slumping imperceptibly back against the comforting warmth of the man's body. She shot upright abruptly and murmured an embarrassed apology. He smiled down at her and, to her surprise, gently drew her head back towards him in a companionable way. With a sigh, she rested her head gratefully on his shoulder and, her last conscious thought registering the fact that his heart appeared to be thumping at a prodigious rate, she fell asleep.

She awoke with a start. "What was that noise?" Moidart had reined in his horse and was listening intently. It was now almost dark, and their way was lit by a full moon. A brilliant harvest moon. The deer hound had come close to Moidart's foot in the stirrup and was snarling gently.

Lucy urged her pony alongside and said, white-faced with horror, "Miss Nell! Did you hear that? Oh, sir, what was it? That howling?"

"Oh, nothing to worry about, Lucy," he replied unconcernedly. "Some old farm dog run wild and howling for his mate. There are packs of wild dogs in the woods—foxes too—and the full moon always seems to excite them. Don't be afraid—old Lupus here is a match for any other dog, and I've got my gun!" Lucy smiled with relief and fell in behind.

He leaned forward as they set off again and said confidingly in Nell's ear, "I wouldn't say so to your maid, but that howl—ah! There it is again!" Nell shuddered to hear the despairing, blood-chilling yell. "There are those in these parts who would tell you that the howling is that of the Werewolf of Lochnagal."

"Werewolf?" said Nell trembling. "What is that? There are no wolves of any kind left in the British Isles, sir, surely?"

"Not a real wolf, Elinor, a werewolf—a shape shifter. A man by day who becomes a wolf by night on the night of the full moon. He tears the throats out of sheep—and sometimes of humans, when he can catch them out late in the forest. There is an old story that, years ago, a tenant farmer of the Lindsays was bitten by a wolf and caught a terrible disease that turned him into a shape shifter. He killed his own wife and three sons by biting out their throats as they slept, but he himself cannot die! He was buried alive for his sins by his neighbours but every full moon, there he goes again!"

Nell gasped and covered her ears to block out the appalling screech. She thrust herself back into the safety of Moidart's arms and, pulling the plaid over her head, clasped her arms tightly round his chest, shivering with terror.

"There, now, there!" he whispered anxiously into her hair. "Och! I should not have so worried you with my daft tales! You're safe with me, my lass, so don't be afraid." He stroked her tangled hair gently, assuring her that if they could but step out a bit faster now the moon was lighting their path they would soon be out of the forest. Her shivering stopped, and her breathing grew less ragged, but Nell was still firmly holding on to him as the horse paced over the rough ground with only the occasional chink as a hoof struck a loose stone.

Her strange escort fell silent too. She sniffed appreciatively. He smelt warm and friendly and of the open air, of grass and heather and a subtle underlying scent, which she found attractive and exciting. She sank within the circle of his protective arm in a dream state between waking and sleeping. She was aware of the rise and fall in the track, of the distant tinkle of a burn through the trees and the drowning fragrance of bog myrtle coming down on the cold wind off the encircling hills, and she noticed, as they moved forward, that the track began a steady downward slope. The noise of the burn increased and, for a while, a brawling torrent ran beside them until, with a rattle of hooves on a stone bridge, they crossed over and the trees began to thin.

Nell lifted a sleepy head and looked about. Dark clouds still massed over the Trossachs and a glow behind them marked the sinking sun. "Red sky at night," thought Nell, "shepherds' delight?"

Her escort, feeling her stir, looked down and, in a strange flash of sympathetic understanding, murmured, "The last of the rain, I believe. We could have a fine day tomorrow." And then, reining his horse and lifting Nell in the crook of his arm, he pointed ahead. "Behold," he said, "the House of Lindsay!"

Nell followed his pointing arm and saw below, shining like a sheet of steel in the bright light of the moon, the windless waters of a loch. The surrounding hills were reflected purely and perfectly in the still water. It was a scene of ethereal beauty and, as she watched, a strong-winged flight of wild geese beat steadily up from the west to settle silently on the water.

From the loch's edge, a causeway ran one hundred yards out into the water, and there—ancient, formidable, but safe and welcoming—the House of Lindsay sprawled across a rocky island. Defensive round towers stood at each corner, a steeply pitched roof between them was decorated with clusters of vast chimney stacks, an entrance courtyard was shaded by gnarled trees bowing to the prevailing westerly winds and shedding a hoard of autumn gold on the dark water in the shadow of the causeway.

Many windows were lit in welcome, and as Nell watched, a square of light broke briefly from the window of an ivy-covered tower where an unseen hand, it seemed, had lit a lamp and closed the shutter.

At last they were clear of the trees, and Moidart stopped the horse and pointed again. "See there," he said. "You're right. It seems Lindsay *is* expecting you." He looked at her in surprise. "A welcome guest indeed! I have not seen so many rooms candle-lit for years. You would think he was having a feast!"

"But it's beautiful!" she breathed. "I had no idea that cousin Roderick was a nobleman! Surely he must be to live in such a house?"

"House? Castle more like. The Lindsays have lived here on the Loch for centuries. They're a well-respected family hereabouts, you'll find. God-fearing people who care for their tenants—hard-working, peaceable, and fair. Aye, it's a pity that all this will be coming to an end," he said bitterly, moving off down the slope.

"Coming to an end? Why, Mr. Moidart? I do not understand you."

"You're telling me you've not heard and you a kinswoman?" he asked in disbelief. "Everyone hereabouts has heard of Roderick Lindsay's bad fortune. He who should have by rights inherited his own house and his own lands from his grandfather Lindsay has had them passed away from him."

"What do you mean, 'passed away from him'?"

"As the only son of his grandfather's only son, he should clearly have inherited the estates, would ye not think, but, oh no!" His voice took on a sharpness of tone as he went on. "Roderick's father was so foolish as to marry an Ogilvie, a clan long enemies of the Lindsays, and his grandfather, in his rage and spite, left his possessions to his eldest child, a girl, Alice, on whom he doted. Alice had married an English lord and had never any intention of returning to Scotland, so she was quite content to leave the estates undisturbed and in the possession of her brother Lindsay during her lifetime. When she died some years ago, they passed to her son, who is, or was, the present Lindsay's cousin, a Lord Hartismere and one of the richest men in the two kingdoms."

Nell was silent, listening intently and awkwardly to this recital of her own family history. The details were accurate as far as she remembered, but she was held back from declaring her interest by the disapproval amounting to hatred in his voice.

"It was always expected that this cousin Hartismere would do the decent thing and restore the lands to their rightful owner, but no, this was not to be! All has gone to Hartismere's daughter, a soft, spoilt, southern Miss, barely out of the schoolroom, so I hear, who holds in her silken hands the lives of scores of honest Scottish folk!"

Nell quailed at the undisguised venom. This account of Moidart's... could it be true? She searched her memory for snatches of conversations about her family. Her grandmother had been a beauty in her day, and Nell still thought with fondness of the soft Scottish voice, the dazzling grey eyes, very like her own, eyes that never seemed to lose their sparkle and the gentle humour and patience she had shown to Nell when she was growing up.

Nell felt suddenly humbled. She had not thought of her inheritance in terms of land with tenants, farmers, ghillies, and shepherds depending on it and upon the benevolence of its owner. It had not occurred to her that one day she would have the power to order Lindsay to leave his ancestral home.

Did this man, Moidart, know who she was? Surely he had guessed? But of course he had! Indeed, that was the point of his story. He was signalling his knowledge. From the bitterness of his words and the steely gleam in his eye, the soft southern Miss he spoke of would have a very bleak reception from him. It became important for her to discover exactly who he was. A kinsman of her cousin? A servant?

A hired assassin?

Unwelcome, there edged into her mind the story of the massacre of Glencoe. A clan of Macdonalds had been shot or hacked to pieces, every last one—men, women, and children—one winter's morning. The snows of the remote glen had been stained with the blood of thirty-eight Scots killed by the fellow Scotsmen to whom they had offered the shelter of their homes. Even the English had been sickened by this deed, and they had held an enquiry, an enquiry that had uncovered the treachery, and the name of Campbell had rung around the world for evermore, bringing dishonour to all who bore it, innocent and guilty alike.

Would anyone hold an enquiry if two Englishwomen disappeared in this forest? Nell reflected that the Lindsays would have all to gain, and her stepmother was hardly likely to raise a hue and cry.

Too late it occurred to her that the blockage on the road, seemingly so naturally occurring, was cleverly placed. The postilions could not have been aware of it until they were upon it. And the figure lurking by the roadside? Had he set himself to wait there, having first dislodged a slurry of loose scree? And who would bear witness to their disappearance? The postilions were the last to see them and, judging by their deferential tone and the way they doffed their caps to this Moidart, their mouths would be stopped by clan loyalty.

None of these Scots would care in the slightest—in fact they would be relieved if Lindsay went on living in his castle undisturbed by any quirks of English law. Two quick dagger blows under the ribs was all it would take, and their bodies would never be found in this wilderness. If they were traced as far as this point, then all would swear that the two silly women had insisted upon walking the few miles through wolf-infested woods to the house of Lindsay and had simply never arrived.

Desolate and terrified by her own imaginings, she put her thumb between her teeth to stop them from chattering. Perversely, in her fear, she could only cling more closely to the man who threatened her, her head on his heart, her senses stretching to feel any change in his movements.

He had begun again to hum his mournful Scottish lament and was plodding on, unconcerned, towards the castle. He had not eased the dirk in its scabbard or checked the knife she had glimpsed in his sock. He had not even flexed his muscles. So, evidently, it was not to be a death in the woods, then. Nell's horror began to dissipate, and she dared to raise her head. She looked searchingly at the castle they were approaching. Dimly seen now in the rapidly fading light, the road wound onwards down before them to the loch's edge. Patches of clear moonlit sky began to show, and a steady wind dispersed the clouds above them. Nell looked up with a start as a flight of mallards whipped across a patch of sky and slanted down to the still waters. Even in the hard grey light, she felt the pull, the attraction, the magic of the place and recognised that here was a place worth marrying for. Worth killing for. If this were her own home, she would fight like a she-bear to keep it.

"But it is yours," whispered an inward voice. "It *will* be yours one day."

The voice added with a twist of cynicism: "If they will allow you to possess it."

4

She became aware that Moidart was watching her carefully under lowered lashes, and her good breeding reminded her that she had been silent and unresponsive for too long an interval, absorbed by her own thoughts and calculations.

"I can see," she said in a low voice, looking up at him seriously, "why Roderick Lindsay would fight to keep possession of such a place. I have never seen its like before. He is a lucky man indeed to have it. But tell me, Mr. Moidart..."

"No," he broke in impatiently, "I'm not Mister! Just Moidart of Moidart or Rorie if you should condescend..."

"Very well, Moidart," she said. "I was just going to ask if Lindsay has children of his own?"

"It seems you know remarkably little of your kinsman, Lady Elinor," he said with suspicion.

"That is true," she admitted, guessing that he would see through any dissimulation or half truth. "I have never met him, and we have never corresponded—until recently, that is," she corrected herself hurriedly. "He is my father's relative and of an older generation than mine."

He laughed shortly and said, "The man has never been married, and ye'll find he has no heirs—luckily—at least none that he is aware of.

44

Fighting is what we Scotsmen are good at after all and hunting and fa-
thering sons for the English to come and murder. Yes, the man counts
himself lucky he has no sacrifices to offer up."

Nell looked away quickly, uncomfortably aware again of his wildness
and the heat of his barely concealed bitterness. Surely he was not going
to hold her responsible for centuries of oppression at the hands of her
countrymen? She longed to reveal that Scottish blood ran in her veins
also, but again, this unpredictable man laughed at his own vehemence
and, unbending at the sight of the hurt in her eyes, he raised his hand
to smooth down a lock of her hair. "There now. You'll be thankful to
arrive and tidy yourself. Mrs. Fraser will think she's opening her doors
to a pair of scarecrows!"

"Mrs. Fraser?"

"Aye, Jennie, the housekeeper. A very decent woman and the best
cook this side of the Tweed!"

"You seem to know the household well,' Nell said hesitantly.

He gave a chuckle. "Aye...none better! I'm the factor, after all," he
said, and then seeing her puzzled frown, he added, "the steward I think
you'd say in England, so yes, ye could say I know the household pretty
well."

The horses clattered over the narrow causeway and across a paved
courtyard, and Moidart halted before an iron-bound oak door. He
paused for a moment with his arms about Nell and seemed about to say
more but then grunted and lowered her to the ground. He dismounted and went to help Lucy, carrying her easily to the door. A small boy
dashed around from the back of the house, stopped dead, and looked
with surprise first at Nell and then at Lucy and back to look a question
at Moidart but, on a word from him, took charge of the horses, leading
them away to the stables behind the house.

Nell, catching a look of terror from Lucy, managed to whisper comfort-
ingly, "It's all right, Lucy, we're with friends." But she wondered, "Are we?
What is this strange place? And these strange people? Where are we going?"

But Moidart was saying impatiently, "Knock on the door will ye,
Lady Elinor! I have my hands full here."

Seizing the great ring knocker and waking the echoes within the house, Elinor hammered with the firmness such a door seemed to expect and was rewarded by the sound of a woman's voice calling, "Who's there?"

"Moidart!" he shouted back. "And I have with me two English maidens come to visit the master. Come on Jennie, open up, we're all starving!"

There came the sound of bolts being drawn back, and the door opened, revealing a dimly lit hall. A pretty, plump, middle-aged woman with grey-streaked brown curls and a branched candlestick in her hand was peering into the darkness with a look of surprised enquiry.

"Rorie? 'Tis yourself Rorie? We'd almost given up on ye for the night, man!"

"Aye. Now move aside Jennie and get me some help. This here's Lady Elinor Somersham," he said, nodding at her, "and this is her maid, Lucy, who has sprained her ankle. Coll and I found them on the road. The rains had swollen the burn and washed out the carriage road with mud. The post chaise and the ladies' belongings too, I'm afraid, have gone back to Vennacher and will have to be fetched later. Jennie, come with me and we'll get this wee thing settled."

With much clucking sympathy, Jennie Fraser swiftly examined Lucy's ankle and gave orders to a girl standing by.

"This is Tibbie," she said to Nell. "I've just told her to take your maid into her room for the night and care for her. But what I think she needs immediately is a cold compress and one of my mutton pies."

Lucy smiled shyly and whispered, "Thank you, Mrs. Fraser! Thank you indeed!"

"Will you wait here a moment, while we bestow Miss Lucy?" said Moidart as he strode off and, still carrying the anxious Lucy, followed by the housekeeper and Tibbie, disappeared through a small door below the great staircase, leaving Nell standing by herself and shivering slightly in the great hall, the dimness of its mighty roof hardly visible in the candlelight. Reared, as she had been, on Gothic romance, Nell's thoughts turned briefly to imprisonments and abductions and spectral appearances, and she was glad to move over to the fireplace, where a large log fire burned brightly, and warm herself by it. She was abnormally pleased to be joined after a while by the deer hound who, by sitting very close to her, managed to displace her gently from what was obviously his hearthstone.

Some minutes later, Moidart, conversing earnestly in what Nell took to be Gaelic with Mrs. Fraser, came back downstairs. Nell sprang to her feet. "Lucy? Is she all right?" she asked anxiously. "Poor Lucy; she didn't want to leave London and must be wondering where she's landed."

"My lady, your maid is not badly hurt and will be on her feet in no time I should say," said Jennie Fraser comfortably. "And now, I am forgetting my manners—I should have bid you welcome to Roderick Lindsay's home, as he is not here to say this for himself."

"Not here? My guardian is not here?" Nell's voice was desperate with disappointment.

"No, he is not." The housekeeper was disturbed by the effect of her disappointing news, but she rallied and said apologetically, "He was away to Glasgow yesterday to consult his lawyer some hours before your letter came, my lady. He had no idea that you were in the country, or of course he would have awaited your arrival."

"Will he be long in Glasgow?" Nell asked anxiously.

Moidart answered her. "He told no one his business. Not even me. Sometimes he is gone for as little as three days and sometimes for upwards of a week. It depends on how demanding his man of law is being—or his mistress," he added with a sly grin.

"Rorie!" snapped Jennie Fraser, much scandalised, and she began to reproach him crisply in Gaelic.

He shrugged his shoulders and then added more helpfully, "He will be back by Friday week at the latest for the Harvest Home dance he gives for the Clan and the neighbours each year."

Nell's heart sank as she absorbed the idea that she was to be stranded with these strange people in this wild place until her cousin should grow weary of his lawyer or his lover. His *mistress*, Moidart had said. Nell was struck by a sudden and unwelcome thought. She must try to ascertain her cousin's age.

"But at least you were so thoughtful as to send us warning, your ladyship," Jennie was saying. "There was quite a bustle here when your letter arrived, but all is ready for you. I've made the preparations I know the Laird himself would have demanded." She smiled at Nell and added with a blend of pride and affection, "Lindsay is unstinting in his hospitality, you'll find. He is known throughout the north country for the warmth of his welcome. Will you come with me now, Lady Elinor, and I will show you to your room. Supper is ready and will be served the moment you descend."

The warmth faded from her tone as she turned to address Moidart. A scolding challenge replaced the deference. "And you, Rorie! Will you be away to your quarters or will you be supping with her Ladyship? Sitting at the head of the table and playing the host, as Himself is not here to welcome her?"

Nell found it hard to account for the asperity in her voice. Had Jennie been her own housekeeper, she would have taken her aside and asked her to speak with a little more respect when she addressed the steward in the presence of important company. But then a further thought, more unsettling, intruded. Perhaps the good Jennie had cause to disapprove of his behaviour in some way? Perhaps this sharpness was intended to convey a womanly warning to herself: "Have a care, your ladyship! This rogue will take liberties!"

Nell decided it was wise to accept the more sinister interpretation. Turning away from Moidart, she gave Jennie a reassuring smile and a nod, which conveyed the message that she had understood Jennie's underlying meaning. Exhausted, dishevelled, and disoriented she might be, but she was determined to give the impression that she was in control of her affairs and her manners.

Nonetheless, Nell found she was waiting for his answer. To her surprise, she found that she would be excessively disappointed if he said no. He smiled his acceptance and looked questioningly at her. She felt an unaccountable rush of pleasure that her acquaintance with the Scotsman was not to be cut short and smiled hesitantly back at him as she prepared to follow Jennie Fraser to her room.

Leading the way up a massive black oak staircase and lighting the way along a sombre corridor lined with portraits, the housekeeper escorted her to a room at the end on the first floor. As the candlelight touched each portrait in turn, Nell contrasted the dark and forbidding warrior faces with their arms and armour with the familiar rosy-cheeked and smiling huntsmen and soldiers that lined the walls at home in distant Somersham Hall. An oak door swung open before them to reveal a room that charmed Nell at once by the amber warmth of its welcome. A fire was glowing in a large corner fireplace, the painted shutter at the window had been closed, and all was snug for the night. The panelled walls were decorated in a faded yellow and white paint, and the wide-boarded pine floor was partly covered with a scatter of Persian rugs of antique elegance. A four-poster bed with hangings of gold, blue, and amber was receiving last minute attentions from a maid who, passing a copper warming pan between the white linen sheets, bobbed a curtsy and went to stand by the door. At the foot of the bed was a cedar wood chest painted in a country pattern with what Nell took to be the arms of Lindsay.

Nell's eye ranged approvingly round the room, and she moved about murmuring her appreciation to the housekeeper. Mrs. Fraser opened a concealed door by the fireplace and showed her into a powder room equipped with dressing table lit by candles on either side of a pier glass, large water jugs and washing bowls, piles of towels, and a hip bath.

"If your ladyship would care to take a bath, I will have the hot water brought up." Seeing the thankful look on Nell's face, Mrs. Fraser called to the housemaid to come forward. "Tibbie will care for you until your own maid is back on her feet again. Tibbie," she said to the smiling, bobbing girl, "you may now see to her Ladyship's bath."

When the girl had gone about her duties, Mrs. Fraser continued, "I understand from Moidart that your luggage has gone back to Vennacher in the post chaise. We will send for it tomorrow, but for this evening, I will look out some things for you from the mistress's wardrobe."

"The mistress? I understood Mr. Lindsay to be unmarried?"

"Och! The *old* mistress, I should say! Mr. Lindsay's mother—she who was an Ogilvie. But a wonderful woman for all that! She was a great beauty in her day and the kindest lady you would ever hope to meet. Her things would fit you—she was tall like you. Ye'll not find them the peak of London fashion after all these years, but they are clean and warm and comfortable." And she whisked off, leaving Nell alone in her room.

She used the moments of solitude to strip off her mud-stained travelling suit and arrange on the dressing table the pitifully few possessions she had been carrying on her person and in her reticule. Laughter along the corridor announced the return of Tibbie shepherding two other housemaids, each struggling along with a polished brass can of hot water. Throwing off her damp petticoats and rejecting an offer of further help, Nell sank gratefully into the hip bath and sponged away with lavender soap the crusted dirt of the journey. She would have liked to linger in the warm water, letting her thoughts roam over her day and especially the last two hours, but her conscience and her stomach reminded her that supper was awaiting her downstairs, as was her strange and intriguing host.

Standing wrapped in a towel before the darkened old mirror and finding silver-backed hairbrushes and an ivory comb, she attacked her dishevelled hair and brushed it until it crackled and glowed in the candlelight. She was so busy with her task that she started slightly as Tibbie reappeared behind her, clucking her tongue and passing a lace-trimmed white cotton peignoir around her shoulders.

"There! Don't you be taking a chill now, my lady. It gets a wee bit raw these September evenings. Shall I be doing that for you now?" She took the brush from Nell's hand and began expertly to smooth and curl the heavy gold strands onto her shoulders.

"Will I leave it loose or tie it up for you, madam? I have never dressed golden hair before—the mistress's was black as a raven's wing."

"Tied up, I think, Tibbie," said Nell, wishing to present a more formal appearance to Moidart than she had so far. "Tell me—your master—Mr. Lindsay—does he take after his mother?"

Tibbie paused in her brushing for a moment to consider this question and replied thoughtfully, "Yes, indeed, madam. Mr. Roderick Lindsay may be Lindsay in name, but in looks he is pure Ogilvie and the image of his mother. A handsome man, ye'll find. In his day, that is."

Handsome? Nell had not prepared herself for a handsome man in his day with a mistress in Glasgow.

"And do you like him, Tibbie?" Nell was embarrassed to hear herself ask. Really! Questioning the servants! What depths of informality she found herself plumbing in this most informal household.

Before she could retract or rephrase her question, Tibbie spoke up. She seemed eager to reply. An affectionate smile lit her face as she said at once, "Oh, that I do, madam! That we all do! You could not wish for a better master. There are those in the Clan as would give their lives for him, and he wouldna have to ask!"

Elinor frowned as she tried to fit this unexpected piece of information with her preconceived ideas on her guardian. Moments later, Tibbie's clever fingers had fastened up Nell's hair with a length of black velvet ribbon, and she had coaxed soft, curling tendrils over her ears. "There, that will do now, I think. And will you now look at the dress Mrs. Fraser has picked out for you? It is a dress Mrs. Lindsay wore but once. The colour was not right for her, and she put it away, though it came from France, but I think it will flatter your colouring, madam. The cut is not fashionable, but the fabric is soft and warm."

She held up a slender dress of fine wool in a subtle shade of mossy green. Nell's heart sank. The dress at first glance was decidedly dowdy, but she instantly spoke sharply to herself. She was not, after all, dressing in silk and satin for the Prince Regent's Birthday Ball tonight, to dine on lobster and iced champagne and dance till dawn! She was about to step downstairs to eat mutton pies and drink ale with her cousin's steward in a remote and draughty Scottish castle. It was with a shock that she realised that she was looking forward to her evening, and the thought came creeping to her unbidden that she wanted to look impressive for Moidart, as cool and sophisticated as might be to redress, if possible, his first impression of her.

Wondering at her own complicated motives, she slipped on the stockings Tibbie was handing her, the straight-cut lawn petticoat and green kid pumps with tiny heels, a little too big but luckily cut for either foot, and held up her arms for Tibbie to slide the dress over her head. At least, she sighed with relief, it was high-waisted and did not require an old-fashioned corset. She did up the four buttons between her breasts, noting with satisfaction that it was a perfect fit, and peered critically into the mirror. Tibbie held a candle close to her head, smiling with pleasure at her achievement.

"Tibbie, that's wonderful!" murmured Nell, enchanted by her reflection. The soft understatement of the dress was a remarkable foil for the vivid colours of her hair and complexion, and the soft, clinging fabric made her feel both sensuous and elegant. Her eyes were glowing with an excitement she had not felt for months, her eyebrows arched coquettishly and her lashes swept down in an enticing regard as she practised her London arts of seduction and then, remembering where she was, burst out laughing at her performance.

"There now. You could go down to dinner, my lady. Moidart will be waiting in the parlour where Jennie has set out your supper. And don't you worry about your own maid, madam. Lucy is fed and fast asleep but had better keep to her room until her ankle is better again. I will wait on you in the meantime. And your ladyship will be requiring a nightgown—I'll see that one is aired for you. If your ladyship will ring when you retire, I will be here."

Nell refused this offer. "No, no. You may dismiss now, Tibbie, thank you. I am quite accustomed to waiting on myself."

Smiling her appreciation of this show of good manners, Tibbie escorted Nell from the bedchamber and bade her goodnight, wishing her a pleasant evening and assuring her again that she was indeed most welcome under Lindsay's roof and what a pity it was that the master was not there to say so himself.

Nell picked up her trailing skirts and walked carefully down the stairs in her borrowed slippers, sniffing appreciatively the smells beckoning her on towards the door of the parlour, which opened onto the great hall.

She crossed the great hall, feeling uncharacteristically hesitant. Surely her heart had not been beating so loudly, her pulses racing so fast, her cheeks so aflame even when she was being presented for the first time at Court? Why was she finding the prospect of a casual supper tête à tête with her kinsman's rough steward, a serving man after all, so alarming? Would he continue, as he had begun, to treat her with that brusque incivility to which she was so completely unaccustomed? A lack of deference seemed to be the style in this household, where they called each other by their Christian names and formality was flown out of the window.

"Don't skulk out there in the hall, Lady Elinor," growled a very informal voice. "I have been waiting for my supper this half hour!"

Summoning all her dignity and affecting a stately smile, Elinor swept into the room and stopped dead, a polite but crushing comment stilled on her lips. The tall figure standing by the fireplace turned to greet her: Moidart—but a Moidart seen clearly for the first time in the bright lamplight. She had expected that he would have changed out of his dirty hunting clothes, but the transformation took her breath away. He was wearing black trousers, a black velvet coat with silver buttons, and a snowy white shirt with a froth of lace at the throat and wrists, looking every inch the gentleman.

She had had a sense that he was an attractive man even in their twilight ride through the forest, but she realised as she stood transfixed and staring openly that she had in no way been prepared for this vivid and distinguished figure, a figure totally different from the languid, good looking men of her acquaintance. Their fair good looks were generally the unformed features of boys whose faces had yet to be given an imprint by life or character, but, in this man, nothing was blurred or unstated, everything clear and decisive. His black hair was swept straight across his broad forehead, and his eyes were sweeping her from head to foot with just the same astonishment as she was herself feeling. The impression of confident power she had sensed in the rough wayside figure of a few hours ago was, if anything, intensified now that she saw him clearly.

He was the first to break the charged silence. "Lady Elinor. I beg your pardon. Once again, I fear I forget my manners. Your appearance is so changed that for a moment I did not recognise you."

"Nor I you, Moidart." She smiled, recovering her poise and adding lightly, "The rough poacher is transformed into a handsome Scottish gentleman. I like well the change."

"And my shrieking hoyden is a demure and courtly lady with neck to rival a swan and eyes the colour of Loch Katrine as I now see. I am not certain yet whether I shall like the change. I had grown accustomed to the sharp-tongued hoyden." His voice was low and, to her surprise, his accent was English with only the faintest overlay of the north.

"The toilette is different, but the tongue is the same," she teased him gently.

"Then I am forewarned. But will you not be seated, madam? You must be hungry indeed after your day's exertions." He indicated a seat at the table laid with two places and, puzzled, Nell looked around for a footman to help her into her place. Moidart closed the door. "No staff this evening," he said cheerfully, easing her chair forward to seat her at the table, "I have told Jennie we will wait on ourselves. You may not be used to such informality, but you will be well served." With careful hand he took up a crystal decanter and poured out claret into tall Venetian glasses. Turning to the sideboard, he removed the gleaming domed tops from two chafing dishes and the source of the mouth-watering aroma was revealed.

At the sight of the brace of golden roast grouse and mounds of buttery vegetables, Nell could not hold back an appreciative murmur. Catching the slight sound, Moidart grinned, "I told you Jennie was the best cook in Scotland. This is what she would call a plain supper. Had she had better notice of your arrival she would have prepared something special."

"This is perfection! I can imagine nothing I would rather be eating." Nell smiled as she contemplated the dish of expertly carved grouse he was placing in front of her. *And when I come to think of it,* she admitted silently to herself, *no one I would rather be sharing my meal with,* and her eyes dropped shyly from a covert inspection of his face.

To cover her confusion, she said lightly, "We have met nothing but kindness since we have been in Scotland, though my maid is, I am persuaded, overwhelmed by all that has occurred. She was in dread as to what unmentionable fate she might be exposed to in the barbarous north."

"And you?" he asked, "Were you not in dread as to what reception might be afforded you?"

Nell considered this for a moment, knowing that there was a deeper meaning to the question than the bland smile that accompanied it suggested. She decided to play the innocent and take his enquiry at its face value, saying at last, "No. I am afraid you will think me overconfident perhaps, but I always expect to be well received in whatever company I find myself."

"But—unprotected and far from your home, amongst people who have no cause to feel a duty of friendship to the English?"

"You forget, Moidart, I am not unprotected. I am the guest of my cousin, who, I am confident, feels a duty of kinship to me." She paused and then went on, "I can sense that you judge it an eccentric and rash thing to do—to undertake this long journey in the company of my maid. And you are right, it is not the usual behaviour of a well-born lady... but then, as far as it is possible for a young female, I'm accustomed to go my own way. It was always so at home at Somersham, and there were many to criticise my father for indulging me. In London, I am always at odds with my stepmama on this score. 'Elinor—do not do this, do not do that...Do not speak so to Lord Tom Noddy...Do not loll so! Preserve a little decorum, I beg!'—You may imagine the tedium! But, at the end of it all, I am either Lady Elinor Somersham who chooses her own friends and goes her own way, or—I am no one."

She wondered if she had said too much to this stranger, but when she looked up she encountered a look so strange, a look blended of surprise and—yes—of admiration and friendship, that she was emboldened to add confidingly, "And I usually get my own way!"

At her words, a shutter seemed to fall between them for, after a level pause, he raised his glass. "Let us drink, Lady Elinor, to the success of your venture to Scotland!"

The simple words brought a chill to Nell's heart. As she raised her glass to his, she was aware again of the calculation in the mocking brown eyes, and she could be no longer in doubt. Could it be that Moidart knew his master's business? She began to fear so, and her pleasure in the meal began to fade. He knew perfectly well the reason for her dash to Scotland then, and was doubtless despising her for it. He must, knowing none of the circumstances, consider her a mercenary little minx, she thought bitterly. A girl who would be willing to undertake this foolhardy journey, as she was beginning to consider it, with the intention of contracting an alliance with her guardian in order to release her inheritance would be hardly likely to commend herself to this passionate Scotsman, whose livelihood also, she must not allow herself to forget, lay in her hands. She wondered briefly what connection she had with Moidart. He thought of himself, clearly, as Lindsay's steward, but if, as indeed they were, the Scottish estates were hers in law, then surely he was *her* man, *her* employee?

This was not the moment to embark on an explanation to him that his position and his future depended on her actions and decisions; she was sure he was all too well aware of that. She began to fear that nothing she could say would endear her to him and, with a pang, she recognised how much she regretted this and how much she did not want to offend him; it disturbed her to be viewed as cold-hearted and venal. Would he be able to see that the money in question was her own? And yet she was too proud to embark on self-justification. Holding up her glass, she gave him her sweetest smile and replied, "To the success of my venture? Let us drink rather to the continued prosperity of the House of Lindsay. Slainté!"

"Slainté!" he replied with a raised eyebrow, and the glasses met and chimed.

They were silent for a time as each ate and drank gratefully, and Nell felt the spreading glow of the good wine flow around her body and sting her cheeks. She noticed that Moidart was not slow to refill her glass, and, anxious to keep her wits about her, she sipped her second glass very slowly, realising that all her sophisticated small talk had deserted her.

She found that she was simply not able to chatter inconsequentially, to tease and flirt with this man as she would have done—as she had been trained to do—in London. She thought with a smile that if she were to attempt to flutter her eyelashes for his benefit, he would probably hand her a kerchief to remove the grit.

He too seemed to be aware of an awkwardness in their situation, as he once or twice began to speak and then thought better of it and fell silent. The grouse finished, he cleared away the plates and produced the dessert, glass dishes of bramble syllabub, creamy but sharp and delicious. Nell sighed as she licked the last trace from her silver spoon and, feeling suddenly satisfied, warm, and almost relaxed, put down her spoon and looked steadily at her host. "Shall we stop fencing with each other? You know exactly who I am and why I have come here, Moidart, I'm thinking."

"Yes, I do. I am privy to most of Lindsay's affairs, but this can hardly be described as business of mine, my lady," he said with a dismissive shrug of the shoulder.

"Good. I'm glad you understand that. I was afraid, from your manner, that you had it in you to condemn me, perhaps, for my readiness to contract a marriage with an unknown cousin in order to take control of my possessions?" she persisted and immediately bit her lip and wished the words unsaid. Why was she raising such a personal matter with this man? It was unseemly of her to initiate a conversation of this kind, but before she could withdraw or pass over her question, he began to answer.

Her words appeared to trigger a strong response that he was no longer able to control. "Then you had it right, your ladyship," he said scathingly. "Since you raise the matter—I despise you for it! I despise you for taking what is not yours to take in the first place, and I despise you even more heartily for the manner in which you are proposing to barter yourself to gain your own ends!"

Harsh words. And from a man who was, after all, in her employ if she reasoned rightly! Her cheeks flushed as though he had slapped her. "The manner? What do you mean?" she asked faintly, recoiling from his open dislike.

"You know well what I mean!" he replied thunderously. "To contract cold-heartedly a marriage with a man you have never even seen and are quite expecting to dislike to unlock your fortune—this is the act of a money-grabbing baggage! 'Tis nothing but greed that moves ye to such a marriage! That would never be my way of it!" His voice had grown rough and Scottish, and his eyes flashed his disgust.

He sensed her shock at his harsh words, and, in silence, he watched Nell measure the distance between her open hand and his flat, tanned cheek and waited, motionless, for the blow. It did not come. She sat back in her chair, assuming an ease and a control she did not feel, smiled, and said firmly, "Well, as you already consider me greedy, you will not be surprised to hear me ask if I may have another helping of this delicious syllabub?"

With some surprise, he fetched another glass of the pink froth and placed it in front of her, and then, glowering, he poured another glass of wine for himself. Sensing that she had disconcerted and in a strange way disappointed him by not smacking him or shouting and stamping and flying into a rage, she followed up her advantage by fixing him with an interested gaze, head slightly tilted and mouth curved softly open, and asked, "And what would be your way of it, Moidart?"

"I beg your pardon, madam, I do not understand your question," he prevaricated. His handsome face had closed up, his long lashes concealing his expression from her, and she guessed that he was regretting his outburst. Knowing that she had the advantage for the moment in a battle of wills she barely understood, she pressed on, "You were saying, I believe, and possibly in defence of your master's interests, that you did not approve of my motives, and you intimated, if I understood you correctly, that you would choose another path to matrimony. I was merely enquiring what that path might be." This was accompanied by a smile so dazzling it disguised any suggestion of inquisitiveness.

"Lindsay is not my master!" he snapped back, evidently not seduced by the sweet tone and the enticing smile. "What do you take me for, girl—a serf? I am my own man! I simply meant that when I decide to take a wife, as—God willing—I hope one day I shall, and that right soon, she will be a lass I know and love and trust and who loves me and wants to bear my children, not a stranger who signs a contract for her own financial advantage and then hurries away with relief to pray for my early demise!"

"How very feeling! How simple and utterly charming! Your speech leaves me quite moist-eyed with emotion. I had not realised," purred Nell with devastating sweetness, "that the circulating libraries had reached these northern fastnesses or that *gentlemen* were so influenced by the mawkish sentiments of Gothic romances."

At once, she wished she had not goaded him. His dark face flushed with anger, and he slammed his glass down onto the table, spilling the claret in a spreading stain on the white damask. "I should have left you in the mud!" he growled through gritted teeth. "My head told me you were trouble the moment I clapped eyes on you! But who would have realised that a face of such beauty, a figure of such grace would mask an empty heart and a calculating mind? And what of your first scheme? To marry that poor, unfortunate Collingwood? You never had any true regard for him, I'll wager. Incompetent, gullible milk-sop that he is, he would never have roused any feelings in a spirited girl like you. No feelings, that is, other than the relief you would have felt on reading that he had been shot to pieces in Spain!"

"Henry? What can *you* possibly know of Henry?" she asked with suspicion and anger.

"I too fought in the Peninsula," he muttered darkly, "where I was unlucky enough to encounter the booby Collingwood...When your cousin consulted me on the matter, I was pleased to be able to share with him my impressions of the Honourable Henry," he added with a smile of satisfaction. "They were not flattering. Lindsay was glad to have the information. I know enough about Collingwood to know that he is not the kind of man you should be considering a suitable match."

So the puzzle was explained! It was to this impertinent meddler that Nell owed her guardian's rejection of her request. She made an effort to keep calm. "On the contrary," she said defensively, "Henry would—perhaps will, for nothing is yet decided—be the perfect match for me! He may not be Viscount Wellesley's most distinguished soldier, but he is the man I have chosen—from among many—to be my husband. He attaches me to him by his many good qualities. He is kind, considerate, and loving and has been devoted to me for years!"

"I could say the same of my dog!" he snarled. "And so, this...this... spaniel has been chosen by you to be your husband and to have possession of all your worldly goods? I canna believe ye have any real affection for the man! And Lindsay? Your second choice, Lindsay? Poor fool! I'm thinking he will need all his native wit about him to avoid being taken in and gulled by you! 'Tis a pity the man is still susceptible to a pair of wheedling eyes. By God, I fear for him."

Nell rose to her feet as gracefully as she could. She was alarmed, indeed even a little ashamed, at the reactions she had provoked. She reproached herself for having let him so far into her confidence, could hardly remember why she had done, and was now, as a result of her carelessness, in the awkward situation of hearing herself abused by her steward. "Sir," she said coldly, "you insult an honourable soldier, you insult the noble lord, your master, to whom I am practically affianced, and you insult me. I bid you goodnight!"

She turned for the door, but in a second he had leapt to his feet and was barring her way. Nell's training had not prepared her to deal with six feet of angry Scotsman, but her pride prevented her from attempting to walk around him. She merely stood quietly, head tilted proudly, eyes averted, waiting with dignity for him to apologise for incommoding her and move out of her way.

He moved at last, but, to her alarm, the step he took was towards her. His brown eyes were inches from her own, searching her face for she knew not what emotion or response. Hypnotised by his intensity she stared back, alarmed but defiant. He seized her by the shoulders and pulled her to him. One arm moved around her, holding her tightly, and his other hand came up to hold her chin firmly, while his mouth descended onto her lips, cleverly anticipating her swift evasive movement.

The shock of the contact with his firm mouth ran through her whole body. His lips began urgently to press against hers, and she waited in horror, breathing through her nose, with the last shreds of dignity, for the kiss—if that was what this procedure was—to end; but to her dismay, he moved his hand up from her shoulders and thrust his fingers deep into her hair, anchoring her face below his. The lips grew more assertive, incited, apparently, by her lack of response, to assault her mouth with an alarming demand. She began to struggle, finding it increasingly difficult to breathe, but the mouth stayed relentlessly on hers, pressing and bruising.

Nell was furious. Kisses in her experience were signs of affection, lightly applied to cheeks like dabs of rouge, but this, she recognised, was far from affectionate in purpose. The man was deliberately trying to humiliate and hurt her. He was using this extraordinary and barbaric method of punishing her for being who she was, she thought wildly, and her anger blazed.

How to break free? She discounted any attempt to call the servants. They had been dismissed for the night and she would anyway much prefer not to have her embarrassment witnessed by a solicitous and possibly garrulous footman. She remembered a device she had used once to good effect in close combat with Rupert during one of their childhood battle games, and, without further thought, she raised her foot and brought it slamming down with all her strength on his. She winced at the contact of his sharp buckle through the thin kid of her evening slipper, but he appeared not to have noticed her attack. In despair, and believing herself in serious danger of asphyxiation, she stopped struggling and stayed still in his arms, having noticed that he increased the tightness of his hold the more frantically she wriggled. Her ploy seemed to work. His grasp relaxed and he removed his lips from hers...but only to transfer them to her ear, where she was shocked to hear his voice, low and urgent, whispering her name.

On a see-saw of emotions, Nell now found her tormentor stroking her cheek, caressing and calming her with voice and hands. In astonishment, she raised stormy eyes to his, desperate to understand him. His eyes too were full of amazement and, drawing in a ragged breath, he brought his mouth down on hers again. She found she no longer had the will to struggle, but now his lips had grown gentle and were slanting caressingly over hers. Surprised by this new tenderness, she decided that this was perhaps even a rather pleasant sensation, and she could quite imagine beginning to enjoy the warm contact with his firm mouth. The scent of his skin and the tightness of his embrace were beginning to disturb her. Wondering at her own reactions, she stirred slightly against him and made a faint questioning sound in her throat. He raised his head, keeping his watchful eyes on hers, and with a thumb delicately stroked her lower lip. She shuddered gently at the intimacy of the gesture and snuggled her head with the clumsiness of inexperience against his chest. He sighed and with swift fingers unknotted the velvet ribbon in her hair, exclaiming softly with pleasure as the silken waves cascaded over her shoulders.

"There," he said in a low voice that caressed her just as his hand stroked her head, "now you're a girl I can hold in my arms and kiss without thinking I should be asking her ladyship's permission."

"What would you do, Moidart, if I refused permission?" she asked, whispering into his chest and adding quickly, "And I do, I do refuse!"

He detached her face from his lace jabot and made her look up at him, eyes crinkling with humour. "Aye, I'd noticed you refusing! What I'd do is take no notice at all and kiss you anyway!" he said firmly and proceeded to do that.

Nell was lost, her emotions swimming in a sensuous daze. A swift, dry peck on the cheek from elderly uncles and a sticky, attempted embrace from the young Henry Collingwood had been no preparation for this. She had never imagined that such a contact could arouse the fierce current in her body that was making her feel dizzy and grateful for his supporting arm.

At last, he raised his mouth from hers, noting her slight movement towards him. She looked at him in fascination, hazily aware of the effort it was costing him to put her down. He steadied his breathing with a perceptible effort and said, "So there is a warm nature under the cold exterior! There is more to Elinor Somersham than calculation, I'm happy to find, and I'll say again—and perhaps this time ye'll hear me—there's no way a girl like you can be marrying for other than love, and don't you try to deny it, or I'll kiss you again! Now, will you come back and sit with me for a while by the fire? I'm thinking there are things you maybe want to tell me..."

Hardly aware of what she was doing, unsure whether she was experiencing relief or disappointment and deciding that, incredibly, it was both, Nell allowed herself to be led back to the table and sank unsteadily down on the chair that he had pulled close to his own. Under his gentle questioning, she found herself talking about Henry Collingwood and admitting that she had no affection for the man she had originally chosen as her husband and confessing that she realised now that she had acted rashly in coming to Scotland, provoked as she was by her stepmother's tyranny into striking out to find her own freedom by the only method open to her.

"Your stepmother's tyranny?" he asked. "Have some more claret, Elinor, and tell me about this behaviour that drove you north." She sat back in her chair and absently accepted another half glass of wine. His concerned, attentive face and the warmth of the claret loosened Nell's tongue, and she found herself telling the story of the state of siege she had been living in before she broke out and escaped to Scotland. She told him of her fear of her stepmother's manipulative plotting, of her disgust at the marriage market that was the London season, and of the increasing isolation and friendlessness she had encountered. She could almost imagine a flicker of understanding in the impassive brown eyes as she recognised that all her actions had been directed to achieving a state of independence for herself, a state of freedom where she might take control of her own life, manage her own estates, and begin really to live instead of moving mechanically to a preset rhythm through her trivial London life.

When she finished, he took her hand in his and said gently, "I fear I have misjudged you, Elinor. You are a brave and resourceful girl, and I can find it in me to admire your resolve."

"No, I have been reckless and silly," she replied in a low voice, "but I will not give up at once. I will at least await my cousin's coming and discuss my affairs with him. He is my guardian after all, and my father's choice, though I have never been able to understand it. It may be that we can come to some conclusion that will be to our mutual benefit."

He was watching her guardedly and then, appearing to come to a decision, sighed and said thoughtfully, "Take care, Lady Elinor, the benefit may not be mutual...If you would take my advice, you will be circumspect in your dealings with Lindsay. He is a good master and, believe me, has the loyalty of all under this roof, but I cannot stand by and see an innocent like you deceived. He has the reputation of being a cool-headed businessman, and he has been known to drive a hard bargain. When he takes a look at you—young and fresh as you are—he could well...it might well enter his head...that he should perhaps be thinking of doing his duty at last to preserve the line of Lindsay and set about providing himself with heirs."

With a furious blush, Nell caught his meaning. "Sir, how dare you insult my cousin's integrity? Besides, he is an old man, is he not? Long past the time when such thoughts would occur to him?"

"Ah well, he may be a good few years older than your ladyship, but the man would tell you himself that he is in the prime of life. And do not be forgetting that he is a Highlander! It is thus with Highlanders, Elinor. Why, old Tam McVeigh of Vennacher fathered a son last spring, and he seventy-five years old!"

Nell turned pale. "Then the notion is quite out of the question. I have no intention of linking myself to an aged, purse-proud, and now I must add *lecherous* Scotsman, who would keep me here, chained like a milk cow to provide money and heirs for his estates! No, never!" Tears were springing to her eyes. She took a deep breath and announced, "I must thank you for your warning, Moidart. I think, perhaps, in the circumstances, it would be wise if I were to return to London before my cousin arrives to find what a foolish ward he has. I would be obliged if you would make arrangements in the morning for my immediate return to England."

Instead of the relief that she expected to see flood his features, he frowned and said slowly, "No. Perhaps that is not such a good idea...But it is late, madam. Let us consider your position in the morning—there is no need for a precipitate decision. And do not forget that your maid will not be able to travel for a few days yet. Come now, before the candles start to gutter, we will use them to light our way to bed."

He put a candlestick into her hand, taking up the other for himself, and snuffed out the lamps. Offering her his arm courteously, he led her from the room and across the great hall where a fire still glowed in the grate and climbed the wide back stairs to the landing, at the end of which she remembered was her bedchamber. Arriving at the door, he opened it and checked the room briefly, noting that the fire was alight, the candles were lit by the bedside, and the bed had been turned down. Draped over the counterpane was a white cambric nightdress trimmed with lace and fastened at the front with blue ribbons.

He nodded his approval. "The room is warm and aired, and I think you will have all that you require, so I will bid you goodnight, Lady Elinor." She half expected that he would kiss her again, but with a smile of mock deference he turned and walked away down the corridor.

Nell closed her door dreamily, warmed by his concern for her comfort. Who could he be, she wondered as she slipped out of her dress and kicked off her slippers. She had told him her life story this evening—had confided thoughts and hopes and opinions she had never shared with anyone else—but he had told her nothing in return. She knew that the upper servants and certainly the stewards in a noble household were often themselves well born and frequently kin to the master...perhaps she could question him more closely in the morning.

She paused as she brushed her hair, remembering his kiss and the way he had untied her hair. With a guilty start, she remembered that the velvet ribbon had fallen to the floor in front of the fire, doubtless to be discovered by a puzzled parlour maid in the morning. Her toilet completed, she looked with satisfaction at the welcoming bed and wriggled her way into the cotton gown. One last thing to do before she threw herself into the downy depths of the feather bed, and that was to open the shutters of the small window. The room was excessively warm now, and Nell liked to sleep with her window open, feeling suffocated if she ever left it closed.

The internal wooden shutters were swiftly flung back against the wall, and she leaned forward to push up the sash window, which had been inserted into the wall's deep embrasure. She caught a brief glimpse of the bright moon riding high and silver now over a range of shadowed hills, and finally surrendering her weary limbs to the soft bed, she allowed herself at last to think unrestrainedly of Moidart. "Though for five minutes only," she told herself. After half an hour, she fell into a deep slumber.

She awoke with a lurch of the heart, and in panic sat up in bed, her eyes straining to see in the dark. There was a dull red glow from the fire, which had burned almost away, and a cold grey dawn light was streaking the ceiling. She had no idea how long she had been asleep, but she was fully awake now and every fibre of her body was stretched and dreading to hear again the shocking sound that had wakened her. Eyes fixed on the window she held her breath. There! Again! It was the voice from the forest! She heard the heartbreaking, keening wail of a lost soul and saw a white face with staring eyes appear at her open window. The creature was tapping and scrabbling to get into her room!

5

esperately, Nell searched about in the darkness and found the heavy brass candlestick by her bed. She threw it with all her strength at the white shape. With a hiss of surprise, it disappeared from sight, and she used the moment to bound from her bed and slam shut the wooden shutters, sliding the fastening into place with trembling fingers.

Her horror grew as she heard a slow rhythmic beating sound and a sinister rustling. The creature was climbing the ivy in another attempt to get up to her room! Gasping with terror she flung herself out into the dark corridor. "Lucy!" she screamed uselessly, and then, remembering where she was and in whose household, she shouted, "Mrs. Fraser! Tibbie! Oh, where is everyone? Help me, someone!" She crashed along the landing, yelping in pain as she cut her shin on a brass coal scuttle and overturning a jardinière bearing a pot, which fell to the ground with a thunderous crash.

A door at the other end of the corridor opened, emitting a shaft of candlelight to illuminate the dark landing, and Moidart's gruff voice called out, "Elinor? Is that you Elinor? Good God, girl, what's with ye?" He strode forward, shrugging into a velvet robe de chambre and was almost knocked over by the force with which she flung herself at him.

"Moidart! Thank goodness! I feared I was alone. Oh, the horror!" she stammered. "It's the Shape Shifter! It's at my window, trying to get in!"

He held her tightly and made calming noises. "There now. It's all right. This is all a nonsense you know, my lassie. There is no such thing as a Shape Shifter, and I'm really sorry I should have told you a story to give you such nightmares..."

"It wasn't a nightmare," she said stoutly. "I really saw it! I had opened my shutters and the window, and the creature was hissing and howling and trying to get in. I threw the candlestick at it, but it came back up the ivy, beating and banging."

"What did it look like, this creature?" he asked seriously.

"White, ghostlike, with great staring eyes!" She shivered again, remembering the awful shape and snuggled her head into his chest. She suddenly became aware that his chest was heaving with suppressed laughter.

"You are mocking me!" she said accusingly. "What do you find to laugh at in my dreadful encounter?"

"I think I know what frightened you, Elinor," he said gently, "and believe me, it was nothing supernatural—not a Shape Shifter nor a werewolf! Now, come back to your room and I will show you what it was." He loosened her grasp and, taking her hand, passed it under his arm reassuringly, making to lead her down the corridor.

"No!" she exclaimed, pulling away from him in terror, I shall sit in the corridor till dawn if there is no other accommodation, but I shall not return to that room!"

He stopped at once, smiled, and said, "Allow me to fetch another candle." Emerging from his room a moment later with a tallow candle well ablaze, he handed it to her, saying firmly, "You may use my room if you wish, but I am going to yours now to check that all is well and to account for this mystery."

He seemed so sure and unconcerned, amused even, that Nell's panic subsided and curiosity began to creep in. She padded hesitantly after him down the corridor. Back inside her room, the pretty things reflected back at her in the candlelight, looking friendly, unthreatening, and completely ordinary. She was beginning to feel a little foolish and wonder whether it had indeed been a nightmare when the noises began. Again came the steady, rhythmic pounding of the ivy outside her window.

"I thought so!" Moidart smiled with satisfaction and started towards the window.

"Pray do not open the shutters!" Nell squealed. "Oh, what is that dreadful noise?"

"Well, now, it is my duty to check that it isn't a bunch of marauding McGregors fighting their way up the tower, but I'm sure it's not! I am sure it's my old friend the white owl though!"

"White owl?"

"Yes, the Scottish white owl! He has a nasty way of keening and hissing that fair makes your skin crawl, and you wouldn't be the first soul to run screeching away from him! You heard him in the woods tonight, and that scrabbling in the ivy you hear—he's getting his supper. He beats the branches with his wings to dislodge the sparrows that nest there, and then he snaps them up! I've watched him do it many an evening."

Nell's fear had almost completely subsided at his rational explanation, and yet she still felt unaccountably nervous as he opened the shutters. No face peered in at her; she saw just the line of distant hills now turning milky grey. He picked something up from the sill and brought it to her. A white bird's feather. She was able in her relief to summon up a shaky smile. "Moidart, I am so sorry to have caused you such trouble! I am mortified to think how I have disturbed your sleep tonight...and needlessly."

"I was already disturbed by you Elinor," he said smiling. "Indeed, I had barely slept all night. You were so much in my thoughts it was no surprise to me to hear you calling."

"I was calling the servants, but I do not know where they are."

"They have rooms above and would not hear you through these thick walls and floors. This is the oldest part of the castle—the old keep—and you and I are the only ones on this floor." He paused for a moment, looking at her carefully in the half light, and then reached out and held up the candle. "But, Lady Elinor, did you injure yourself in the corridor?" he asked with concern. "That crash?"

She followed his gaze to her knees and was aware of a trail of blood from her aching shin staining the front of her nightgown. "I fell over a coal scuttle," she said guiltily.

"I will summon Tibbie to attend to you," he said, making for the door.

"No, pray do not!" she said quickly. "I would not have Tibbie disturbed on account of my foolishness. I am perfectly competent to attend to my own cut leg. It is nothing."

He nodded, approving her decision. "Sit down," he said, pointing to a chair. "I will dampen a cloth for you." With a deft hand he poured fresh water from the ewer into the bowl and dipped a facecloth into it. A moment later, he was on his knees by her feet, solemnly moving aside the hem of her nightgown and dabbing gently at the blood oozing down her bruised shin.

Elinor was too shocked to move or protest at such treatment. She gasped with astonishment, though he took it for a gasp of pain and apologised for hurting her. She was abruptly aware of her situation. Alone in her room at night with a stranger, a stranger who, with all the calm and detachment of a doctor, was holding her ankle in one great square hand and attending to her leg with the other. But what could she say in the circumstances, she reflected—"Unhand me, sir!"? The man was showing the kindness and concern he would have shown to a fellow officer wounded in battle, and she would have felt it an act of gross ingratitude to ask him to desist or to suggest that there was anything unsuitable in his conduct. He was only here thanks to her foolishness after all.

"There," he said, inspecting his handiwork. "It's a bad bruise but luckily not a deep cut and has stopped bleeding already."

She looked down at him gratefully but with considerable agitation. Only moments ago she had flung herself into his arms in her terror, knowing that she would be safe there, feeling for him a trust she had no way of knowing that he deserved. She had no good reason to trust him; she had only just met him. Yet the primitive impulse to run and shelter in his arms had been overwhelming.

Even in the hour before dawn and after a sleepless night, Moidart was a handsome man, she was thinking. Trying not to be caught staring, she looked at the dark, ruffled hair of his head bending over her ankle, and her eyes slid down to his strong neck and shoulders, clearly visible where his dressing gown fell open. She looked away quickly, her senses alert and stirred by his closeness. In trepidation, she wondered what words she would find to explain the scene if Mrs. Fraser were, belatedly, to come to her aid. The sight of a man in his dressing robe giving intimate attentions to a girl with her nightgown up to her knees in the middle of the night would be enough to ruin her for life, however unblemished her reputation had been.

She cast an anxious glance at the door, ensuring that it was indeed fully closed, and her gaze was drawn inexorably back to the man before her. She had never seen a nearly naked man so close to her before, though the male anatomy held no secrets for her. She had often watched her brother Rupert and his friends swimming naked in the mill pool on the Home Farm in Suffolk, until her governess, laughing with mock reproof, had dragged her away.

Those shouting, splashing, fair and slender youths had not struck her as looking physically much different from herself, and she had been only mildly intrigued to note the differences in structure. But this dark male body in front of her was a magnet to her eyes. This body, she concluded, was far more like the idealised and gracefully masculine sculpture she had glanced at slantingly in the park. The sleek, strong muscles of the hero Achilles, lounging naked but for a classical vine leaf hastily added to preserve decorum, had turned many a female head and raised many a gasp. She felt a strong urge to reach out and touch Moidart's firm flesh, to slide her hands under his velvet robe and caress his strong shoulders. Had he noticed her slight shudder?

"You are cold, Elinor," he commented. "I have finished now. You have been a good patient!" He tweaked her big toe in a friendly way and pulled down her nightgown. "Now, back to bed for a few more hours. Tibbie will attend you at eight o'clock. Your new friend the owl will have gone away to his roost, I'm thinking. I've heard nothing from him for a while now, but just in case he makes another appearance at your window, I'll close it, all but an inch or so."

He arranged the window to his satisfaction and returned to Nell who was standing forlornly at the foot of her bed, the intimate spell of the last few minutes broken. Sensing her uncertainty, he paused on his way to the door and came to stand by her, looking down at her but not touching her. "Will you be all right now, your ladyship? You're looking a little pale..."

The gentleness of his enquiry, on top of the terror of the past half hour and the sense of her isolation in hostile surroundings, pushed her over an emotional precipice, and to her own alarm, tears began to roll down her face. "...not to go," she heard herself saying indistinctly, "don't want you to go for a while, Moidart...please, will you not...oh!"

The words were hardly uttered when she found herself enveloped in a tight embrace, almost lifting her off her feet, and a strained voice whispered in her ear, "Do you imagine I want to leave you, lass? I've been awake all night thinking of you with fire in my veins! I've been thinking of the speeches I'd make, the things I would do if you were not the heiress you are. If you had been the servant girl I took you for when I first caught sight of you struggling with the coach horses, you would be in my bed warm and purring right now, and I wouldn't be wandering about at dawn shooing owls out of the ivy! But you are Lady Elinor Somersham and soon to be one of the richest women in the country and I may not touch you."

"But you are touching me, Moidart," she sniffed, snuggling into his armpit.

"Not as I want to touch you," he said grimly, "but it will have to suffice." Then brusquely, "You're shivering! Come, my lady, I will introduce you to an old Scottish custom!" He put an arm behind her knees and swept her up. A second later she had been flung back into her bed and he was stretching out his long length by her side.

"Moidart! What are you about? Go away, sir!" Nell's shaking voice betrayed her confusion. "You go too far!"

"Don't worry! I'm not about to harm your person or your reputation," he said reassuringly, eyes twinkling in the half light. "This is often done by the country folk in these parts. They call it bundling. If a girl cannot make up her mind about a fellow who fancies her, she might well consent to spend a night in the same bed with him—in all honour—and, by the morning, she has generally made up her mind one way or another. An essential ingredient of this process is this," he said, cheerfully tugging the bolster down between them. "The rules are simple—you must stay on your own side, but if hands or feet should happen to touch, that's all right. Though God knows why I torture myself like this!" he added ruefully.

He demonstrated by searching out her cold feet and enveloping them in his own. He took one of her hands in his and squeezed it gently. "There, you'll soon warm up now, and if there are any more unwanted visitors in the night, you have my sword arm at your service, my lady. Goodnight."

"Goodnight, Moidart. Thank you," she managed to whisper back.

She was unable to fall back into sleep, such was the agitation caused by his close presence. She had never slept with another person in her bed, let alone a strange and attractive man. She knew that what she was doing was wrong and that if it were ever generally known that she had slept alongside her cousin's steward, however innocently, she would no longer be able to take her place in English society. But London seemed suddenly so remote, and besides...who would ever know?

Still, she resolved to wake up early to remove all traces of his presence from her room. What would Mrs. Fraser think if she encountered the trail of devastation she had left behind her this evening—the abandoned hair ribbon, the overturned pot stand and its scattered cargo in the corridor outside her room, and, most telling of all for those with a speculative turn of mind, her bloodstained nightgown. Nell struggled to repress a hysterical giggle at the interpretation that might be put on events and felt lighthearted at the ease with which she was able to put all feelings of guilt and impropriety aside. This was Scotland after all, and she was heady with the excitement of the strangeness and informality she had encountered. Yes, Scotland suited her, she was thinking contentedly as she sighed and fell asleep, clutching a warm, work-roughened, and reassuring hand.

She was unaware that brown eyes were open for long after her sleepy sigh and searching her undefended features with hungry speculation.

She awoke to the clatter of a horse's hooves below and the chatter and subdued laughter of maidservants. She stretched lazily and then shot up in bed, patting the space beside her. She was alone. The bolster was on the floor, and the place where Moidart had lain was cold, the sheet smooth. She blushed to think that she had dreamed or imagined the scene in her bedroom that night, but raising her hands to rub her eyes, she found that she was still clutching a white owl's feather. She smiled with satisfaction and lay back on her pillows to indulge in the luxury of thinking about the dark Scotsman and his glowing words to her before he had swept her into bed.

He had made it perfectly clear that he found her attractive as a woman and yet had acknowledged that there was no possibility of a romantic relationship between them with a frankness that she found at once beguiling and frustrating. Analysing her own body's reactions to him, she admitted to herself that she had yearned for him to take her in his arms and make love to her with scant regard for the consequences. As long as she remained under the same roof as Moidart without the chaperonage of her ancient relative, she realised that she was in danger. In danger from her own unbridled behaviour and from her own forward rush towards him. The man had shown himself considerate and honourable, but could this state of affairs continue if they found themselves thrust into each other's company evening after evening? With her head, she looked forward to the return of her father's elusive cousin; with her heart...she hoped...that he might yet be delayed for a day. Or two.

With a sly smile, Nell conceded to herself that an enforced closeness was exactly what she desired. She wanted the man, and that was very plain to her. She would not deceive herself; that was what it amounted to—these strange feelings, the excitement of being close to him, hearing his voice: she was falling in love with him. "Choose—don't be chosen!"

Well, she had made her choice, and it was a cruel blow of fate that her choice was an impossible one.

Impossible? Never one to give up easily in anything, Nell thought hard, plotting and planning. She would have him, she concluded.

But how was this to be accomplished? So much depended on her obtaining her cousin's good will. She sighed at the difficulties of her situation. Now, if only she were Mrs. Roderick Lindsay, whose elderly husband was mouldering away a thousand miles distant from her, or Mrs. Henry Collingwood, rich, free, and left to her own devices while her husband soldiered in the Peninsula; then, she calculated, she could do as the titled, married ladies of her acquaintance all did and take a lover. Why not?

She thought with amusement of her neighbour in Suffolk, Lady Maria Lowestoft, who had three children—each of whom, it was suspected, with a different father. And the rumours surrounding Kitty Laidlaw and her son's tutor could not be ignored, though her husband gave every appearance of complacency. His attitude might well be one of indifference, however, Nell reasoned, when one counted the number of *his* mistresses! The rules of fidelity and propriety were much less rigid for women of her rank, particularly for those who had a great personal fortune and a puppet-like husband to give them countenance! They were beyond the opprobrium of the middle classes and would be judged by their own consciences alone. Discretion, for these ladies, took the place of morality, and all was permitted provided that open scandal was avoided. Recrimination, jealousy, and duelling were very much frowned on; so long as the surface of life was observed by all to be smooth, one could behave as one liked.

Well, once her marriage was assured, she would take Moidart as her lover, she mused, playing with the notion, as soon as she could get her affairs in order, but she was suddenly struck by an uncomfortable thought...This was not a stallion or a ram she was contemplating acquiring—would her chosen lover ever follow her to Suffolk? She thought of the uproar Moidart's swinging kilt and abrasive manners would create in her douce Palladian home. And how to explain to Henry the presence of a captive, wild Highlander at Somersham Hall? And to Kenton—'You will be retiring in a few years, Kenton, and, against the day, here is your replacement to train on." The imagined introductions and explanations made her begin to laugh at the ludicrous path her thoughts were taking.

More soberly, she recognised that whatever her feelings for Moidart, he was a man who would not survive transplanting from his native soil and, she suspected, a man who would never accept to become her lover, her dependent, in any way. And what was more, she admitted to herself, if—and Heaven forbid—she should choose the alternative of marriage with her cousin, her chances of persuading him to transfer the services of his steward to his new young wife were slender. Unless, of course, Lindsay was prepared to bargain with her. And bargain with her is what he would have to do—after all, she held the trump cards in this game, did she not? She held what he wanted above all: the title to these lands. Perhaps, if she had judged his character aright, he might well be manoeuvred into entering Moidart into the balance?

She began cheerfully to practise her speech to her guardian when he should return. And when would that be? She wondered. She must question Moidart more closely on his master's movements. A few minutes alone with her guardian could well change her prospects completely.

6

Nell was still smiling with pleasure at the plan she had just made when she heard a clatter along the corridor and her door was flung open by Tibbie to admit Lucy, clad in the dark green dress of the Lindsay household and proudly bearing a breakfast tray, just as if they had been in Park Lane.

"Lucy!" Nell exclaimed in delight to see her maid. "But what are you doing? I thought you were to stay abed for a day or two?"

"Nothing would keep her in bed a minute longer, ma'am," said Tibbie, grinning. "I think you'll find she's as good as new, but we've put a bandage on the ankle just to be on the safe side." She bobbed and left the room.

Nell jumped out of bed in a flurry of lawn and with an indecorous display of bare leg and took the tray from Lucy's hands. She was glad not only to see her maid again but also to be spared the solemnities of breakfast in the great hall, warm and welcoming enough by candlelight and firelight but bleak perhaps in the cold light of an autumn morning.

"Well, you were right about the porridge, Miss Nell! Are you really going to eat all this?" said Lucy, dubiously eyeing the contents of the tray. "And these things—oat cakes they call them—are a bit gritty. No wonder these Scots girls have such bad teeth! But the bread's fresh made and the coffee's as good as at home, and under this cover are smoked haddock—haddies, they call them." She shook her head indulgently.

Lucy had hardly set the tray down before she began to chatter. She chattered about Mrs. Fraser and how kind she had been. She chattered about the other girls and how difficult they were to understand and how impressed they had been by her London ways and her society stories. She was obviously enjoying her role of the London sophisticate amongst these northern barbarians. Not, it would seem, that they *were* barbarians, as they had extended a warm welcome to Lucy. As her brimming account drew to its close, she recollected herself and said, "Oh, and I was to say, 'Would the lady care for her steward to show her around the castle after breakfast? Mr. Moidart will attend her in the parlour.' They've washed and dried your russet travelling dress and your petticoats, Miss Nell. Will you put them on?"

Nell smiled to herself, pleased at the thought of spending the morning with Moidart and poked about on her breakfast tray, trying a little of each of the dishes presented, declaring the porridge tolerable but the haddies delicious. She drank up her coffee and bounced happily out of bed to prepare for her day. Delighted to see the overnight change in her mistress's mood, Lucy busied about brushing her hair until it flowed like a golden waterfall over the shoulders of her chestnut tunic and finally was satisfied that Nell was suitably prepared to make her appearance before the Scottish household.

"You may take away the tray Lucy, and then inform Moidart that I will join him in the parlour directly."

When Lucy had hurried out, Nell loitered for a moment in her room, suddenly nervous at the thought of encountering Rorie Moidart again. Last evening all had been moonshine, romantic rescue, claret, and candlelight. In this crisp autumn morning, perhaps her steward would appear no more than that—simply her Scottish steward. He had invited her, very properly, to inspect the castle. Her castle. Would he be able to put out of his mind the kiss he had forced upon her last evening, the bed they had shared in the grey dawn? She was not certain that she could. Telling herself that she should be prepared to find him completely impersonal, businesslike, and even dull, she ventured out of her room and along the corridor.

She noted, with a guilty smile as she passed, that the plant holder had been put back in place and the broken pottery swept up. She paused by the door through which she remembered he had come to her aid in the night. It was ajar. On an impulse, she stood still and listened, her senses alert. Domestic noises, the laughter of maids, the rattle of cutlery downstairs—but on that corridor there was no sign of movement.

Impelled by curiosity, she pushed the door open a little further and, driven to find some indication of the kind of man he might be, she told herself that if she were to spend the coming days in his close companionship, she ought, sensibly, to attempt to discover as much as she could about his character and preferences. To her surprise, the door creaked open on a short flight of stairs leading to a further door.

Somewhat wondering at her effrontery, Nell quickly mounted the flight of shallow, rough steps and looked about her. It was clear that she had now passed into an older part of the castle, or at least, a part of the castle that had not been improved. Walls were in rough, unplastered stone; doorways were low. The floor was flagged in stone. Ahead of her was another deeply embrasured window—an arrowslit, no less. On her right was a door uncompromisingly shut, but to her left was a door ajar. She pushed it open with her foot, glancing anxiously over her shoulder as she did so, eager not to be caught prying.

The room into which she looked was square and vaulted, a ribbed and domed ceiling rose above her. The walls were roughly plastered and had been lime-washed many times, so many times that their outline was blurred, giving the space a warmth and an informality. Ahead of her was a transomed and mullioned leaded window with massive oak shutters, which must surely have dated from the earliest time of the castle. There were, obviously, corner turrets, approached from the room, each designed to give an all-round field of fire to defending bowmen.

Looking further about the room, she saw a fine fireplace in which the pine logs of yesterday's fire still smouldered on a mound of white ash. A picture hung above, a picture of two children standing hand in hand in a formal pose, painted in a conventional way by a not greatly skilled hand, but in spite of its shortcomings, Nell couldn't help smiling back at the two little figures, wondering who they were, wondering what moment in their lives the painter had caught, and wondering, indeed, how this picture came to be in Moidart's room.

Catching sight of a desk under the window, Nell advanced on it, her attention drawn by a muddled pile of papers. Pretending to herself that she was not doing so, she glanced surreptitiously at the sheets. To her surprise, the shortness and spacing of the lines written there showed, it seemed, that what Moidart did when he was alone was write poetry.

Poetry? Much intrigued, Nell decided to investigate further. She stepped quickly back to the door and propped it open, the better to hear the sound of anyone approaching and as a signal to any upstairs maid busying about her duties that Nell's occupation of the room was above board and fleeting.

The handwriting was neat and well formed but clotted with crossings out, interpolations, and corrections. Muttering to herself, Nell managed to make out three verses of four lines each and a chorus under the title of "MacLean's Welcome." The words were largely English. Squiggles of a musical notation in a strip along the bottom of the page gave her the clue that this was a song she was looking at—a song in midcomposition.

Nell could play and sing many old Scottish folk songs, learned from her grandmother Alice, but this one was unknown to her. She hummed the musical notes, finding there not the rousing marching song she had expected but a dancing tune, lilting and repetitive. She tried linking it with the words of the chorus:

> Come o'er the stream, Charlie, dear Charlie, brave Charlie.
> Come o'er the stream, Charlie and dine with MacLean.
> And though you be weary we'll make your heart cheery
> And welcome our Charlie and his loyal train.

Ah. Well, this cleared up a question she had asked herself regarding the author. Moidart was a Jacobite sympathiser. A Scottish rebel. A wearer of the White Rose. The sworn enemy of all things English. A deluded supporter of the Bonny Prince Charlie, who had "crossed the stream" from France and landed in Scotland, bringing down devastation on both countries.

Nell, with her mixture of Scottish and English blood, had made it her business to learn a good deal about the disastrous wars of the previous century. Her grandmother, a child at the time, had, indeed, been sent south to London to escape the uncertainties and slaughter of the rebellion of 1745. Whenever the old lady had spoken of the doomed attempt by Charles Stuart to seize the throne of the two kingdoms, Nell noted that the bare facts of the story, plainly and truthfully told, were always accompanied by a trickle of tears down the powdered cheeks.

One day when Nell, with her pragmatic sense and reliance on figures, had sought to establish the strength of the English victory at Culloden, she had asked how many men had fallen. The answer came at once: "English redcoats fighting with cannon and musket for King George: one thousand dead. Scotsmen fighting in their shirts with claymore and fist for the Bonny Prince: ten thousand dead."

"Hurrah for England!" the young Nell had exclaimed without thinking.

"Ten thousand brave Highlanders," Alice had murmured. "Loyal to the last man. Shot to pieces and left to rot in the heather." She had burst into sobs and run from the room, leaving behind her a very puzzled child.

Anxiously, Nell read on through a piece of writing that in an earlier—and not that much earlier—age would have condemned its author to execution at the Tower of London.

We'll bring down the red deer, we'll bring down the black steer,
The lamb from the breckan and doe from the glen.
The salt sea we'll harry and bring to our Charlie
The cream from the bothy and curd from the pen.

And you shall drink freely the dews of Glen Sheerly
That stream in the starlight when kings dinna ken

And deep be your need of the wine that is red
To drink to your Sire and his friend MacLean.

MacLean, whoever he was, was extending a fine welcome to the Pretender, most probably on the eve of battle. The best the country hereabouts could provide: venison, beef, fish, and cream were on the menu. And all washed down with the finest of spirits. She savoured again the mention of red wine and the mysterious "dews of Glen Sheerly." An elegant reference no doubt to the strong spirit these Scots seemed to conjure up from the very peat bogs they walked upon.

But it was the third verse that arrested her attention and caused her to bite back a cry of dismay.

Our heath-bells shall trace you the maids to embrace you
And deck your blue bonnet wi' flowers o' the brae.
And the loveliest Mari in all of Glen Garry
Shall lie in your bosom till break of the day.

"Oh, Mari, my love!" Nell whispered with the sudden fellow feeling of one who'd lain in a Jacobite bosom only the previous night. "God bless you!"

Behind her a floorboard creaked and a cough, quietly accusing, came from the doorway.

"So your ladyship has decided to start her tour of the castle here?" said an ironic voice behind her.

With a supreme effort, Nell hid her surprise, turning to the light from the window, the better to pretend to read the sheet of paper in her hand.

"You must allow me to show you the library, milady. If you are thirsting for a book to read, you need not be reduced to scavenging from your steward's desk."

She flushed with shame and, goaded by his tone of mock servility, stuck her chin in the air and replied haughtily, "I accept your kind offer—I should not wish, during my stay, to confine myself to the perusal of sentimental doggerel! *Cheery, weary, red deer, black steer,* indeed! Who can be the author of such repetitious versification? Too simple for such a mind as yours, I'm guessing, Moidart."

"You see nothing of value there?" he asked coldly.

"Oh, don't misunderstand me—I was struck by its voluptuous barbarity! Indeed, it might be taken for a passage from Homer's *Iliad*. Who, pray, was the MacLean who offers these Highland delights? A man who could have dealt on equal terms with any of the ancient Greek chieftains: Agamemnon, Menelaus, or Nestor! 'You're welcome to our hearth with meat and drink and the finest of our maidens to keep you warm.' I had not prepared myself for a stay in a country that celebrates a pagan culture three thousand years old."

He sighed. "A simple man, but well educated, a friend of mine, is a shepherd from Ettrick in the Borders. He had the fine notion of collecting together all the ancient Gaelic songs he could find from those who still remember—and sing—them and publishing them in a book. He has asked his friends to translate them into English. The sheet you are holding in your hand is my attempt at one of them."

Nell was ashamed of her outburst. "A commendable endeavour. I wish your friend well of it," she murmured. "What became of him? No, not Charlie! The Bonny Prince scrupled not to duck off back to Europe choosing inglorious exile above loyalty in defeat. He proved unworthy of his followers. I enquire after the so-generous MacLean who was gulled into supporting him?"

His eyes darkened. "The last verse will answer that I'm afraid," he said, and he growled out from memory:

> If aught will invite you or more will delight you
> 'Tis ready a troop of our bold Highland men
> Shall range on the heather with bonnet and feather
> Strong arms and broad claymores three hundred and ten.

"Maclean and his men fought bravely...In the front line at Culloden," he finished.

Nell had listened to his words, enchanted but sorrowful. No further explanation was needed. Clan MacLean had feasted its last, and she held in her hand the record of its final flourish. With the knowledge, the three simple verses had taken on the grandeur of Prince Henry's speech before Agincourt. "Perhaps it is my English voice that reduces the quality of the verse," she whispered. "I find I can hear its beauty when you speak the lines, Moidart."

He eyed her, on the watch for the slightest flicker of cynicism and, seeing none, conceded, "Aye, ye're right."

He recollected himself and began to speak in formal tones. "And now, as you seem to have started the tour without me, perhaps I can catch up with you. This is, as you see, one of the turrets of the oldest part of the castle..."

Nell was listening to his discourse on the origins of the castle, its defences and the sieges it had withstood, while attempting to hide the attention she was giving to him. His abrupt appearance in the room had disconcerted her, and she was unaccountably saddened that he had swung back into his attitude of barely concealed resentment combined with a spurious show of deference. Here was a man, she was convinced, who had never deferred to anyone in his life. His smooth tongue called her milady, but the bold insouciance of his eyes contradicted any impression of respect. The man himself, she was alarmed to register, was as handsome in the broad daylight as she had supposed him to be in the evening light. His tall figure appeared to advantage in what she assumed to be his working clothes—riding breeches and shiny black boots, white shirt, and jacket of grey duffel. Her eyes slid up from his muscular legs, narrow waist, and broad shoulders to fix on the smooth brown skin of his throat. He had stopped talking and was looking at her enquiringly. "I see I am boring her ladyship."

She looked away quickly. "No, no! Not at all, Moidart. It is just that...I am...I was..." How could she explain that she had been lulled and fascinated by the sound of his low voice, drawn magnetically to watch him as he moved around the room? Angry with herself for her unaccountable loss of poise, she turned and walked to the window, leaving her sentence unfinished.

"Ah, yes, of course, Lady Elinor. You are perhaps trying to tell me that it is less than seemly for us to spend so much of our time in each other's bedchambers?"

His voice was teasing, but nonetheless she blushed furiously, swallowed, and said stiffly, "If you are ready, Moidart, we will proceed with the inspection."

"Very well. If I had known that an *inspection*," he repeated the word carefully, "is what we were about, I would have had all the servants parade for you in their Sunday best, the silver polished and the horses' tails plaited..." He froze as he caught the full force of her scornful gaze.

"Do you imagine I would be taken in by such devices?" Her words were cold. "Half an hour with your books in the business room will tell me all I need to know about the running of these estates. But I will postpone that pleasure until last. Shall we proceed?"

"Indeed. I suppose you have inspected possibly the least interesting room in the castle, and if you would now like to look further?" He bowed by the door, and Nell preceded him onto the landing. At once he opened the opposite door and, to Nell's considerable surprise, she found herself in the open air, on a walkway behind the battlements of the castle and at the foot of a little winding stair leading upwards.

"While we're here," said Moidart, "we might as well start our visit from the top. This, after all, in ancient days, was where a lookout sentry would have been permanently posted and, indeed, the field of vision is good. No one in all its history ever took the House of Lindsay by surprise, and here"—he pointed to an iron basket perched on the battlement's edge—"is a cresset where, in times of trouble, a fire would burn to warn the surrounding people of raiders."

Nell leant her elbows on the rough parapet and gazed down the full length of the loch, her eye travelling the circling hills and turning about to look towards the wood in which she had first encountered this strange, poetry reading man who chose to hang in his bedroom a picture of two long-forgotten children.

"If your ladyship can manage this narrow stair," he said, "we could return by the west tower. This was the keep of the castle, but there's nothing left now but the encircling walls—the roof fell in many years ago, and the floors followed."

They stepped out onto the battlemented walk, encircling the now-ruined keep, and Nell looked down, and down. The floors had gone, but fireplaces and windows remained. It was a mysterious place—perhaps even a haunted place. Nell shivered a little and looked up to see Moidart eyeing her closely.

"You feel it too, do you?" he asked. "Not everybody does, but perhaps I may say it, the brightest do. It's an uncommonly dreary bit, is it not? The floors have gone, but it's never empty of folk, so it seems to me..."

"And to me too," said Nell. And then, hesitating she added, "I could almost imagine I saw people down there..."

"You're not the first to say it! But come—there are better parts of the castle than this old pit to be looking into. Let me show you some other things."

Nell was glad to leave the ruin of the keep and to follow Moidart down a narrow staircase to a further battlemented wall, under a small archway in a defensive turret, and, to her total surprise, into a small garden. Her gasp of astonishment was so complete that Moidart began to laugh. "I didn't do this on purpose," he said. "But perhaps that's a good way of showing you. Your great grandmother was not well at all towards the end of her life and could not get out of the castle easily. Her husband, John Lindsay, made her this little rose garden, where it would always be warm and where she could sit in shelter even when it was raining. They say the roses do better here than anywhere. And there's hardly a time of year when there's not something blooming. But that's always the way when a garden is planted with love."

He stopped abruptly and laughed self-consciously, adding roughly, "It would probably mean very little to one used to the fine gardens of England."

"It means a very great deal to me," said Nell sincerely. She was quite conscious of her great-grandfather and of the act of love it had been to create this garden for a wife whose closing years had been illuminated by it. Absent-mindedly, she picked a small white rose and, hardly aware of what she was doing, tucked it into the neck of her blouse. Moidart contemplated her for a second, a wry smile on his face and his eye, it seemed to Nell, shining with humour.

Both became embarrassed by the silence that had fallen between them, and he shook himself and said, "Let me lead on. Perhaps that is enough of ancient days. If we go through this door, we find our-selves back in what I may think of as the more civilised parts of the castle."

"Don't mistake me," said Nell, "I think it is wonderful, what we have seen."

In silence, he led the way down to open a small door, which, to Nell's further surprise, opened onto a wide passage. "It seems I never know what I am going to find behind a closed door," she murmured. They were in a wide corridor with golden pine floor boarding, panelling to the ceiling painted pale green, and a long line of sash windows through which the panorama of the hills continually unfolded. Each pair of win-dows was separated by a portrait and, as they walked, Moidart explained each painting for her.

"This was Mary Cameron. She married Douglas Lindsay in 1562. This was his son, who took a ship to sea in the time of the Armada. This is a cousin, Lindsay of the Hill, who was killed at Sherrifmuir. Not killed by the English, you understand, but killed by a canon exploding. This is Helen Lindsay, 'Virtuous Helen' they called her to distinguish her from her sister. And this is she—sister Margaret, who, they say, was the original 'Muckle-Mouthed Meg' in the Burns poem, though, of course, you would not recognise it as a poem!"

He stopped in front of a portrait of a handsome but stern-faced man in a powdered wig. The dark figure was wearing, she noticed, a large emerald ring on his finger. Moidart's eyes narrowed with dislike. "Your great-grandfather, John Lindsay," he announced briefly and moved on without further comment.

"And who is this beautiful girl?" asked Nell moving on quickly to the next painting. "Could it be?" Startled, she peered closely at the formal portrait of a fair-haired, grey-eyed girl, smiling shyly at the painter, her slight figure tightly corseted and clad in powder blue velvet.

"Yes, indeed," he laughed down at her. 'Tis as though you were looking in a mirror, Lady Elinor! That is your grandmother Alice. And no wonder that I thought I already knew you when I met you on the road yesterday!" Allowing her time to absorb the painting and to feel, for the first time, that she did have some connection with this foreign place, he moved on.

"And this is the prize of our collection—this is a glove left behind by the Young Pretender at the time of the Forty-five. He must have been a man with many gloves, as there's hardly a house in Scotland that has not got one of them if we are to believe all the legends!"

"Tell me something, Moidart," said Nell. "With all the resources of the house, it seems, to choose from, what made you choose the painting of the two small children hanging in your room? Who were they?"

"Who were they? I don't know who they were. I found the portrait in the attic. It's not very much, I know, but there's something about them... I never had any brothers or sisters and always wished I had, and sometimes I used to pretend they were my family. In this old house, you need a bit of young company."

They walked the length of the long gallery and, taking a turn, proceeded down a further reach of the castle. On this side, the view was across the loch. One by one, Moidart opened doors and showed her the interiors. "These are the company rooms," he said. "They are very little used now, but ready when needed. Perhaps the appointments seem spartan to your ladyship, but that's the way it is in Scotland."

Once again, Nell said, "I think they are all beautiful, each more beautiful than the last, and truly, would not any room be perfect where you could see down the loch and over the hills?"

"So it has always seemed to me," said Moidart.

Their way led them onwards and into disused lumber rooms with ancient furniture, even with a suit of armour, and with a basketwork cradle suspended on a sling. Moidart paused by this and thoughtfully set it swinging. "No child has been born in the House of Lindsay this many long year," he said, shaking his head.

Nell made no comment and followed him onwards and down to the main rooms of the castle, through the familiar great hall, into the library where Nell ostentatiously chose a book of Wordsworth's poems, past the great staircase, and out into the endless kitchen quarters. They proceeded up a little flight of stairs to a dormitory under the roof—"Servants' accommodations," Moidart explained—and out to a further battlement and to a cooing dovecote.

"We have fan-tailed pigeons at Somersham," said Nell, reacting as to an old friend to the gentle cooing.

"We can't afford fan-tails," said Moidart, "they don't make good eating. These are the common cushat of the Highlands, and we'll see if we can put a cushat pie before you while you are here. With some mushrooms off the hill and perhaps a little bacon, it is as fine as anything you can find."

As they walked back through the kitchen, they encountered Tibbie, tray in her hand, with a silver coffee pot and its accompanying silver jug, basin, and cups. Awkwardly, she bobbed a curtsy behind her burden and said, "Mrs. Fraser said to be putting the coffee in the business room to recover her ladyship after traipsing through the corners of the castle."

"And to fortify her ladyship for her inspection of the accounts," he said grimly. "Thank you, Tibbie." He relieved her of the tray and led the way into the business room.

The square, book-lined room, with its one comfortable chair before the fireplace, was neat and uncluttered. Moidart set the tray down and pulled a straight-backed chair forward for Nell, who was glad enough to sit down after her tour. She looked about her with interest at the central writing table, covered as it was with dockets neatly tied with pink tape. She looked also at an enormous estate map hanging on the wall and noted various alterations that had been inserted in a neat hand. Moidart politely put a cup of coffee at her elbow and went himself to sit in the large armchair by the fire, settling his outstretched feet on a stool. Linking his fingers behind his head, he settled lazily to watch her as she looked about the room. She was inspecting his stewardship of her affairs, was she not, so why, she wondered, did she have an uneasy feeling that she herself was under inspection?

A line of leather-bound account books with marbled covers and each with a date in gold stamped on its spine took Nell's eye. "Do you mind?"

she asked, reaching out a hand for the last of these with its emblazoned date of 1814.

"No. No, indeed," said Moidart, somewhat surprised, "Who, after all, has better right than yourself? If, of course, you understand such things..."

Nell drew the heavy volume down and sat with it in her lap, noting that on one side it recorded monthly expenditures and on the other monthly receipts. She compared with something between pity and amusement the monthly rents on the Lindsay estate with the monthly rates she remembered from Somersham. She noticed a croft called Cros na Buckie and the tenant, Alexander Neal (younger); his monthly rent was four shillings. "A shilling a week," she thought, "that's probably a lot of money for these people."

On the line below, she read "Glen Foot" Andrew Baird—two shillings and, in the margin—"Remitted." Interested, she turned back a month and saw again "Andrew Baird—two shillings, Remitted." Running her eye down the expenditures column, she noted that ten pounds and fifteen pence had been spent on rebuilding Andrew Baird's chimney stack, with a little note in brackets following this—"October gale."

From time to time, she noted the considerable income from stock sales, from wool sales, even occasionally from the sale of venison. Completely absorbed, her coffee growing cold beside her, she read on, caught up in the world of frugal and, at times, fragile husbandry. From the stillness in the room, she became aware that Moidart was leaning forward and watching her intently. "I'm sorry," she said, "I do not know where are my manners! I became so interested..."

"Interested? Do these dry, dusty bones interest you?"

"Oh, yes, yes indeed," said Nell. "I am familiar with all the accounting procedures at Somersham. Kenton, my steward, taught me a lot. I have always been interested in such things. And they are not dry! Oh no, they tell a story..."

"What do they tell you?" he asked, a defensive shutter falling over his eyes.

"They tell me that my estates are being run efficiently but hardly profitably by a romantic, who has, apparently, a head for figures."

He inclined his head with a slight smile. "Thank you for the compliment, your ladyship. My professor of mathematics at Edinburgh would be gratified to hear your praise."

She blushed at the jibe but continued, "What is Andrew Baird's problem? The man would seem to have been something of a burden on the estate for quite a while..."

"Ah, there! So you have rootled out that one! Poor Andrew broke his leg last June. It has set badly, which is an inconvenience for a shepherd as I think you would agree, and he has a wife and four bairns. What would you have me do? Put him out? Put the family on the next ship for the Americas?" he asked coldly.

"Certainly not. You must fetch a doctor to treat him, and then you must give him work to do off the mountains, in the folds, until he is healed."

"In the folds?" he said, mystified. "Our Scottish sheep live out on the hill all year round."

"Then that explains it," she said and waited for his enquiry. As he continued to look at her with mistrust, she went on cheerfully, "I have been examining the figures for the sale of wool. Your income from the sale of wool is high, but comparing the price of raw wool with the numbers of sheep kept on the estate, I see that the price for each sheep is low—much lower than it would be for our Suffolk sheep. Also, it appears that you lose many ewes at the lambing season—I assume because they are kept out on the hill? Kenton has, for the past few years, taken to folding the ewes for the lambing, and we find that we have far fewer losses. My advice would be to acquire a better quality of sheep—I can have sent up a pair of my prize rams from Suffolk to improve your native stock—and make much better efforts to pen the sheep at lambing time."

Seeing his surprised approval, she said defensively, "I would be ashamed to take all this for granted and not to understand the foundations. I am not just a society Miss, you know!"

"You are full of surprises, Lady Elinor," said Moidart, rising to his feet to bow formally. "There are some old things that might interest you," he said, taking a bundle of papers from a shelf. One by one, he began to put before her tenancy agreements, each with the Lindsay seal in the corner—Patents of Arms with their gay heraldry, maps and plans delineating boundary agreements, all in the most meticulous order, and finally, on parchment sealed with the Royal Arms of Scotland, a summons to the Lindsay of the day to join the Young Pretender, dated Glenfinnan 1745.

"What happened to him?" asked Nell.

Moidart laughed. "Well, luckily, of the two brothers Lindsay, one joined the Prince and one stayed at home. For the first time, perhaps, in the history of the family, they had a foot in both camps, and Lindsay survived."

"What happened to the boy who joined the Prince?" she could not help asking.

"Culloden," said Moidart. "He didn't survive Culloden."

"He does not add," thought Nell bitterly, "'slaughtered by the English,' but I know that is what he is thinking."

It would have seemed petty of her to remind him that he was speaking of her ancestor. He seemed to identify her so fully with the despised English side of her family. She sighed. This morning had not gone well. She was not entirely sure what she had been expecting, but this cold, ironic formality was hard to bear. She was beginning to imagine that she had, after all, dreamed the closeness and the excitement of the previous evening.

In an attempt to say something flattering about the estate and fearing that she might have insulted him on the subject of the wool sales, she drew his attention to a pile of tenancy agreements, all duly signed by a variety of tenants from the humblest shilling a week shepherd to the grander five pounds a week tacksman. "Explain this to me, Moidart," she said with a puzzled smile. "Every one of these agreements is signed and annotated in the most beautiful, flowing copperplate handwriting. Now, in Suffolk, you would find that more than half of such documents would be signed by a cross, for the humbler tenants cannot write."

"Then 'tis a shame on you and your English system," he said roundly. "Here all children in the village go to the Parish school and receive a good education. The Laird's son sits on a form with the shepherd's son, and they learn together. The brighter ones can go on to grammar school and then on to university in Edinburgh, which is accounted among the finest in the world. You probably do not know that half your doctors and scientists in England are Scots. And it is Scots who are running many of the armies of Europe, good fighters that they are!"

"I should like to meet some of my tenants and herdsmen," she said thoughtfully.

"Aye, and they will be very curious to meet you, my lady. We will start tomorrow. You are acquainted now with your castle; you must begin to get to know your lands."

A light tap at the door interrupted further plans as Tibbie entered. "Moidart, your horse is ready, Coll says, and Jenny has prepared a bite to eat in the kitchen before you leave; begging your pardon, my lady." She bobbed, gathered up the coffee tray, and left.

Before she could stop herself, Elinor had burst out with a disappointment that was audible even to her own ears, "You are leaving, Moidart?"

He turned to her with a questioning smile playing on his lips. "I am sorry, I forgot that I must now ask your ladyship's permission to absent myself," he said provokingly. "I have a business meeting in Callander. As a magistrate, it is my duty to take my turn to act as Judge's Marshal in the Quarterly Assize. I usually stay overnight with my friend Doctor Jameson, but as the owls are being a particular nuisance here, I shall make my excuses and return tonight...in case I am needed," he added. "Can it be that you do not wish me to go?" he asked, moving over to her and looking intently into her eyes.

"Not at all," she said, recovering herself. "I had not realised that you were such an important personage in this part of the country. Of course you must do your duty. And pray do not concern yourself for me, Moidart. I shall sleep well tonight, and undisturbed."

"All the same," he said thoughtfully, "I shall not leave you unattended."

He opened the door and leaned outside. Nell heard a sharp whistle and, a moment later, the hound came slipping and sliding into the room. Moidart spoke crisply to the dog in Gaelic and pointed at Nell. "There. You have your companion now, Lady Elinor. Lupus will not leave your side until I return."

Nell looked down dubiously at the dog, wondering if this was the good idea Moidart seemed to think it was. She could have sworn that the dog was equally uneasy with its task, but nevertheless, it settled down grumpily by her right foot and, licking its lips, whined pathetically at its master. Such was the dejection in its eyes that they both burst out laughing.

"I fear I am being a great nuisance to the whole household," said Nell.

"Nay, lass, never think it!" he said surprisingly and, taking a step closer, lifted her hand and kissed it. Feeling her fingers tremble at his touch and seeing the smile fade from her face, he gathered her into his arms with a sigh and gently touched her lips with his.

"Two and a half hours," he murmured. "I have been within kissing distance of you for two and a half hours and have not touched you. Am I not a good and self-sacrificing steward?"

As she made no attempt to pull away from him but stayed quietly in his arms, his next kiss was more serious and left her trembling and yearning for—she hardly knew what—for his closeness, for his warmth, for his continued presence. She knew with a clear certainty that she did not want him to leave her side even for the half of a day.

Gently he held her away from him and looked at her steadily. "I shall hasten back, never fear. Ask for anything you want or need. Remember, you are at home here." And, with a warning word to Lupus, he was gone.

Nell felt for the dog as it scurried to the closed door and sniffed underneath, whimpering and listening to the retreating footsteps, and then ran back to her, pleading for the door to be opened. Hardening her heart, she waited for several minutes to allow Moidart to ride clear of the castle before leaving the business room and taking the staircase to her bedroom. The dog shadowed her and, to her amusement, settled down in front of the fire, looking up and watching her with sad but alert eyes every time she moved about the room.

"Lupus, I don't know which of us is keeping guard on the other, but perhaps we should both break out!" And, taking pity on him, she was just promising him a long walk across the hill to while away the afternoon when Tibbie tapped at the door and entered. She was grinning conspiratorially and holding out a small silver bowl of roses.

"Last of the summer, Miss," she said, placing them by the bedside. "Moidart said I was to pick only the white ones, seeing as how you liked them so much."

7

Nell woke the next morning to find the door ajar and the dog gone from his post at her threshold. She assumed with a smile of pleasure that Moidart must have returned and called his dog off duty. Her five-mile tramp through the sodden heather with Lupus streaming ahead like the wind had left her exhausted, and after an early supper, shadowed at every step by the hound, she had gone up to her room, where she had fallen into a deep and undisturbed sleep.

She stretched pleasurably in anticipation of her day. He had said that they would ride out together to inspect her lands, and she acknowledged that her eagerness to do this stemmed largely from a desire to be at his side for as long as she could. She wanted to be near him, to hear his voice, share his thoughts, tease him, be annoyed by him. But where was this exciting urge going to lead her? Straight into the pit of iniquity, she told herself grimly. The Prayer Book warned her and other inexperienced maidens of the dangers of toying with the affections of men, who were, for the most part, like the Devil, a "roaring lion, seeking whom they might devour!" Would Moidart devour her if she did not take care? The thought made her shiver with anticipation.

Of the physical relationship between men and women, she knew rather more than most girls of her age and rank, since her old governess,

Thérèse de Bercy, was a French émigrée whose adored husband had died during the Revolution. Thérèse, with Gallic frankness, had not only passed on to Nell a grounding in the physical facts of love but had also given her a glimpse of the spiritual closeness that could and should exist between lovers.

Lovers? She savoured the word, saying it softly to herself. Was this what she wanted then—to be lovers? But it was not a simple physical attraction that drew her to him, and it was here, she acknowledged, that the danger truly lay. She was becoming fascinated by the whole man. She had never met his like before. He did not pretend to even a conventional veneer of good manners. He spoke his mind clearly, even when he knew she would not be pleased to hear his words. He treated her with considerable—and well deserved, she had to admit—rudeness one minute, only to be gentle and loving the next. And she found much in him to admire. Under the tough outer skin was a man who would defend his decision to go easy on his distressed tenants, who would sit wakeful in his room and write poetry, who would think of sending her a little bowl of white roses, though she decided, with a rueful smile, that the thought had not been without its thorns.

Her whirling thoughts came round full circle again, as they had a hundred times since she had met him, and still without resolution. The only thing of which she was certain was that she wanted the man and was determined to attach him to her by whatever means should come to hand. So—what was she to do? And the answer, the only one that occurred to her was, as always, be near him, seek him out, and the way forward would become apparent.

Hearing a clatter of dishes in the distance, Nell became suddenly acutely aware of how hungry she was feeling. She was relieved to hear Lucy's pert voice along the corridor and delighted to see her come through the door with a breakfast tray, laden as before.

"Message for you, Miss Nell," she said, "before I forget what it was...I was to say, 'Would the lady care to ride out the day? Mister Moidart has to ride to Achill (she stumbled over the unfamiliar word), and maybe you'd like to ride with him?' Mrs. Fraser has sorted out some clothes for you."

Tibbie bustled in close on her heels, arms full of clothes. A dark green riding habit, a cloak, a hat and several pairs of boots were carried in for her inspection.

Her breakfast disposed of, Nell jumped from her bed and ran to the window to look out over the loch and over the encircling hills and surrounding rolling moorland. Her eyes picked out the white walls of crofters' houses dotted here and there across the mountain slopes, each surrounded by small stone-walled fields, each with its attendant black cattle, and from the chimney stacks in the turf roofs of each a plume of smoke flattened by the wind. It was a peaceful scene and a busy one.

Turning to look in the other direction and down into the castle courtyard, she saw Coll emerge with two fine saddle horses, one black and one roan, and as she watched, she saw him fit a sidesaddle to the roan.

"Come on, Lucy! Obviously Moidart didn't expect no for an answer!"

"From all I hear," said Lucy, rolling her eyes suggestively, "the steward never expects no for an answer! He's no Mister Kenton, Miss Nell! He'll bear watching!"

Nell considered this for a moment and decided not to pursue the remark.

Washed and brushed, she dressed herself in her borrowed clothes and stood in front of the long mirror. As on her first evening, this morning's collection fitted surprisingly well, and she found she was satisfied with what she saw. She went to stand for a moment with Tibbie at her side looking down on the stable courtyard below. The scene had changed, and she smiled to see black head next to redhead, Moidart and Coll, adjusting the harnesses of the two horses. Not, perhaps, strapped up to the peak of Park perfection that Turvey would have demanded, but fine horses all the same—plenty of bone, Nell decided, and well coupled up. Just the horses for this country.

As she watched, from an open stable door a third horse was led out in the hands of a man so old, so bent, so crabwise in his gait and forming a contrast so marked with the vigorous men and horses that Nell was for a moment tempted to laugh. "Who's that, for goodness' sake?" she asked.

"Why, that," said Tibbie, "that would be auld Angus, if you please."

"And auld Angus—who's he?"

"Well, it was this way, milady. When Mr. John—that is John Lindsay the younger, you understand—came out in Forty-five—came out for the gude cause—auld Angus, him below that's now eighty-four, was just a wee lad. Fifteen, would he have been? And he like a little tyke that would run always at Mr. John's heel to do his bidding and the way people would laugh at the pair of them...But when Mr. John rode out to join Prince Charlie, he said, laughing of course, because that was his way, they say, 'Lock him up if you have to, but this is one time when wee Angus'll no follow me!'"

Aware that she had the full attention of her audience, Tibbie made a histrionic pause before resuming, wide-eyed, "And what did this wee Angus do? Why, he slipped away and wandered on in search of Mr. John and in search of the army. But he'd not catch him but on dark Culloden field." Her voice wavered for a moment, and Nell saw a tear gather in her eye.

"Good heavens," Nell thought. "This was seventy years ago! But to Tibbie it might have been last week!"

"And wha' did he find? The battle lost. But wee Angus searched the corpses where they lay thick on the field, and he found Mr. John there dead, his good broadsword in his hand! And the red soldiers caught wee Angus, and he lay two days with four wounds in him out in the cold, while the crows were hopping round him and with the foxes barking for two nights. But he strapped himself up and walked back to the house of Lindsay, hiding by day and crawling by night. And that was the first the gude folk knew for sure which way the battle went. He brought away Mr. John's ring—as a token like—and whiles the Laird will wear it to this day.

"The folk cared for him and hid him, but young though he was, he was a bent old man from that day, for the broken bones—ill-set—that was in it, though he's always had the touch with horses. The Laird gave him shelter and food and the wee room over the stable arch, 'for as long as he should need it, and Angus McColl shall ne'er lack for shelter while Lindsay has a roof over his head,' he said. And so it was and so it is and there he bides, God bless him!"

Nell looked from the eager face beside her to the bent figure below and felt a lump rise in her throat and knew a tear was in her eye.

"But there," said Tibbie practically, "he's a blithe man! Nothing whatever will fash him, as your ladyship will discover."

Thoughtfully, Nell made her way downstairs, and as she did so, words from one of her grandmother's songs came into her head:

> *On dark Culloden's field of gore, Hark! Hark!*
> *They cry, "Claymore! Claymore!"*
> *And bravely fight—they can nae more*
> *Than die for Royal Charlie.*

So, singing sadly to herself, she passed through the low arch and into the sunlit courtyard. She stood for a moment at the head of the steps, outlined against the darkness within, listening to the badinage between the three men: badinage in which Angus gave as good as he got. At Nell's appearance, he turned to face her and at once the toothless smile faded. He seemed to stagger and, for a moment, needed Moidart's steadying hand under his elbow. With his curious sideways walk he took two steps towards her, paused again, wiped his sleeve across his eyes, and reached to take Nell's hand between his.

"Gude sakes!" he said. "I thought it was the mistress come back to us! When you ride out on the hill, I think the folks will think the gude times is come again to see the mistress out and about!"

Moidart approached and looked at her, she really believed, with approval. "I thought," he said without preamble, "that you would like to look at this outlandish place where you have fetched up for yourself. I thought you would like to look at some of the people you've landed yourself with too. You may as well begin with Angus." He bent and strapped a pair of spurs round his boots, and with these jingling on the pavings, walked off to his horse, pulling a blue bonnet on his head as he went.

Angus brought the roan over for Nell and held it by the head while Coll, extending cupped hands, received her booted foot and swung her easily into the saddle. In silence, Moidart mounted the black horse, gathered up the rein, and, ducking under the low archway, clattered in the lead down the ramp to the bridge and along the causeway.

The wind stirred the surface of the loch, which broke in little waves on either side of their path until they joined the mountain track that led through a stand of rowan trees, blazing in autumn gold and crimson. Trails of mist still curled languorously at waist height over the flat meadows and marked the paths of the burns where they spilled down from the heather-covered hills.

The horses trotted on and upwards, Moidart in the lead and Coll on his pony bringing up the rear. As their way led out onto the hillside and without a further word to Nell, Moidart broke into a canter, and Nell urged her horse forward until she was riding at his side. The path led upwards on a stony track within low walls and to a stone-built, turf-roofed cabin with a flock of clamouring geese, and a wide-horned Highland cow with its hairy calf at heel gazed over the wall at their advance, blowing a disdainful welcome. At their approach, the half door of the cabin opened and three small kilted children ran out barefooted and bare-legged to greet them. Moidart reined in and addressed them cheerfully in Gaelic, and shyly they replied.

Wiping her hands on her apron, their mother appeared with a baby on her hip. She, it seemed, had a word or two of English, for Nell was able to hear that "Himself is away over the hill." Nell smiled down at the children and slowly they smiled back. She essayed a few words, but it was clear that they hardly understood what she was saying, and with a few more commonplace greetings, they went on their way. Nell had an impression of cheerful friendliness, hard work and rough comfort, independence and courage.

She said as much to Moidart. He looked at her searchingly, and at last he said, "Aye, it's a rough life, but it's a fine life. Things have changed since the Forty-five. The Lindsays no longer need—could no longer maintain—a clan of fighting men, which is what these people have been. They can't any longer, when things get hard, raid cattle from the Grahams. The Grahams can't any longer raid cattle from us. Peace on the border after perhaps a thousand years of bloodshed—I can't regret it—but whiles I fear for these people now, the old ways are gone."

Nell pondered this, and they rode on for a while in silence, passing other crofts as they made their way up the hillside, its mantle flaming purple heather. Distantly, the lowering Trossachs barred the horizon.

"Are you up to a breather across the hill?" asked Moidart. "The going's firm and the horses could do with it."

Not to be outdone, Nell banged her heel into the roan's flank, gathered him short by the head and spurted away, urging him on to gallop ahead across the hill.

"To the right," shouted Moidart, hastening in pursuit. "Bear away to the right a wee while!"

Nell did as he said, loving the thunder of drumming hooves, loving the muscular ripple of her horse's flank, and breathing with delight the cool wind and feeling the warm sunshine on her face.

Their way led upwards to a saddle in the hills, and here Moidart reined in his horse and looked down. "Look south," he said. "That's all Lindsay land as far as you can see. Look north—that is Achill Water, and beyond that we do not own."

Not for the first time, Nell was secretly amused by his possessive words—*we do not own.* But Moidart was shading his eyes ahead. "Do you see any difference," he said, "when you look back and when you look forward?"

Nell looked about her and, after a moment's reflection, said, "Yes. Why does nobody live the other side of Achill Water?"

He gave her a level glance and said at last, "Do you know what I mean by the Clearance? You don't? Black shame to those who have done it! With the breakup of the clans, many have cleared their land for sheep and dispossessed the men who used to fight for them! Even their own tacksmen are priced off land they have farmed for centuries! The Devil's work if ever I saw the Devil's work! Ten years ago, and I mind it well, that hill was as full of people as the hill behind us, and if you look you'll see from where the folk have gone."

Nell did look. The landscape was not, as she had supposed, empty. Here and there, roofless gable ends were to be seen, and she could also see evidence of stone walls having been thrown down. Evidence too, in the blackened ruins, of houses having been burned. Sheep there were in quantity, but cattle she could not see. "But...the people...where are the people? What happened to them?"

"Exiled," said Moidart grimly "Some here, some there. Driven out of their homes, most by force, by beatings and burnings. Some have wandered south, even into England, but for the most part, they have gone overseas, to Canada and to the Americas."

"And who has done this thing? And why?" asked Elinor, scarcely able to believe her ears and eyes.

"The why is more easily answered. For profit. Of course. The owners of the land see more profit from sheep than from men and, accordingly, they clear their lands of the inhabitants and bring in ever more sheep from the Cheviots. And who are they, these profiteers?" He paused for a moment, ordering his thoughts. "I'd like fine to say it was only the Incomers, the Englishmen and those who bought up the forfeited estates after the Forty-five, but there are chieftains too who have sold off their men and broken down their houses and shipped them like cattle overseas in coffin ships. An entire way of life has disappeared over thousands of miles of Scotland. So what was Clan friendship worth when it came to the pinch?"

He brooded on in silence before resuming his way, saying as he did so, "The Bridge of Achill. It's partly Lindsay responsibility and partly the responsibility of our new neighbour, an English Lord..." he could not keep the scorn from his voice, "who has never graced his estates with his presence. It was damaged last winter, and there's work to be done."

They trotted on downwards into the wind and towards a sturdy and graceful two-arched bridge, an open gate at either end. "Hounds?" asked Nell tentatively. "Do I hear hounds running? Would they be running the deer?"

Moidart stopped abruptly and cupped his ear with his hand, calling to Coll as he did so in Gaelic. Coll ranged up alongside, and both men gazed ahead in seemingly angry conference. "It's not the deer they're running, I'm afraid," said Moidart. "Not everybody agreed to leave their homes. Some hide up here and some there, and not a few on Lindsay land; they hunt them down..."

"*Hunt them?*" said Nell, much shocked. "Are you saying it's men they're hunting?"

"Men, women, boys...they're not choosy...and look there!"

Running over the hill came a small figure, perhaps half a mile away. Even at that distance, it could be seen that he was running desperately in the last stages of exhaustion and, as they watched, he fell, only to claw his way to his feet again and, despairingly, run on. As he rose to his feet, four horsemen appeared on the hilltop and faintly on the wind came a "View halloo!" Two great hounds ran before them.

"Come!" said Moidart, and swinging his horse round, he and Coll slithered and scrabbled in a rattling gallop down the hillside to the Bridge of Achill. Moidart leapt from his horse, threw the reins to Coll, and strode to the centre of the bridge. Nell ranged up, watching eagerly and with dismay.

"What will happen?" she said to Coll.

"They'll no cross the Achill burn while Moidart holds the bridge, that's for sure," he said grimly, and as he twitched his plaid to one side, she saw the dull gleam of a cairngorm in the hilt of a Highland dirk concealed amongst his clothes. Hardly realising what she was doing, Nell reversed her riding crop and gripped it firmly in her right hand as a weapon. A gleam of approval from Coll was her reward. "I see you're ready to stand with us," he said with a fierce laugh. "Three of us and four of them, they'll maybe find the last battle on Achill Bridge has not yet been fought!"

By now, the fugitive could be plainly seen. He was little more than a child. His clothes were ragged, and he was woefully thin. Desperately, he drew deep rasping breaths as he staggered onwards towards the bridge.

"Here!" called Moidart. "Over here, Robin Oig!"

The little boy looked up, heartened, and picked up a burst of pathetic speed as his pursuers closed in behind him.

"Here!" called Moidart again, and scarce twenty yards ahead of the hounds, the boy staggered onto the bridge and into the protective arms of Moidart. The hounds stopped, each gazing ahead, each with one paw raised, each ready to attack. The huntsmen gathered behind.

"Rorie Moidart!" said one. "Is it yourself?"

"Aye, so you'll find. And perhaps you'll tell me what brings you to the Bridge of Achill and into the land of Lindsay?"

"We're to pick up the lad and ship him awa'," said one. "Aye, his family were taken up a week ago. He's been lying up in the heather," and then, turning to the child, he said, "but that's all Robin Oig!"

Inexpressibly moved, Nell slipped from her horse and ran to take the child from Moidart. Panting and coughing, his eyes hollow and luminous with fatigue and hunger, the boy looked up at her, trying to pull his ragged shirt together in embarrassment across his naked, narrow chest. "You're safe! You're safe, little man!" whispered Nell, throwing a fold of her cloak around him.

Nell's intervention appeared to provoke the huntsmen further. Their leader, a tall, rangy man with red hair and arrogant blue eyes, looked at her scornfully and leered at Moidart, "So Rorie Moidart looks for help to his bit o' muslin! And where did ye find this flaunting slut, I'm wondering? Not in the stews of Glasgow, I'll be bound. Better get your bawbeejoe away from here if you know what's good for her!"

The jibe went home, and Moidart's voice was icy in reply. Haughtily, he snarled, "I'll have ye know the lady is a Lindsay, and as your great-grandfather found out to his cost, Tam McGregor, the Lindsay women ken fine how to deal with slights on their honour!"

At the words, McGregor stiffened, and his eyes coldly fixed on Nell. She sensed that the feeling between the two men had changed from one of rough banter to something darker and more personal and that, in some way that she did not understand, she had become a pawn in their game.

McGregor spoke in a voice tight with rage.

"Enough of your interference, Moidart! You go too far! Ye canna always be defying the master. Now just hand over what is his, or it's maybe we'll have to force a way past you, and it's maybe your Lindsay woman will find herself paying for your obstruction!"

His lieutenant took up the challenge, calling out, "Give up the boy, Moidart! Give him up and we'll be on our way. Ye canna give shelter to every sneck-draw on the Trossachs!"

Moidart strode forward, his face dark with anger, and in a voice with all the stiff menace of an unsheathed claymore he addressed them almost formally. "I'd gart ye to ken," he said, "that this bridge is held by a Lindsay! Ye'll no pass the Bridge of Achill without leave! So go your way and do your dirty business elsewhere! The lad is with me. Move another inch, and ye'll find ye've a braw pirn to unwind! Your fine southern gentleman may have cleared the hill north of the burn, but there are still some brisk birkies at my back, as ye'll find!" And, turning to Nell, in a low voice, he asked, "You must get away from here as fast as you can. Can you find your way back alone? Will you take the lad?" His eyes betrayed his anxiety.

"Yes," said Nell, "I can do that, but what about you?"

"It wouldn't be the first time this bridge has been held for the Lindsays. Go you now, and don't delay!" He said a few words in Gaelic to the boy, who looked from him to Nell and back again and, finally, confidingly, held Nell's hand with his grubby fingers. She mounted the roan swiftly and hauled the lad up in front of her, tucking him up in folds of her cloak, and at once spun her horse about and forward and upwards on the castle road.

Above the drumming of her horse's hooves, Nell heard the insults hurled by each side resume and intensify, and she wondered whether this ritual exchange of threats and abuse was harmless—a replacement for the blows and bloodshed of earlier days. But then, remembering the tension in Coll's body and the barely controlled anger in McGregor's face, she feared she was leaving a situation on the verge of violence and danger. While a confident Moidart held the men off by the force of his arrogant words, Coll was watchful, all his attention focussed, it seemed, through a clear blue eye on the figures of the huntsmen. His hand, lightly placed on his right hip, looked posed and swagger, but Nell knew that it was hovering over the hilt of his dagger.

She turned her head briefly on reaching the crest of the hill and looked back, noticing with apprehension that one of the horsemen was riding like the wind away from the bridge, while his friends remained gesticulating at Moidart and Coll. She pressed on, gathering speed, wondering at Moidart's cool courage and his confident, soldier's bearing.

As they rode, Nell did her best to piece together the boy's story. It was no easy task; he was tongue-tied with shyness and his English was very uncertain. When at a loss he would interpolate a word or phrase in Gaelic, but from the soft Highland voice, often not much above a whisper, she learned that he and two friends had travelled south together, "to the edge of England, Mam!" to search for harvest work. But word had come to him that all was not well at home. And, speaking of his father, he said, "Himself would always fight, and where would I be but at his side?" In desperate haste and abandoning his friends, he made the long journey back to the Trossachs. "Wi' nought to sup but cauld neeps, it was a weary road," he whispered.

His worst fears were realised. Only a blackened ring of stones marked the site of his family's croft, and there was no one left save the agents of the new landlord to tell what had happened. "Where awa' was himself, ma mother, and ma twa wee sisters?" He was peremptorily directed to the Firth, given a few pounds Scots, and ordered aboard a great emigrant ship that lay there "wi' folk greetin' and wailin' for to be goin' west awa' from Scotland." He searched the ship for his folk, only to find—when the ship was underway—that they had departed for the Americas on another boat two days before. "I'm no one to be hassled by anyone," he said almost apologetically, and he had slipped overboard and swum ashore to walk back to the only home he had ever known.

"Oh, poor, poor lad," thought Nell, her heart constricted with pity. Her arm tightened about him. "Poor babe! Nothing to eat but turnips for days, swimming the icy waters of the Solway Firth to become, in the end, a bedraggled fox cub in front—and not far in front—of a pack of hounds."

A quarter of an hour later, Nell rattled over the bridge to the castle. Mrs. Fraser and Lucy, who were walking in the garden, looked up in surprise and came hurrying to greet her.

"Robin Oig?" said Mrs. Fraser. "What's with you?"

Nell rapidly explained, and stablemen and others gathered round to hear the tale, translated from time to time into the Gaelic and, to Lucy's astonishment, "Feed him and clothe him," said Nell and, after an appraising glance, "and wash him too. Care for him. I'll ride back and see that all is well with Moidart. I must hurry. I fear the McGregors were sending for help as I left. I think they have it in mind to teach Moidart a lesson for thwarting them."

"You'll take some men with you," said Mrs. Fraser firmly, and there was a murmur of agreement. There was a brief, purposeful flurry of activity, and, miraculously, the dusty men who had been working peaceably in the yard with shovel and broom were suddenly crowding round her, eyes gleaming with anticipation, fists clutching cudgels. And so it was with an escort of five kilted warriors that Nell found herself minutes later, trotting out of the stable yard.

One, who looked so like Coll that she took him to be his brother, caught her bridle as they passed through the gate and put in her hand a straight stabbing dagger. "Ye'll maybe be glad of a skian-dhu, my lady," he said grimly.

Nell nodded her thanks and tucked it away in the side pocket of her habit. Events had unrolled with such rapidity that she had not, until then, had a chance to consider what had happened to her, and so matter-of-fact had Coll and Moidart been that only now did she realise that pampered Lady Elinor Somersham, heiress to thousands of acres, was riding with singing heart and a black knife into battle. Yes! Truly battle! On a quarrel not her own.

"But," she thought, "it *is* my quarrel! I'll make it my quarrel!"

8

The men, running with extraordinary speed and the determination of hounds, kept up with her trotting horse, but there ever flashed into her mind the picture of the huntsman riding away from the bridge, she was convinced, to fetch help. Arriving at an abrupt decision, Nell shouted to the men, "I'll ride on ahead and let them know that you're coming." And she spurred the roan forward, ignoring the shouted warnings and cries of concern from the Lindsay men. Riding at a canter and then swiftly breaking into a gallop, Nell had drawn half a mile ahead of the men when she topped the rise above Achill water.

"Last time I galloped a horse—good heavens!—it was in Rotten Row!" In spite of her rising excitement, she could even giggle at the memory of the Prince Regent's quivering cheeks.

The scene at the bridge below made her gasp with foreboding. Moidart and Coll remained sitting on the bank at the entrance to the bridge, motionless in the saddle and seemingly unconcerned, but on the opposite bank, the three McGregors were, as she looked, being rejoined by the fourth, who was now flanked by five more rough-looking men of the hills on foot. Nell frowned in dismay as she counted the odds of nine to two and, looking back towards the oncoming Lindsay men and forward to the pack of McGregors now advancing triumphantly and in sinister silence towards Moidart and Coll, she wondered what on earth she was to do next.

No etiquette book she'd ever read told her how she should proceed. What was a well brought-up young lady to do in a brawl on a bridge? Go in? Hang back? Have a fit of the vapours? With a surge of elation, she spurred without further thought, down the slope to the bridge, reversing her crop as she drew near.

The sight of her raised a shout of dismay from Moidart and a yell of triumph from McGregor. Without warning and completely taking the momentarily distracted McGregors by surprise, Moidart and Coll charged. Simultaneously, they drove their horses straight at the mounted huntsmen, catching the two leaders, who were now over halfway across the bridge, full in the shoulder. Their horses staggered back and, quick as lightning, Moidart and Coll each leaned low, grabbed the struggling riders by an ankle, and hurled them down from their mounts.

One fell with a scream and a splash over the parapet and into the burn, the other—the odious Tam McGregor, Nell noticed with satisfaction—rolled himself into a ball as he fell onto the bridge and under his horse's hooves.

The riderless horses snorted and panicked and attempted to back and turn, bumping clumsily into the two mounted hunters behind them. In the confusion, Moidart spurred his gallant black horse forward, parrying blows and flailing with his riding crop, harrying them as they struggled for control. As Nell approached, two Highlanders on foot ran forward through the mêlée, caught Coll's pony by the bridle, and lunged at him, hitting him brutally with their short sticks. A streak of bright light flashed in Coll's hand. It was accompanied by a sharp oath from one of the men, who leapt backwards, clutching at a stream of blood jetting down his forearm.

At the sound and sight of their companion's wound, the rest of the men on foot yelled together and closed in through the milling horses to throw themselves on Coll, reaching up to beat him with their cudgels. Seeing one creep up on Coll from behind, Nell called out a sharp warning: "Coll! Behind you!" and hesitating no longer, urged her horse forward. Leaning perilously out from her sidesaddle, she hit the man smartly across the back of the head. She lifted her arm for a second blow, but Coll twisted in his saddle and caught him as he stumbled, hurling him with ferocious strength and agility off the bridge and into the deep cold pool below.

"Three down, six to go, that's two each," Nell counted excitedly and looked about her for another target. Before she could press forward to assist Moidart, who was surrounded like a bear baited by snapping dogs, she felt a first spurt of fear as hands tugged at the thick stuff of her skirt from behind. Turning, she looked down into the savage, bloodstained face of Tam McGregor.

Bruised but undaunted by his roll under the hooves of two horses, he had come up behind her and, grasping her firmly about the hips with his dirty hands, he was dragging her inch by inch from her saddle. He dodged the first slash of her crop, but the second brought out a red weal on the side of his face. His only reaction to the pain was to redouble his efforts to pull her down. His eyes shone with murderous fury, and his narrow mouth leered with triumph as with a last despairing smack at his head, Nell found herself dragged onto the planks of the bridge.

Silently kicking and struggling, she was easily overpowered by the huge Highlander who forced her arms behind her back and began to haul her off the bridge and away to the river bank. "You'll pay for this, Lindsay slut!" he spat into her ear. "And it's not the only debt you'll make good for your arrogant clan!"

But at that moment, a fierce yell exploded from the hill behind them and Moidart's men burst over the crest. "Lindsay gu brath!" The battle cry rolled down the hill before them as they swept, running with desperate speed, towards the bridge.

McGregor cursed and looked over his shoulder towards the hill. The second of inattention was enough for Nell. Her booted foot crashed backwards into his shin, the spur making contact with hard muscle and bone. Hearing his scream of pain and outrage, she wriggled down and sideways, twisting her right arm free. Her fingers closed over the hilt of the dagger in her pocket and pulled it free. Vibrant with fury, she rounded on McGregor, slashing at the arm that still held her. The dagger came naturally into her grasp, its small size an extension of her hand. She struck out with the speed and precision of a cornered cat.

McGregor stumbled back from her with a hiss and a foul oath as the blade tore once and a second time through his sleeve, drawing a spurt of blood from his upper arm. As he crouched to attack, he was roughly seized from behind by two brawny, panting Lindsay men, who threw him face down onto the ground. The larger of the men sat down firmly on McGregor's back, holding his arm twisted up behind him in a bone-cracking lock, while the other, aghast with anxiety, hurried to Nell to ask if she was hurt.

"I'm all right," she gasped. "Look to Moidart! He is hard pressed!" And she watched with a mixture of concern and pride as the reinforcements swept, yelling with enthusiasm, onto the bridge.

At the sight of them, the tide of battle turned in favour of Lindsay. It was clear to Nell, watching every movement and trying to keep her eye on the figure of Moidart, who had remained mounted throughout the skirmish, that although the huntsmen brought a keenness sparked by ancient enmity to the fight, their foot followers were inclined to hang back when they saw that the odds were no longer in their favour. The Lindsay men, defending their lands and their steward, had no such reserve, and soon, Moidart and Coll were relieved of their attackers and clear of the bridge. Charging together, they sent the remaining horsemen flying while their discouraged men tried to run off across the hillside. Those who were captured were dragged back in triumph to Moidart and tossed into the burn.

Moidart spun his horse around and trotted back across the bridge, searching for Nell. He caught sight of her where she stood, dagger in hand, by the prone body of McGregor, whose head was being banged into the ground every time he cursed with a gentle reminder from the giant astride him that there was a lady present, and he should mind his tongue. Moidart, dark and frowning, rode over to her and slid from his horse. In a cold, tight voice, he asked her if she had been harmed.

Nell's relief to see that he was himself uninjured buoyed up her already elated spirits, and she laughed triumphantly. "Harmed? Not in the least! I would not have missed it for the world!" she said, and then, remembering a gesture she had often seen her brother and his friends use in their war games, she bent and wiped clean her dagger on a tussock of grass.

In disbelief, he looked from Nell's laughing eyes to McGregor's blood-stained sleeve and back again, and his face grew tense. He moved towards her and held out his arms to seize her by the elbows, looking down into her face. At the edges of her vision, Nell was amused to see his men delicately turn their backs on this intimate scene and begin to busy themselves clearing up all signs of the skirmish. She began to feel, as he glowered down at her, like an unrepentant child who is about to be reprimanded for something it did not perceive as a misdemeanour, and the thought made her laugh again.

He stared at her eyes, still glowing with excitement, her soft mouth now curving into a devilish grin, and her hair tumbling uncontrolled around her face and, as he gazed, his expression softened. "Lass, you look like a wildcat kitten that's just made its first kill," he whispered. "But you were foolish to return...there was a danger...you did not understand..." He broke off, dropped her arms, and in a louder voice for the benefit of the men said crisply: "Lady Elinor, this is not seemly! I was never more shocked than to see you in the forefront of the battle!" But then, relenting, and with the edge of laughter, he added, "But there—I had no idea we had such a moss-trooper on our side!"

"The lady did well, whatever!" said the man sitting on the writhing McGregor and nodded his head.

Nell wondered whether she had ever had such a compliment. *Well,* she thought, *wherever the rest of my life leads me, I shall remember that when it came to the point—I did well, whatever!*

Nor was her elation dashed to hear one of the men say, shaking his head with regret, "You could hardly call it a battle, Moidart. More in the nature of a wee spat. But, all the same, they'll think twice before they try that again!"

Moidart returned to his men and walked among them, laughing and slapping their backs. Nell looked at him in admiration to see him so in his element. A fighter, a natural leader, he swaggered about on the bridge with unconscious grace. In his baggy riding trousers, thick cloak, and jaunty blue bonnet, he would have been a figure of fun in the sophisticated society in which she moved, and yet, here in this wild country, he was as natural and, it seemed, as grand as the hills.

He looked round, seeking her out, and with sudden mischief, said, "Shall we resume our ride, my lady? The lads and Coll can clear up this rabble."

The lads were amusing themselves hauling their opponents out of the burn, administering a kick up the backside to each, and sending them on their way, dripping, shivering, and shouting defiance.

"What happened after I had gone?" asked Nell curiously as they rode together.

"Well," he said with satisfaction and flushed with pleasure at his victory, "after a bit of a bluster, one of them was sent off, we guessed to fetch reinforcements. It wasn't necessary, and it could have all ended in a reasonable way, but I'm afraid yon Tam McGregor is a bad man. He believes he has things to avenge, and such a vindictive spirit will never be at rest. He grows bold under the orders of his English lord. Coll and I thought they'd be back in strength and, indeed, we were right. After a while, the man returned with five more to help him teach the two of us a lesson! If you hadn't arrived with our lads, I don't know what the outcome might have been. But you did, and all's well, and Robin Oig is safe in the House of Lindsay. But," he continued, "what was that? Just a skirmish! It doesn't change the position. There are other poor, houseless folk wandering the hills, and yon McCann was right when he said I couldn't take them all in."

He brooded on a while in silence and then said, "While Lindsay can hold what Lindsay held, folk hereabouts are safe enough, but what of the future?"

"You are devoted to my cousin, I observe," she said hesitantly.

He threw her a look of enquiry mingled with—could it be suspicion—and then answered in a level tone, "He would be my kinsman and my Laird, would he not?" as though that was the answer for anything.

She laughed, reminded of the scene at the bridge, before the battle when he and McGregor had exchanged ritual snarls. "So if you can claim also that I am a Lindsay woman—we must be related."

"That's right enough," he admitted slowly.

"And tell me, Moidart, what was the significance of your boast to the odious Tam McGregor? He turned quite pale, I thought, at the reminder of his great-grandfather's encounter with a Lindsay woman! Do you really remember what happened all those years ago?"

"Of course!" he said in surprise, "as though it were last week! It was a deed so foul we will never let the Gregora forget it!"

He paused, and Nell waited eagerly.

"A young girl, sister to the Lady Lindsay of the time, was overtaken on the hill one day by a dirty McGregor who scrupled not to besmirch her virtue. She escaped and, being a brave lass, told no one. But she bided her time and, discovering where he lived, entered his bothy at dead of night and attacked him with a pair of sheep shears."

Nell felt an uncontrollable urge to laugh, but Moidart seemed so earnest and so scandalised by this ancient tale of vengeance that she swallowed and asked carefully, "And did she kill the man?"

"No," he replied and then added, "But he fathered no more bairns after her visit!"

Nell could no longer hold back her peals of laughter. "No wonder Tam McGregor turned pale at the sight of a Lindsay woman!"

Moidart refused to join in her laughter but turned to face her and said seriously, "Memories and lust for revenge are ever keen in the clans, my lady. If Tam McGregor had forced a passage over the bridge and things had gone badly with us, we would have been unable to come to your aid when he dragged you into the woods, where he would perhaps have had it in mind to avenge his ancestor..."

Nell fell silent, understanding at last the danger to which she had exposed herself, but she rallied and replied with spirit: "And perhaps

Tam would have experienced the same shearing as his lustful great-grandfather! I may be a soft southerner and, indeed, a lady of fashion unfitted to take part in such primitive scenes, but I am a farmer's daughter as well and..." She hesitated a moment but concluded boldly, "and it would not have been the first time I'd seen a hog gelded!"

She smiled impudently, taking the dagger from her pocket and offering it to him. "One of the men gave me this. He called it a skian-dhu, I think."

At the sight of the mischief in her eyes, Moidart allowed himself to laugh, and, once started, he could not stop and fell forward on his horse's neck, rising at last to give her a look so strange, so concentrated—a blend of admiration and speculation—that she felt suddenly that she had passed a test she had not been aware she was taking.

"Well, put your dagger back in your pocket, then, my lady," he said. "This is lawless country still, and it's not only from the McGregors you might be needing to defend your virtue!"

9

Their tired horses walking in step, they rode gently side by side down the track by the burn. He seemed to be disposed to ride on in silence, and this was very welcome to Nell, absorbed in her thoughts as she was. She recalled all that had been said of the Clearance and contrasted the empty hillside beyond the Bridge of Achill with the busy, traditional life on the lands of Lindsay. She thought with pity of the waif-like fugitive and felt once more in her imagination his skinny body shivering inside her cloak as she carried him back to the castle and saw once again his grateful eyes looking up at her. She remembered the men running back with her to the bridge and the end of the battle. She hurriedly dismissed from her mind her own rash intervention, and above all she was conscious of the strength, pride, and purpose of Moidart himself. Memories of the night they had shared and a sense of the fear and fascination he inspired in her caused her heart to beat faster, and she kept her gaze determinedly on the path before her, avoiding his eye.

After a while, the path wandered away from the burn and set out across the hillside. Without a word and by common consent, they let the rested horses out and, trotting on at first, cantered together over the hill. Curlews called plaintively from the surrounding bog lands and, as though a warning shot had been fired, a pack of grouse whizzed across their path. The westerly wind was strengthening behind them and, it seemed, blowing them on, and with it came menacing clouds packed densely above the surrounding hills.

Nell's thoughts scampered back to Park Lane and the refinements of Hyde Park and to Suffolk and its lavish corn crops, its peaceful fields, the cattle, and the lush water meadows. In her mind she contrasted the easy, smiling people of her home, in their security, with these Highlanders— poised in danger between an old and familiar and a new and threatening way of life. Several times she tried to put her thoughts into words, but the taciturnity of her companion stopped her, until at last he reined his horse and turned to look at her with a regard so strange she was taken aback. For a moment, he seemed to calculate, and then he said, "Rain is coming up from the west. We might be wise to turn aside for shelter till it's blown over. Just over the hill is a bothy..."

For a moment, his face was illuminated by a smile so friendly and affectionate that Nell was amazed. He continued, "We can shelter ourselves there, and we can shelter our horses. I have not, I'm afraid, been a thoughtful cavalier this morning, dragging you into our primitive squabbles and putting you into danger, but at least I have a venison pastie in my bag, and I have a dram of the coarse peasant spirit that we northern primitives depend on in such situations. You could rest in shelter before the return journey."

Nell paused and looked at him carefully before nodding her acquiescence, and they swung aside to slant across the hill. As they reached a ridge, he pointed downwards with his riding crop and said, "There— see—until a year ago, a wee family lived there, but I was worried for them. They have two children; the wife has not been well. The house is sound, but the good man works for the most part in the demesne, and with a good croft house falling empty, they moved to something better, where the wife would have a bit of company in the glen."

As he spoke, the rain indeed began to fall, blowing up with Highland suddenness, and the last half mile of their journey was undertaken at a splattering gallop down the muddy track. On arrival, looping the reins over his arm, Moidart pushed open the door of a small croft house with his foot and, gathering up the reins, led both horses off into what, it seemed, had been a cow byre.

"Will you go in?" he said.

Nell ducked under the low doorway and into the gloom of the little cabin. As her eyes grew accustomed to the darkness, she became aware of roughly harled stone walls painted with faded lime-wash, a beaten earth floor, and at one end a stone fireplace—still holding the ash of the last fire lit over a year ago. There was a pot hook and, still, a stack of turf and a basket of heather root kindling. On either side of the fireplace stood a sturdy settle. At the other end of the single room, an open shutter revealed a built-in bed where children had obviously once been accommodated in bunks.

The place was primitive, and Nell could hardly imagine a simpler dwelling for a man, his wife and two children, but all the same it was clean, it was neat, and it was welcoming. After a moment's struggle, she forced open the shutter on an unglazed window and looked out across the moorland, now dazzling with the quickly falling rain.

Moidart stooped through the doorway, threw his saddle bag down in a corner, and without a word gathered up an armful of heather root and threw it into the fireplace, kneeling with clicking flint and steel in his hand and, blowing on a tinder box, set it alight. Soon, as the drumming rain darkened the little room, a blaze leapt up in the blackened fireplace. He observed it for a while and then threw on, one by one, neatly squared bricks of turf, and then he finally turned to Nell and said, "Welcome to Lis na Brucka! Ten years ago there must have been a badger living here and the croft has always been called *Lis na Brucka*—"the place of the badger." So here we are! Like two badgers in our set! The accommodation is not smart for Lady Elinor, perhaps, but the welcome is no less warm for that."

He drew from his pocket a silver flask and handed it to her, running his hand over her shoulders as he did so. "You are wet and cold, I am afraid," he said. "This will warm you internally at least, and perhaps this may restore your strength."

"This" was a venison pastie. He broke it in half and handed her a piece. "Share," he said with a grin, "as good moss-troopers must." Pointing towards the settle, he invited her to take a seat. It was rough and country-made, but surprisingly comfortable. She sat gratefully down on it, tugged off her wet boots, and extended her legs towards the blaze.

While he had been speaking and as they had ridden the last half mile to the bothy, Nell had been calculating. It seemed to her that if it was shelter they had required, the House of Lindsay was nearer to the Bridge of Achill than this remote outpost—nearer, she reckoned, with her trained eye for country, by the best part of a mile. She had a feeling that the horses had been of the same opinion, that they had had the scent of their own stables in their nostrils and had turned unwillingly aside to cross the hill. *If he had had my well-being close to his heart,* she thought, *we would have returned to the castle.* Her heart began to thump furiously, and her mouth went dry at the realisation that she was cut off from the world by several rain-sodden miles of heather and quite alone with Moidart. She looked a question at him, and he seemed to read her thought.

"The house," he said, without apology, "is ever in such a bustle, a body can never exchange two words with another in private. It seems to me that here we can eat and drink—perhaps even be merry—and anyway improve our acquaintance without interruption."

Politely, Nell lifted the silver flask to her lips and drank a mouthful of the liquid. She was at once reduced to coughing and spluttering. "What was that?" she said, returning the flask to him.

"Whisky."

"Ah! The dews o' Glen Sheerly! At last I sample them. It is very fierce," she said, but feeling the rush of warmth through her chilled body, she accepted the flask again and drank once more.

"Have a care," said he. "It is not without its effect if you are unaccustomed."

"I am unaccustomed to everything that's happened to me today," said Nell. "I have never cracked a man's skull before, never stabbed a man, and I have certainly never found myself alone with a man in the middle of a wilderness before. One drink doesn't make my situation appreciably more odd, you know." She realised that the battle of the bridge had left her strangely and wildly elated. She had seen men possessed by primitive passions and felt a primitive ferocity in herself that left her hungry for more.

They ate and drank in silence for a while, until, emboldened by the strangeness and perhaps by the fiery spirit warming her blood, Nell said challengingly, "Moidart, I am wondering why I am here. It is obviously not the stimulation of my conversation you are seeking..."

For reply, he peeled his cloak from his shoulder and let it drop to the ground. He knelt across the space between them, taking her hands in his. For a moment he looked into her face, and then he suddenly slipped his hand under her arm and, to her surprise, lifted her to her feet.

"Can you seriously doubt why I have brought you here?"

His voice was teasing in some measure, but there was now a rough intensity that caused Nell to shrink from him. "Please..." she began, but her voice faltered away.

"Please?" he said. "Please what? What would you say? Please don't touch me...Please take me home...Please don't love me?" His hands slid round to the small of her back, and he pressed her to him with an urgency she could not resist; a strong hand took her chin and turned her face up to his. He was searching her face, she knew intuitively, for a response that would either encourage him to further advances or stop him short. Wild and unpredictable he might be, alarming and foreign to her, yet she felt that, even now, in this remote situation, it would take but one look from her to restore their relationship to that of mistress and steward.

She met his hungry gaze, her cheeks colouring with embarrassment but her eyes ablaze with determination. "Wait! A moment, Moidart!" she said with a firmness that surprised her, and she pushed herself free of his close embrace. Swiftly she took the dagger from her pocket, and he tensed and drew in his breath as he caught sight of the steel blade pointing menacingly towards his ribs. With a smile full of challenge, she tossed the dagger in a glittering arc through the air, and it fell, quivering, point downwards in the earth floor.

Soft arms stole up around his neck, and she whispered, "I feared you could not be at ease making love to a Lindsay woman in possession of a skian-dhu!"

With a gasp of mixed astonishment and delight, he swept her up again into his arms, and she shivered uncontrollably as the wet cloth of her habit clung to her cold flesh. Instantly reacting to her shudder, he whispered urgently, "Your habit is soaking wet. You must take off these damp things and put them before the fire to dry. Come, my lady, I will assist you."

"You would be my maid now, Moidart?" she said through teeth clenched and chattering with cold but also with apprehension, "Is there no end to your skills? Poacher, poet, factor, fighter...I wonder what I shall encounter next?"

He realised that she was talking to release her tension and, smiling, he gently bit the lobe of her ear and whispered, "Lover?" His searching hand deftly unbuttoned the stiff stuff of her tight bodice and eased it from her shoulders; her damp blouse followed, and her riding breeches were tugged down from her waist and put on the mantle rail before the fire with all the deftness she might have expected from Lucy. She stood before him, shivering and as though hypnotised, wearing only her chemise and her stockings.

"And the shift!" he murmured.

She realised that no further permission was going to be sought and that she had gone too far to retreat, even had she wanted to do so. The thought made her shiver with delicious dread, and at the last moment she was overcome by the shame of showing her naked body to a man, and in the half light. In her imaginings, such a scene had always taken place under cover of darkness and several layers of bedclothes.

He caught her shyness and said, "My shirt is still dry—you shall have that." He pulled the silk chemise up over her head and allowed his hungry gaze to slant over her naked breasts for a moment before removing his rough cotton shirt and wrapping it, still warm from his body, about her shoulders. "We must keep each other warm as best we can," he said. "Stay by the fire." Moving over to the sleeping part of the cottage, he returned with an armful of bracken and boughs and then fetched another and a third. "Lucky for us, Rab left his beds behind," he said by way of explanation, and then, kicking and smoothing the tufty bracken into place, he spread his thick cloak over it. From his saddlebag he took a plaid and came back to stand in front of her.

Nell's hands reached up and tentatively caressed his naked shoulders, as they had done many times in imagination, running down over his hard chest to his narrow waist, amazed and fearful at the strength she felt there. Nervously, she snatched her hands away, fearing that she was going too far and that perhaps this was something she should not do, but he appeared not to be displeased by her caresses and, catching her hands, firmly placed them back again around his shoulders. With growing confidence and curiosity, she stroked the silky skin of his brown arms, following the lines of his bunched muscles, and exclaimed gently when her exploring fingers discovered the line of a deep scar along his upper arm. He smiled in response to her questioning look and said roughly, "A bullet. No, not an English one, don't be concerned."

He bent his head and kissed her, the gentle pressure increasing, willing her to respond. Remembering the exciting way he had kissed her on their first evening, she dared to trace the line between his lips with her tongue and jolted with surprise and pleasure as he gasped and deepened his kiss.

With a despairing sigh, he broke off and stood away from her. He kicked off his boots in a jingle of spurs and, while Nell looked hastily away, removed his stockings and breeches. She felt her legs being swept away from under her, her back supported by one strong arm, and she was lowered gently onto the roughly assembled bed. He lay down beside her and pulled his plaid over their bodies, cradling her closely in his arms.

After a few silent minutes together, her shivering ceased and a blessed warmth began to relax her limbs. Feeling there was no comment she could possibly make in these strange circumstances that would not sound trivial and out of place, Nell stayed quiet in his arms, round-eyed and hardly daring to breathe. All her senses were alert, every inch of her body in contact with his was sending her messages. The roughness of his chest, his hand about her, cupping her breast, his lips pressed gently to her forehead and, above all, the smooth muscled thighs against which she felt herself moulded, expressing the mysterious threat of his hardened body, were arousing in her the same strange sensations she had felt on the evening she had met him. The urge to strain herself even closer to him, to seek release from the tight and barely understood yearning she was feeling, was becoming unbearable. His all-too-evident intentions towards her were making her shake with fear and, incredibly, she was looking to him for comfort. But she recognised that her situation now was very different from his teasing, nonthreatening presence in her bed when she had been frightened by the owl.

"I'm sorry I have no bolster today," he said, as if reading her thoughts.

She stirred and moved slightly towards him, reaching up to touch his cheek. "I'm thinking I prefer our situation without it, Moidart," she whispered.

His whole body grew tense at her words. A gentle hand parted the shirt and slid inside to caress her, shaking with surprise and delight. With an exclamation of joy he bent his head to her nipples, teasing and kissing. She pressed his dark head to her, breathing in the peat smoke scent of his hair, and recognised that she was incapable of stopping the lovemaking that had begun. With a rush of emotion very like triumph, she knew she had no wish to stop it.

"Don't fear me, Nell," he whispered. "You're safe with me, my lass. Truly. I won't harm you." When her trembling had stopped, his hand moved abruptly downwards again over her hips to stroke and part her soft thighs. Fighting back her instinctive fear and an almost insuperable urge to clamp her legs together, Nell opened wide eyes and looked into his strained face, seeking reassurance there, wanting desperately to trust him.

She whimpered softly, nuzzling her head against his chest. His exploring hand became aware of the ready welcome her body was offering him and, for a moment, Moidart's advances were halted. He lifted his head and, looking at her questioningly and speaking deliberately, he asked, "Do you know what we are about, Elinor? I'm sorry, but I don't know whether you know...what kind of innocent you are...Oh, dammit, lass, I'm going to make love to you!"

Nell laughed quietly in surprise, charmed that he should have at the last moment summoned the restraint to issue a warning. "I had begun to suspect as much, Moidart!" she said. "And I should like it very much if you were to make love to me. You will find I have done no such thing before, but I was ever a quick learner, and I see that you are a willing tutor." She snuggled against him and began to plant a row of soft kisses along his throat, murmuring indistinct endearments.

The unexpected warmth of her passion made him start and look down at her wide-eyed. "Oh my God! What have I done? What am I about?" was his surprising reaction to her show of affection. He rose on one elbow, his face frozen and aghast. "Elinor, I should not have done this! It is unforgivable! Could it be that? Surely not? I think you love me?"

Puzzled by his reaction, she looked back at him and said gently, "Yes, Moidart, I think I do. Have you not been trying to make me love you? Was this not what you were intending? I had thought that you had brought me here to love me...is that so dreadful?"

"I think perhaps it may be. I have taken advantage of your innocence in bringing you here, in tricking you into coming to this bothy with me. And now I find I cannot abuse your trust. It is not too late..." he added, miserably. "Elinor, can you forgive me?"

In the gloom, her eyes were huge pools of distress as she tried to understand him. She put out a hand to stop him, but he rolled determinedly away from her and moved over to kneel by the fire, busying himself putting on more kindling and then more peat. The blaze lit up his face, which she saw was uncharacteristically confused. The handsome features were a mask of indecision, the black eyebrows drawn into a tight line, his mouth narrowed. His strong limbs gleamed golden in the firelight, and she felt a wrenching loss that she could no longer reach out and touch him. Her body was shocked and unwilling to accept the distance that had abruptly arisen between them. He spun round to look at her in astonishment on hearing her shout of scornful amusement.

"My trust, you say? Why on earth should you suppose I trust you, Moidart? On the contrary, I think you are very likely a rogue and a cunning seducer and quite the last person in the world I should trust!" Propped up on one elbow, hand under her chin, her eyes laughing at him invitingly, she insisted, "I'm not a ninny! I came here of my own free will, I assure you, knowing quite well that you were taking me out of our way and being hardly in doubt as to the purpose of your detour!" Her voice sank to a low, seductive tone as she added slowly, "I have *chosen* to make love with you." She sat up lazily, with all the easy grace of a fireside cat, the plaid falling away from her shoulders to her waist, a curtain of thick, fair hair swinging and shining in the glow of the burning peat, and held out her arms to him. "Innocent I certainly am, as you will discover, but I know what I want, and—as I told you—I usually get it. Now stop fiddling with the fire, which is doing very well by itself, and come back here. Your mistress is growing cold!"

An hour later, Nell swam back to consciousness from a sleep that was more in the nature of a swoon. She was lying on Moidart's cloak, folded in his arms with her head resting on his chest. Outside the rain pattered down, but less strongly now, and at her side the heaped red-hot glow of the fire gave the only light in the darkening room. Almost unable to believe how she had reached this point, Nell buried her head in his shoulder and remembered how, with heart almost breaking at his desertion, she had, in anger and frustration, found the words to lure him into returning to her.

Without moving her head and under lowered eyelashes, she scanned the room and smiled to see her scattered clothes mingling most indecently with his. She remembered the hardness, the gentleness, and the ultimately undeniable demands of his body. She remembered the ecstasy and release of abandoning herself to his passion. But now it seemed that he—that strong face peaceful—was the defenceless one.

The warnings contained in so many of the romances she had read, with their paraphrase and their innuendo, came into her mind. Explicitly she thought, *I am undone!* And she waited for the hand-wringing remorse of the seduced maiden to overtake her. She waited in vain. All she could feel was a total warm and animal satisfaction. *I was a stranger when I came here*, she remembered. *I was perhaps even a hostile stranger—and certainly this man greeted me with hostility—but now? What now? These frowning hills and these wild people with their warlike memories and their timeless loyalties—has this made me a part of them? It could be so. It seems that, in being possessed, I have taken possession.*

He stirred sleepily in her embrace and moved about until his head was nuzzling against her breast. She stroked his hair gently and, on impulse, began softly to sing a lullaby she had learned many years before. It was in Gaelic, and she could barely understand the words, but she had always been moved by the haunting, lilting tune.

As her low voice died away, he spoke. "I think I have died and gone to heaven...Surely this is the warrior's reward—a good fire at my back, a willing wench in my arms, and a Scottish lullaby in my ear? I shall never move from this place again!"

"I fear you must, for my arm has gone quite dead under your great weight, and my nose tells me that my riding habit is beginning to char."

"Then you must rescue it. I find myself unable to move after my day's exertions. The battle of the bridge and the battle of the bothy have quite done for me!" He released her arm and watched her with a lazy smile as she scampered out of bed and tugged the dress off the rail. She looked back at him uncertainly and began to search around for her chemise. "The rain has stopped, I think," she said brightly, holding her clothing this way and that in an only partially successful attempt to hide her nakedness from his amused gaze, "and the afternoon must be well advanced. I think perhaps we should be getting back to the castle before they send out a search party..."

"They'll know you are safe with me," he said with an ironic smile.

As he spoke, a pale shaft of sunshine briefly burst, slanting through the cloud and, shining clear through the small window, illuminated her as she stood in the centre of the room. Moidart, who had raised himself on one elbow, the better to follow her movements, gazed spellbound. With her rain-washed hair now dried but unbrushed and standing out in a flying golden cloud about her pretty face, and her naked body slim and pale against the prevailing dark of the little cabin, it seemed to him that he had captured one of the mysterious nymph daughters of the Sea Kings of Orkney, a sweet figure from the legends of his childhood.

Muddling distractedly around the room, Nell was unaware of the fanciful thoughts she was inspiring, unaware that his expression was changing from one of playful mischief to one of gathering desire, unaware, indeed, that after the total, wracking lovemaking of the afternoon it was possible to rekindle the flame that had consumed them.

"Elinor!" At the sudden sharpness in his tone, she looked at him questioningly, her surprise turning to a slow smile of delight as she interpreted the intensity of his look, his outstretched hand, and the need in his voice as he said roughly, "Now put down that shift and come back here, my lady. Your steward is growing cold without you."

10

The sun was going down in a fierce display of orange, pink, and violet, reflecting off the high-massed clouds of a mackerel sky as they rode together back towards the castle. Warm now in her stiff and scorched but dry habit and snuggled into Moidart's plaid, Nell felt that the vivid bonfire colours of the world around her exulted with her. She too was alive, alight, and rejoicing. She glanced across constantly at her smiling companion, with no attempt now to hide the love in her eyes. His mood too had changed, and he had begun to talk to her easily and confidingly, all wariness, it seemed, vanished.

By common consent, they reined in their horses as they topped the rise overlooking the valley in which the castle stood and gazed at the beauty of the scene.

"What a thing it is," murmured Moidart, "to be able to look down on that and say, 'There lies my home.'"

"You are devoted to your land, are you not?" asked Nell quietly. "Would you never consider living anywhere else, Moidart?"

She listened intently for his answer, realising now how much her happiness depended on how he chose to reply. She was in no doubt that he would have understood what she was really asking him. He looked at her directly and answered the thought behind the question. "No,

I would never consider it. I have travelled abroad and lived for short whiles in many places, but it's here I want to be and nothing, Elinor, and no one would persuade me to leave this valley. I was born here, my bairns will be born here, and, like as not, I shall die here."

She had suspected as much but had gone on planning a future for him with her in her imagination, and now he was telling her with unmistakable finality that her hopes were never to be fulfilled. The dark shadows lengthened in her mind as they lengthened along the valley.

"And what would you do if Lindsay were no longer able to retain his lands? Could you exist independently of him? Do you have any land of your own?"

"A field or two that come to me from my mother's family—enough to earn me the blue bonnet of a Laird," he said with a disparaging smile, "but not enough to live on. And Lindsay? I think you forget, Elinor, that he owns none of this anyway. It will be yours to do with as you wish."

"I have been thinking deeply about my situation," she said hesitantly, "and it becomes very urgent that I speak with my cousin. You say he will be back by Friday?"

"He must! Tradition insists that he open the Harvest Home in the early evening, so you may count on seeing him at some time during the day. He will expect you, as the guest of the house, to take part in the evening's merrymaking, and it may afford him some sly satisfaction to present the new owner of the lands to her tenants and tacksmen on that occasion. You'll be needing a white dress. Do you have one in your luggage?"

"Yes, indeed, I have," she said, surprised at the turn the conversation had taken.

"Then wear it. I'll get Jennie to fix up for ye a sash of the Lindsay tartan, and then ye'll not look so much of a stranger."

"You still despise me, Moidart, don't you?"

"Aye," he replied easily and at once, "but I'm fond of ye too, so it's a fine mess I'm in, and it's havoc you're causing for me!"

"Don't judge me yet, Moidart. I may yet surprise you," she said with a wry smile and urged her horse forward.

A gleam of fading sunshine illuminated a stone building by the side of the river west of the castle, a ruined building that caught Nell's attention and caused her to catch Moidart's sleeve and point to it. "Is that a mill down there?" she asked.

"That, why yes, it's an old water mill. Disused these ten years."

"What kind of mill was it? What did it produce?"

"They were weavers who had it," he answered, in some surprise that she should be interested. "They produced woollen cloth, the tartans and the tuile."

"Why did they abandon it?"

"They decided to try their luck in the Americas, like so many others," he said.

Nell was thoughtful for a moment. "Moidart. The stuff of your cloak—is it made of tuile?"

"Yes, it's a local tuile, though some would call it tweed after the river," he said, puzzled as to where her thoughts were leading.

"Where does the wool come from to make the cloth? No! Answer me!" she said seriously, sensing his impatience at her simple question.

"From the sheep you saw swarming all over the hills of our neighbours. You must have seen above a thousand today."

"And the dyes for the cloth?"

"From the plants on the hillside we're standing on."

"And the power for the looms?"

"From the river."

"And the workers to tend the looms?"

"All about you. Not so many as the sheep, but too many."

"Then Lindsay could solve his problems," she said eagerly. "With materials and power and labour aplenty here in the valley, he could build a woollen mill to rival those of Glasgow. At the Saracen's Head, where we spent a day resting on our way here, I listened to the talk of two merchants in woollen cloth who were staying there whilst they did business with the mills. They were very pleased with themselves and declared their goods sold so readily to the English and the Dutch markets that they could not come by sufficient quantities of cloth to satisfy the demands."

He was listening to her attentively with a slight smile curving his mouth. "If cousin Roderick were but to build himself mills," she pressed on, "and buy wool from his neighbours, he might provide employment for his surplus population, might he not?"

He looked down into her excited face with a loving and indulgent smile. "Elinor, I don't know another girl to whom the idea would have occurred! And yes, of course you are right, but there is one question you have left out of your list..."

"What is that?" she asked, sensing a disappointment.

"The question of money! How is Lindsay to pay for the mills—for the designers, the builders, the machinery? He does not have the where-withall even to repair the old mill you are looking at." His face darkened, "And if we have another bad winter, the Laird will not be able to fill the empty bellies of his clan. It's a beautiful inheritance you will have, Elinor, but a poor one!"

They approached the castle in silence, each wrapt in thought, and clattered into the courtyard as the last of the light faded from the sky. At the sound of their hooves, the door opened and two concerned faces looked out—Lucy and Coll, each relieved that master and mistress were safely home.

Moidart did not offer a reason for their late arrival, merely ordering supper for her ladyship and himself in the parlour in an hour's time.

Nell soaked herself thankfully in a bath fragrant with cloves and rose petals and listened in a steamy daze as Lucy chattered on about her day. The portmanteau had arrived and its contents had been unpacked and ironed, so Nell could once again be dressed in the height of fashion. Lucy herself was prinking about, Nell noticed, in her best uniform of lavender dress, frilly white apron, and lace cap with streamers flying down her back.

She had had a busy and absorbing day, it seemed, getting to know the routine of the castle. The routine had been much disturbed early in the afternoon when Coll and the men had returned in triumph with stories of their success in the battle for Achill Bridge. The frequency with which Coll's name cropped up in Lucy's conversation did not escape

Nell's notice, and she smiled to herself, losing no time in giving her own eyewitness account of the doings at the bridge and speaking warmly of Coll's part in the defence.

"And that Mr. Moidart who found us on the road—did you know, Miss Nell?—he isn't just anybody! No—he's a Laird, Coll says! And that's why he wears that floppy blue hat. Is that the same as a lord in English? I had taken him for the steward, like Kenton at Somersham, but Coll laughed at me and said—no, not at all, he's aristocracy really—the Moidart of Moidart and his master."

Nell attempted to explain, as far as she understood it, the social fabric of the Highlands and who owed allegiance to whom, but she quickly ran out of information herself.

"So I suppose, then, it's quite proper for you to go down and have supper with his Lairdship, though you wouldn't dine with Kenton at home, Miss Nell?" asked Lucy, still striving to understand.

"You have it, Lucy. Moidart is acting as my host until my cousin should return." A picture of herself dining tête à tête with portly old Kenton almost made Nell laugh out loud. She had a far different scene in mind. "And now, Lucy, will you put out my dark red dress and shawl, my best silk stockings—the ones with the pink rosebuds, my satin garters, and my kid slippers? Oh, and did we bring my French eau de cologne?"

"Yes, Miss Nell," said Lucy, giving her a long look.

"Oh, and Lucy—you may dismiss when I go down to dinner. I will put myself to bed."

As Lucy turned to the drawers to find the stockings, she smiled secretly to herself. If Tibbie's gossip were to be believed, Miss Nell had had assistance from an unusual quarter in putting herself to bed the very first night at the castle. Indeed, the whole household was buzzing with it, and Lucy had found herself mounting a stout defence of her mistress's virtue, saddened by the looks of indulgent amusement being exchanged behind her back. Her instinctive smile of pleasure at the thought that at last her mistress had fallen in love faded as she called to mind Moidart's handsome features. The man was a heartbreaker if ever she saw one, and not at all what Miss Nell was used to. He quite reminded Lucy of a wolf among a pack of sheep, compared with the London gentlemen her mistress was accustomed to flirting with. And that was another thing—this man didn't flirt with Nell at all. Indeed, Lucy had not liked to see the concentrated calculation in his stare. She had not liked the way he had handled Nell on the coach road on the day of their arrival, and if she had not heard from Tibbie that things were decidedly otherwise, she would have thought Moidart disliked her mistress. Ah, well, he had been considerate to *her*, she had to admit that, and Coll was devoted to the factor. And Coll, well...Lucy's secret smile returned. Coll...was a good man, of that at least she was certain.

There was the same welcoming scene in the small parlour, log fire well ablaze and, stretched before it, the hound lifted a disdainful nose and marked her entrance with a thump of his tail. But there was a different welcome from Moidart. He strode forward eagerly, closed the door, and enfolded her in his arms. Three knee-buckling kisses later, he released her to her supper, pouring the wine and serving the fragrant venison stew left by Mrs. Fraser.

Nell had expected to find herself embarrassed and tongue-tied in his company after the intimate scene in the bothy, but to her relief, Moidart was relaxed and completely charming and seemed determined to draw her out. He talked readily and with all the ease of one of her London friends, but with twice the perception and educated good taste of any of them. He appeared to have read widely and to have a shrewd, though—in Nell's view—unorthodox, perception of the social and political systems of their two countries. She was amused and intrigued by the difference between the elegant figure before her, lightly setting out his objections to the Lakeland poets (deliberately to tease her, she recognised) and the rough, strutting Highlander who had kept the bridge of Achill.

He would pause frequently to ask her a question or her opinion and listen carefully to her reply. She had a clear impression that behind the warm, amused eyes there was an intellect that was scrupling not to test her out, to explore her mind as he had explored her body that afternoon. This was a situation that Nell could react to and enjoy. She was well educated for a girl of her class and had been encouraged by Thérèse, a woman of wider experience than most Englishwomen, to think for herself and not simply to parrot the views of her menfolk.

She led him from a discussion of literature by way of Wordsworth to an exchange of opinions on the outcome of the revolution in France, eager to see whether he would take the side of the monarchists and bemoan the fate of the aristocracy or regard himself as a man of the people and welcome the toppling of the most corrupt régime in Europe. Predictably, this many-faceted man could clearly see both sides of the problem and, on balance, regretted that so little of worth had come out of the struggle and that so much blood should have been spilled for so little progress.

"Progress?" she questioned, affecting surprise. "That is surely an odd word to come from the mouth of a bonneted Laird who talks about the Forty-five as though it were yesterday and who encourages and lives by the outdated customs of a past age?" She held out her glass for more claret, pleased with her challenge.

"Ah, well, you see," he replied unabashed, "the Revolutionaries made the mistake of sweeping away the whole of the past, including much that was good, and the new political edifice, lacking foundation, collapsed in spite of its laudable aims. But me, Elinor? I value tradition and the security of our customs, yet I see that we must move forward. I will show you our—your—lands, and you will see for yourself that we are poised between two times and we must go forward. This is a time to destroy or a time to build, and many hereabouts have chosen to destroy. If I could I would change and expand and build on the firm foundations that we..."

"If *you* could? Don't you mean if Lindsay could?"

"Of course," he said, impatient with her interruption. "We speak, all of us, of Lindsay as a clan. You will come to understand that. It is well known that the Laird has not two brass farthings, however, and can do nothing. Every spare penny he earns is leached away to London, and he has no reserves to develop the land in the way he would like."

He held her in a steady gaze, and she knew that, despite the warmth that had arisen between them this day, there was still a hatred of her position and her power lurking behind the thickly fringed watchful eyes.

"You know well, Moidart, do you not," she said tentatively, "that, as I hold something that Lindsay wants and he holds the key to my independence, we might possibly strike a bargain?"

"I was wondering exactly what kind of a bargain you had in mind," he said slowly. "I am sure that he will listen carefully to any proposal you put before him. You are right, Elinor, you and your kinsman have much to offer each other and must come to a mutually satisfactory arrangement. But tell me...would you still seriously contemplate marrying Lindsay...or even Collingwood? You may speak freely—after all that has passed between us," he added, seeing her hesitation.

Elinor was silent for a moment, feeling acutely the awkwardness of discussing her marriage with the man she was convinced she was in love with. "Yes, with certain stipulations, I believe I would marry either of them," she said finally and defiantly. "For the freedom that's in it."

"But not for the love that's in it?" he questioned.

"I thought that we had established that I was not marrying for love. I want to achieve an alliance that will make no demands on me so that I may look elsewhere for love." She glanced fleetingly up at his impassive face. Surely he was understanding her aright. "But I do see that there are dangers in marrying Lindsay. By so doing, I would place myself fully in his power and, as my husband, my entire fortune would be at his disposal, to plunder as he chose. My entire fortune!" she repeated with emphasis. "The revenues from my Suffolk lands and the considerable sums my father had amassed during his lifetime."

He nodded silently and turned his attention to his wine glass, sensing she was following a thought through and had not yet finished.

"There may be a way, in law, of preventing this," she concluded. "I do not know. For this reason, I would much prefer that he agreed to my marrying Collingwood."

He snorted in disgust, and swiftly she tried to explain—"Henry was a very careful, particular choice. I can control him. I have known him for years; he adores me and will do whatever I tell him to do. When we are married, he will go immediately back to Spain, and I shall live my life as I wish to live it, in freedom by myself or...or with a...companion, if I so choose." She looked up at him, desperately wanting him to understand her meaning, unable to put her dearest wishes into blunt words. She knew no way of making her proposition clearer.

An icy smile was her only response.

"You think me spoilt and wilful, do you not, Moidart?"

"I do! I would think that you are a girl who is accustomed to having whatever and whomever she wants as soon as she wants it. And I can't help wondering what you are intending to do with your great wealth when you have it. Fritter it away on modistes and mantua makers in London and Brighton? You have been bred for little else, clever girl though you be."

So this was his verdict on her character? This was his finding after the close scrutiny to which he had subjected her—spoilt, selfish, and extravagant. She had hoped for better, and disappointment kindled her anger.

"It is none of your business, Moidart, what I choose to do with my own money!" she said stiffly. "And do not think to assist me with my choice of husband—it is none of your concern whom I choose! I consult my steward on the mating of my prize ewes, not my own!"

Tears started to her eyes. How could he treat her in this fashion? How could he discuss in this unconcerned manner a marriage between herself and his employer after what had passed in the bothy only a few hours ago? Was this not unnatural and unfeeling? Why was he deliberately refusing to consider or respond to her blatantly clear suggestions? Had he any idea of what it was costing her to so deny her upbringing, her position, and her nature to approach him in this way? She wanted him to be warm and loving, to take her in his arms again and repeat the sweet things he had said to her in the afternoon.

In a moment, he was by her side and, kneeling, put his arms around her waist. "Forgive me, Elinor. I am tormenting myself with these thoughts, and I see I am tormenting you also. Do you think I can easily contemplate the picture of you in another man's arms, whoever he may be?"

With a sob, Nell pulled his dark head towards her and buried her nose in his hair. He stood and drew her up close to him, kissing her wet cheeks with a sigh. His hand brushed her breast, and she felt a shock of desire run through her body. Would he want to make love to her again?

She had heard that some men, having taken a girl's virginity, had no further use for her...Some men, but evidently not Moidart. His kiss left her in no doubt that he wanted her. He watched her anxious grey eyes melt into seductive pools of enticement, her damp lashes lowered onto her flushed cheeks, and her hot breath teasing his skin. With a sound halfway between a groan and a laugh, he held her away from him and said in a tight and formal voice, "It is late. Will I light your ladyship to bed?"

Reaching the door to her bedchamber, he held the candle aloft and, taking her hand, raised it to his lips and kissed it. "Will that be all, your ladyship?" he asked quietly, his dark eyes reading hers.

Again Nell had an impression of pressure being taken off, a conviction that whatever happened next would be at her instigation, and that if she chose to do so she could leave him here at her door without another word.

"No, Moidart," she said firmly. "There is something more—I wish that you would make certain that the owl is not banging about in the ivy tonight."

With a low laugh he flung the door open and followed her into her room. He made no pretence of opening the shutter but walked to the bedside, lit another candle, and placed his own down on the dressing table. In the gentle candle glow, his face looked stern and thoughtful.

"You have dismissed your maid?"

At her nod, he walked to the door and pushed across the heavy bolt. Nell's heart thumped at the sound, which signalled so clearly his intentions. He returned to her and stood for a moment caressing her with his eyes. Nell made an impatient move towards him.

"My lady must allow me to be her maid once more," he said.

There followed a succession of golden days during which it seemed the storm of rain which had, for better or for worse, driven them for shelter to the bothy at Lis na Brucka had served only to usher in a golden Saint Anthony's Summer. The heather covered moorland was emblazoned in autumn purple and the stands of ash and birch and scrub oak enfolded in the secret places of the hills blazed with autumn gold and autumn crimson.

Daily, Nell heard the sound of horses in the stable yard and, daily, a smiling Lucy or Tibbie would bring a message with the breakfast tray - 'Will her Ladyship care to ride out, the day?' and Nell sent a message back signifying her assent. She and Moidart rode out together unaccompanied under the stable yard archway and onto the causeway bridge and out into the hills.

When she was alone, Nell sought earnestly to understand her situation and to understand what had happened to her. She realised that she had left London determined to have her own way, determined to create a freedom for herself by means of a marriage of convenience, caring little for anybody but herself. Sadly, she recognised that not only had she still not succeeded in negotiating her freedom, she had actually embarked on a totally unforeseen new enslavement. His physical presence, his lovemaking, drugged her senses and were grown essential to her, and the emotions he aroused in her were far beyond any she had imagined or heard described.

Against the reality of these days, Nell decided that her early information had lacked an important ingredient. Nothing had prepared her for the wild, the ferocious elation that Moidart had brought to her. Nothing had warned her that she would find in herself a passion that would equal his own. And where, she often asked herself, was the tide of shame and remorse in which, if she had read aright, Nature had designed to engulf her?

When, during these days, she looked back on the bothy at Lis na Brucka, she couldn't even tell herself that, in the literary tradition, she had fallen victim to the seductive wiles of an unscrupulous man. It seemed to her, in truth, that seductive wiles had been employed evenly between the two of them and that, against all tradition and contrary to all expectation—outside, indeed, the bounds of her wildest imaginings—she had welcomed him.

They came home from their expeditions flushed and cheerful. Sometimes they rode the last mile or so in companionable talk, and sometimes they let the horses have their heads as they drew near the welcome of their stable, rattling over the causeway at a gallop and to the disapproval of Coll.

On these occasions, Nell withdrew without a word to her room, ringing her bell for Lucy and ordering a bath, dropping her muddy clothes around the room. Wrapping herself in a peignoir and warming her toes in front of the fire, she would answer Lucy's questions as to where she had been and what she had seen. As she sat in her bath, Nell planned each evening how, from the limited resources available to her, she could present herself in a new and teasing light at the supper table. In these manoeuvres, she was aided by Lucy, who was puzzled and intrigued but eager to assist.

Every evening, Moidart was waiting to receive her as she descended the stairs, and every evening, his eye took in the details of her toilette with smiling appreciation. Their conversation ranged far and wide. Moidart spoke of his childhood and of the friends of his youth, of his school days and the Peninsular war. Nell spoke likewise of the penalties and compensations of London, of her perplexing and antagonistic life with her stepmother, and of her happy childhood at Somersham. She discovered in herself a frankness she had not found before, but perpetually, it seemed that her frankness was not matched in kind by her companion. There seemed ever to be a reticence. She saw much, but she did not see all. Nor could her gentle probing elicit more than he was prepared to say. A shutter came gently down between him and his past, and nothing Nell could say would penetrate it.

After supper, and with a formal apology, he would withdraw to the business room, explaining that if the correspondence of the estate was allowed to lapse for twenty-four hours, he seemed never able to make up for lost ground. Nell would withdraw a book from the library, usually a book of history or poetry, for the Lindsay library did not descend to the frivolities of the novel. These were, for the most part, gold-backed, red leather volumes, each stamped with the arms of Lindsay. Nell opened each in turn, read her way conscientiously through a page or two, and found in no time that she had let the volume fall shut and was content to sit gazing dreamily into the fire.

In her heart, she knew that she was waiting until she could decently retire to her room, where she would find an attentive Lucy ready to help her out of her dress, brush her hair, envelop her in the soft and lacy froth of a gophered lawn nightgown, and, finally, troubled but unquestioning to the last, bid her a whispered goodnight.

Nell would lie, happy but tremulous, awaiting Moidart's certain coming. The candle at her bedside threw a clear spire of light within the bed hangings, and the firelight flickered against the ceiling. And so she would lie, dewy and enticing, until the inevitable moment when the door would open and the dark figure of Moidart would stand in the door, take three paces across the room, impatiently drop his dressing gown to the floor, and, kneeling on one knee at the bedside, blow out the candle, only to loom, dark and golden in the firelight, above her for a moment before descending to crush her in his arms and be met with an ardour that equalled his own.

It seemed that under the passion that consumed them both, they would wrestle for a while as adversaries but, inevitably, the high tide of passion would ebb and a humorous tenderness would supervene, and they would cling together till Nell fell asleep at last, head pillowed on his chest. When she woke in the morning, he was invariably gone, and Nell would find the bedclothes straightened and the shutter slightly ajar to admit the early morning sunshine and to admit, likewise, the cheerful early morning clatter from the stableyard. And so she would lie in dreamy contemplation until a discreet tap admitted the always anxious face of Lucy. *Lucy knows*, thought Nell. *Of course she does. How could she not? But what does she think? Respectable Suffolk farmer's daughter that she is! Oh, dear, she has become more of an accomplice than a maidservant! I suppose many would say I don't set her a good example!*

It seemed that Lucy's look of anxiety would clear as soon as she had established that Nell, although perhaps languorous, was at least alone, undamaged, and apparently happy. And so another day would start with the customary enquiry, "Will her ladyship ride out, the day?"

11

"I am ashamed," said Moidart as they took breakfast together, "to have so neglected the affairs of the estate. You will think I'm a frivolous steward to spend so much time dallying with you, and today I must lock myself away."

"To make all straight before cousin Roderick returns tomorrow?"

Moidart eyed her quizzically for a moment and said finally, "Yes, you have it. Make all straight before the Laird descends on us and claims your attention."

The morning was cool and fine and, refusing Coll's offer to accompany her, she ordered the roan horse to be saddled and set off to ride over the hill.

"It's not fit," Coll had said reprovingly, "for a young lady to ride out by herself. Moidart will not be pleased."

Nell bit back a sharp rejoinder. She found herself torn between an indulgent amusement at the flattering way Moidart hardly ever let her out of his sight and an irritation with the way she found her movements circumscribed at every turn. The truth was that Nell was glad of the chance that solitude offered, away from the distraction of Moidart's presence, to consider for the first time what had become her position.

Her mind was buzzing, and it seemed to her that she had become two people. Somewhere in the background was a girl who had set off from London, determined to engineer a marriage with the pliable Henry Collingwood or the dry and mysterious Roderick Lindsay. Somewhere in the background, indeed, was that same Henry Collingwood, an increasingly forgotten figure. Somewhere in the background, likewise, was the comfort and splendour of Somersham Hall, the fashionable elegance of Park Lane, and the chattering company of her London friends, where all was silk and muslin and all, it seemed to her as she viewed it from Scotland, was gold and silver.

Here in the foreground, though, was girl of a different sort, a girl increasingly possessed by a country where the dark shadows of a bloodstained past still stretched across the land and by a people whose hereditary enemies might have been disarmed but were now in danger of enslavement by forces that they did not understand. A passionate yearning to fight with and for the people who had made her so welcome possessed her as she rode. *And yet,* she thought, *who am I? A stranger—and worse than a stranger, if all were known. Lindsay blood there may be, but what would they say of a girl to whom the steward had but to crook a finger for her to give herself to him? Why—a drab from the streets of Glasgow could have done no more! And perhaps that is exactly what I have become, a—what did McGregor call me?—a bawbeejoe!*

Try as she might, the wild splendour of the last few days could not be gainsaid. "I am not Lady Elinor Somersham any longer," she said. "I have become Nell Lindsay, it seems. At least for the time. But for so short a time."

Her ride had taken her towards the ruined mill, and on an impulse, she swung her horse aside and trotted down to the burn's side. Throwing her reins over a hitching post, she walked into the dark building. Accustomed as she was to the oak-framed buildings of Suffolk, this stark granite fortress seemed alien indeed. Nell stood for a while, looking upwards through the dusty rafters to the ruined roof. Pushing a little window open, she gazed down into the burn and onto the remains of a ponderous waterwheel. At first it seemed that all the endeavour that had created this building had passed into history, but then she became aware of fine tie beams and a stout floor, and, above all, of its fortress-like walls.

It could breathe again, she thought excitedly. *People could work here. Money could be made.*

Stepping outside into the sunlight once more, she viewed the line of ruined cottages. *Roofs and roof coverings...that's all they need. The walls are there...This glen could be full of people once more.*

Musing and planning, she walked slowly down what must once have been a little street in the wilderness. Here and there a door remained drunkenly askew, here and there were the remains of a window, but otherwise window and door openings stared blindly at her. Blindly at her, that is, until she reached the end of the line, where one cottage appeared to have partially escaped the general ruin. About half of its roof under its heather thatch remained. There was a door in the front doorway; the window was covered with sacking, which was tacked across it.

Curious as to what was the nature of these little dwellings in their heyday, Nell advanced to the door, only to stop dead in her tracks. There were sounds from within. A corner of the sacking twitched. There was someone inside. Nell backed off in alarm. The Gregora? Her hand closed over the skian-dhu in her pocket. To advance and investigate or to retreat? She took a hesitant step forward and called, "Who's there?"

There was no reply, but she was sure someone had moved inside the little house. "Is anyone there?" she called again. She was answered by a thin, wailing, childish voice, which gave way to an uncontrollable hack of coughing. Nell advanced more confidently. She lifted the door latch and pushed the door open into a dim interior.

At first, she could see nothing, but as her eyes grew accustomed to the gloom, she saw a woman seated on a bench of heather bushes covered with a plaid. Her little girl sat beside her holding her hand, and on her lap was an infant, who, on Nell's appearance, began pathetically to cough again. Nearby stood a dark man, large-eyed and sunken-cheeked. His wrists and ankles, Nell noticed, were skeletally thin, but on seeing her, he drew from his clothing a black knife and, with this in hand, bore down upon her, addressing her in a flood of Gaelic. He was angry and frightened. Nell stood her ground.

"I don't have the Gaelic," she said, as she had repeated so often over the past week.

The man turned helplessly to his wife, who began to speak in a sing-song English. "The good man," she said, "does not have the English, but he would say, 'For pity's sake, for the love of God, dinna ye give us awa!' The wee boy can walk nae further. He needs this night to rest before we gang on our way."

She rose to her feet and thrust the little boy into the arms of her husband and, crawling on her knees, she seized Nell's hand. "For the love of God, have pity, fine lady!"

"What...What do you fear?" Nell began desperately, pulling her to her feet again. She did not understand.

"We are turned from our home," the woman went on. "We have no home to return to—naught but a ring o' blackened stones."

Nell looked from one to the other and back to the little boy. "That cough," she said, "He should be by a good fire."

"Good fire?" said the woman bitterly. "Where would we find a fire that we could sit beside? Folks struggle to care for themselves without caring for the likes of us." Tears began to run down her cheeks, making white rivulets in the grime, and she continued, "God save us—another night in the open will be his last, I'm thinking! Oh, my bairn!"

Nell didn't pause to reflect. Her duty had never been clearer before her. "Can you yet walk two miles more?" she asked. "If I carry the bairns for you? You shall spend this night in the house of Lindsay. I come from there."

The woman looked at her with large, wondering eyes. "But we're none of Lindsay's folk," she said dubiously.

"I'll answer for the House of Lindsay," said Nell firmly. "I choose my folk."

In voluble Gaelic the woman turned to her husband and to her children, saying at last, and in English for Nell's benefit, "Come ye, we're going with the lady."

There was a protest from the man, who still stood, knife in hand, and an argument ensued between the two, with the woman saying finally to Nell, "He doesna ken how we can trust ye, begging your pardon."

For reply, Nell held out her arms to the little girl, who went to her willingly enough. She kissed her dirty cheek, picked her up, and carried her through the door. She waited outside, and first the woman with her infant and then, reluctantly, the man emerged, carrying in his hand four small potatoes.

"Oh, God," thought Nell. "That's all they own in the world! Four small potatoes!"

They walked back down the little street to Nell's horse. Jumping clumsily, Nell hoisted herself into the saddle and held out her arms to the little girl. Trusting at last, the man lifted his daughter to her. Nell cradled the thin body in its bundle of rags, looking down with speechless pity at the small scratched feet as they dangled on either side of her horse. She held out her arms to take the little boy too, but the man shook his head and they set off.

They looked with awe as at last they drew near the House of Lindsay, and evidently the man's fears returned. For the last time, the wife turned beseechingly to Nell and said, "Promise ye'll no ship us awa'." With tears in her eyes, Nell shook her head and led the way into the stableyard where they were greeted—as always—by auld Angus and by Coll.

"What have you got there?" Coll asked roughly.

"A family," said Nell. "Poor folk."

Coll addressed them fluently in Gaelic and listened carefully to their reply, saying at last to Nell with a bitter twist to his mouth, "Och, they're no poor folk! Why they've only travelled forty miles in the last three days, and look—they've got four potatoes. What more in this world would you be wanting!" He laughed grimly and, beckoning them to follow, led them to a door at the end of the stables and pointed their way to a little staircase that led to an upper room. "They can rest there awhile until the Laird can see what he can do for them. I'll have food sent across from the house. There's a pump in the yard, straw in the wee room—it's by way of a hayloft. They'll come to no harm."

"Oh, Coll," said Nell, "have I done the right thing?"

He looked at her solemnly. "I don't know about the right thing," he said, "but you've done the only thing."

"But Lindsay—there's a limit to what the House of Lindsay can do."

"Limit there may be," said Coll, "but the bad times will have come forever when Lindsay turns away such as those. God's curse on the times we live in!"

Deeply moved and thoughtful, Nell gave her horse over to the care of auld Angus, who seemed always to be gladly on hand to greet her returns and oversee her departures, and walked over to the castle. During her absence, the whole aspect of the great hall had changed. For one thing, it was swarming with people, many of whom Nell had never seen before; trestle tables were being set up here and there; sheaves of barley were being arranged in the window embrasures, and, she noticed, a pyramid of apples had been set up on the table in a bower of crimson rowan.

"What is this?" she asked in puzzlement as Moidart emerged from the business room, smiling a welcome.

"Making all ready for the Harvest Dance," he said. "I don't interfere— I wouldn't be allowed to interfere! The Harvest Dance has been arranged like this for years beyond count. The barley sheaves go here because they have always gone here. We have a pile of apples on the table because that has always been so, and Rob McColl has arranged them because that's the way his father used to arrange them. If I tried to change any of this, all would listen politely because Highland folk are polite, but none would take the slightest bit of notice of me! And see there," he continued as two men staggering under the weight of the most enormous iron cauldron Nell had ever seen came through the door from the kitchen quarters, "they'll make the punch in that. They'll make the punch as they always have—lemons, cinnamon, honey, whisky, ale, all in due proportion—a proportion, I dare say, worked out hundreds of years ago."

The entry of the cauldron and its bearers had released a blast of cooking smells from the kitchen, and Moidart sniffed appreciatively. "Come with me," he said, "if you want to see industry!"

Nell followed him into the kitchen to find Mrs. Fraser in command of a roomful of country women. Ranks of pies and pasties were forming up on the long table, and a great cake the size of a cart wheel was, under Mrs. Fraser's directions, being decorated by Tibbie and Lucy with cherries and nuts and sprigs of angelica. Nell smiled to see Lucy, the elegant London lady's maid, sleeves rolled up to the elbow, absorbed, in happy equality, in this menial task.

They've captured Lucy as well! thought Nell.

In the middle of all this purposeful activity, she was relieved to see a young boy being sent across the yard to the hayloft with a basket laden with food from the tables. Her little family would eat well that day.

Turning to Moidart, she asked, "Cousin Roderick will be here tomorrow?" And as she spoke, the question came insistently into her mind: "And what then?"

He eyed her speculatively for a moment and said at last, "Yes. He has sent no word, but the Laird would never miss the Harvest Dance. He will be here. So—tomorrow it is!"

Aware that her question had created a tension between them, Nell endeavoured to change the subject. "And how many people are coming to your dance, Moidart?"

"Well it's hard to tell exactly," he said. "Perhaps a hundred? Perhaps more. All the folk from the estate, and that would be about fifty...but then there will be their bairns...Our neighbour Fergusson of Donuil, his wife and his three strapping children, McPherson of Doune, and I forget how many he's got...Doctor Jameson and Mrs. Jameson and the Misses Jameson...I think that's five...Oh, and our English neighbour, young Rob Kintoul, whom you may well have met in London with his new wife, I believe."

"Lord Kintoul are you saying? Robert Kintoul? Yes...I believe we have met before...And where will you put them all?"

"This is a big house when all is said and done, and Mrs. Fraser and her girls have been opening and airing the company rooms for some while, but for the humbler folk, well, they mostly live hard by and they'll walk to their home. The Fergussons will drive home I dare say, and Kintoul and McPherson. Doctor Jim and his wife will stay—they've a long road—but for the rest, well, they'll sleep just here and there. There's always a few whose legs wouldn't carry them over the bridge, so you'll find some in front of the fire, some in the hay, you know the sort of thing...As I say—some here and some there!"

Nell's mind flashed back to the last Servants' Ball she had attended at Somersham, with Poulson the butler formally leading her stepmother onto the floor to open the dance and with the other servants following in strict order of precedence; Mrs. Maxwell, the housekeeper, was tightly corseted in black bombazine, her gimlet-like eye roaming the room for any possible breach of decorum on the part of the younger staff. Evidently, the Harvest Home at the House of Lindsay was to be of a different character.

One of the men entered, requesting Moidart's presence in the stables, where arrangements for the accommodation of the guests' horses needed his attention. He went off, leaving Nell to poke about in the cherry jar and steal the almonds. She had always loved kitchens, and as a child had spent many hours trailing around behind the cook, delighting in making herself useful, and it was almost more than she could bear not to roll her sleeves up too and join in the preparations. But all was so well organised and industrious that she realised there was little she could do to be of practical help, and she wandered back into the great hall.

A moment later, she was joined by Lucy, the cake finished, and they walked around together, admiring the decorations. Fingering a display of barley sheaves crossed and tied with red ribbons, Nell said dreamily, "I wish I could remember how to make a corn dolly like the ones we have at home. Cook taught me how to do it years ago, but I don't know if my fingers would still have the skill..."

"Oh, I can do corn dollies," replied Lucy, the farmer's daughter. "That's easy. We could have a go, Miss Nell, if you like, but they've only got barley straw here. You need wheat straw for a good corn dolly. I wonder if? I'll go and ask Coll."

Coll, who was never far away, it seemed, was consulted and agreed to go and fetch an armful of wheat straw from the big barn. He returned in triumph a few minutes later with the right kind of straw and was instantly dispatched by Lucy to get a bucket of water to dampen it. Lucy checked the length, the pliability, and the hollowness of the straw with a knowledgeable eye and pronounced it satisfactory, and they settled down on the floor and started, with much argument at first, to twist up a big corn dolly, dampening, bending, and plaiting.

Lucy began to shape the body and the skirt, while Nell took on the simpler task of forming the head and arms. A crowd gathered and murmured their admiration as the nimble fingers, swiftly gathering confidence, moulded and teased the stubborn stalks into the whirling skirt and rounded bosom of a female figure. They decorated her head with trailing velvet ribbons and berries and stood back, proud and slightly surprised by their own skill, to inspect the result of their efforts.

Coll was loudest in his praise, to Lucy's dimpling pleasure, and in response to a general call to display the ladies' work, he climbed a ladder and fixed it with care in pride of place over the great fireplace.

When Moidart returned, Nell took his arm and said teasingly, "Now what would you say, Moidart, if anyone wished to make a change to the harvest ritual here?"

"I'd say, as I said before, that they wouldn't have a hope! I moved a dish of pickles one year, and it was put back again five minutes later. Every year I try to get the music down the other end of the hall, but it's a useless effort!"

"Well look behind you!" she laughed. "This year you have an addition to your ritual—you have a Suffolk corn dolly looking down on your Scottish feast!"

His face showed astonishment followed by pleasure, which quickly faded as he said, "I think your corn dolly is beautiful, but just wait until Mrs. Fraser sees it! I'm afraid it will have to come down…"

"Don't be so sure now, Rorie!" said a cheerful voice behind them. Jennie Fraser had come out of the kitchen, wiping her hands on her apron, and stood looking up admiringly at the decoration. "There it shall stay! I think a time has come when the south shall be joined with the north, and who knows? Perhaps we shall all be the better for it."

She smiled fondly at the corn dolly. "I mind when I was a girl in Angus...we had such a one each harvest. The lads would cut the last bundle of standing corn in the last field and bring it home for the prettiest girls in the village to plait it up into a figure. The Corn Maiden, she was called, and it was said that she would bring fruitfulness and prosperity to all in the coming year. There would be food aplenty, the ewes would all have twins, and there'd be babies in the cradles before the next Harvest Home." She sighed dreamily. "Yes, the Corn Maiden was accounted a sign of fertility—as, no doubt, Lady Elinor is aware..." she finished with a parting glance at Elinor.

Nell had sprung instinctively away from Moidart at Jennie Fraser's appearance, but her indulgent glance back towards them as she walked away left Nell in no doubt that she knew more than she was supposed to know about their relationship. Moidart gazed tenderly into Nell's agitated face and asked gently, "What are you thinking?"

"I am thinking, Moidart, that Mrs. Fraser knows that we...that..." she stammered in confusion, turning her glowing cheeks to the fire.

He did not need to consider his reply. "Why, yes, of course she knows! How could you doubt it? A house can never keep secrets from the housekeeper, you know! And I will tell you that everyone in this house and probably for miles around is gossiping about nothing else. Are you disturbed?"

Nell found herself gasping at his frankness. "Of course I am disturbed! What must they all be thinking? Oh, Moidart! I must leave the moment I have seen my cousin tomorrow! I cannot attend the ball knowing that everyone is whispering."

He stood close to her, captured one of her hands in his, and held it tightly.

"But 'tis no shame, Elinor! They are happy for us! They all know me and respect and trust me and, though you have been with us for but a few days, they have come to love you. You are a proud woman, Elinor, and do not hesitate to crush me with your noble birth and freeze me with your hauteur, but I have remarked that in your dealings with my people you are all sweetness and concern."

She looked up at him, beginning to smile again, "Crushed? Frozen, you say? I will never believe that! But tell me the truth, man. Are you saying that, truly, *your*," and her slight emphasis on the word made him look sharply at her, "your people no longer mistrust me, although it is certain that they all know who I am and the part I might play in their lives?"

"I know that anyone having any disrespectful word to say about your ladyship would find himself being brought to account by auld Angus and Robin Oig," he said mischievously. "Courage and loyalty, Elinor. If you have these two qualities, be you the devil himself, you will win the heart of a Highlander, and after your intervention on the bridge, I fear that, whether you like it or not, you are forevermore in their eyes and in their stories, a Lindsay. They know what we are to each other, of course they do, down to the smallest shepherd boy, and, they would reason, if we make each other happy, where's the harm?"

But Nell was more shaken than she had believed she could possibly be and needed time by herself to put her thoughts in order and make her plans for the coming interview with her cousin, an interview that she was growing increasingly to dread, she realised. Suppose a whiff of the scandal reached Roderick before she could see him? How would it change his attitude to his ward and, indeed, his plans to marry her, when he discovered that she had been conducting a love affair with his steward under his roof during his absence? She took the opportunity when a footman entered of saying, "I have preparations of my own to make for tomorrow, Moidart. I will retire early to my room and have a light supper brought to me on a tray. Mrs. Fraser has quite enough to do today without having to prepare a supper for me. Will you please arrange that?" And she hurried upstairs to the haven of her bedchamber.

There Nell settled down with a novel and a small book of Scottish history, found for her by Moidart and pressed into her hand with an urgent wish that she acquaint herself with an unbiased account of the events of the Forty-five. He had seemed uncommonly eager that she should be well informed about her surroundings and the history and traditions of the land, she mused. Her attention to the comings and goings of the Bonny Prince Charlie was desultory to say the least and, although normally a quick and eager reader, she found her thoughts wandering more and more frequently to her own Scottish Odyssey.

After a final excited account from Lucy of the last of the preparations below and a list of the dishes she had helped to prepare for the feast, Nell dismissed her early, suggesting that the girl was quite exhausted and would need to recover her strength for the morrow's festivities. Nell prepared herself for bed, assessing for the hundredth time her situation, analysing her thoughts, and planning a speech to her cousin.

All day she had been happy and busy and caught up in the excitement. She had relished the sense of purpose and community and tradition that radiated from these people and had been warmed by their approval. In contrast, her London life appeared artificial and meaningless. With a smile, she wondered how she could ever begin to explain to her smart city friends the total happiness she had felt, sitting on the floor of the great hall of a Scottish castle, plaiting up a corn dolly with her maid. How could she explain the sense of freedom and the intoxicating whiff of danger when she rode out by herself on the moor this morning, dagger in pocket, in case she encountered a McGregor? The most alarming thing that could happen to her out riding in London, she reflected, was a chance meeting with Jemmie Fanshawe! With surprise, she realised that this was the first time for days Fanshawe had swum into her consciousness, so distant was she beginning to feel from her Park Lane life. And the destitute family she had brought in to add to the already overstretched estate, she saw as her personal responsibility. She would make certain that her cousin was in a position to support them.

She had been looking forward with as much pleasurable anticipation as anyone to the ball and yet...and yet...Hard on the heels of her pleasure came the thought that tomorrow could well be her last day in the House of Lindsay. If her cousin proved, in the flesh, to be the cold, unsympathetic old reprobate she had every reason to expect him to be, she would have an uncomfortable interview with him and be at once on her way, perhaps even before the ball started, leaving undone the many things she wanted to achieve.

This thought was swiftly followed by the reassurance of the trump card she held. She had decided on her first morning at the castle that she would bargain with Roderick Lindsay. If the cost of acquiring independence was high, she was prepared to go high. She had decided that if her cousin's hostility to her plans was founded on the simple fact that he would lose his lands if she had her way, then she would trade these lands for her freedom. She would agree to make no claim on them ever, in return for his cooperation in the matter of her marriage. They were not hers, these wild hills, this castle, these people; they could not be and never should be hers, however much she had grown to love them since her arrival. How strange that only by knowing and loving them had she learned that she must give them up! And did this hold true for Moidart also? Must she have known and loved him only to give him up?

And who, after all, was Moidart? Nell had often smiled at the proprietorial airs that he assumed. Did her Suffolk steward's demeanour change when she was absent? Did Kenton parade about like the cock of the walk? She didn't think so. But there was something special about Moidart's deportment, his deep love of the place and the people and the honour in which they so obviously held him, that argued a connection with Lindsay closer than that of servant and Laird. Not for the first time, a polite phrase often heard in London came to her mind—born on the wrong side of the blanket. Were Moidart an illegitimate son of the house of Lindsay, that would account for much!

Bastard sons never inherited. Moidart could only wait and watch while Lindsay struggled to keep the clan afloat. How far did he approve of his master's plans to marry the unworldly young heiress? Perhaps these plans were the product of the steward's own resourceful and devious mind? What had he called her jokingly when he'd rescued her on the road? A braw, plump dawtie, flighting north. A well fleshed but brainless bird, an easy catch in the Lindsay nets.

Her mind twisted this way and that, still struggling to find a solution. Surely her proud cousin would never give his consent to her marrying his steward? The possibility only entered her mind to be ruefully dismissed. She might lower herself to such a liaison, but Roderick

Lindsay would never countenance it. And Moidart had not mentioned marriage to her anyway. Indeed, he had not said a word about any future they might have together. He had not even said he loved her. He had talked freely of making love but had never uttered the words she yearned to hear.

Perhaps awareness of the gulf between the Lady Elinor Somersham and the steward on a remote and impoverished Scottish estate had held him back but, dully, the thought crept into her head that perhaps she had, after all, been deluded, deceived. Perhaps she was no more to him than a passing fancy, and he might even arrange her post chaise back to London with some relief tomorrow. An innocent remark of Lucy's that first morning flashed with clarity into her mind. Sharing the gossip of the servants' hall, she had said, "No one ever says no to Moidart!" Could it be that the steward of the house assumed that he had the right to bed any visiting maidservant? And he had, as he had freely confessed, taken a fancy to her on the road when he had thought her to be a servant.

There had been nothing in her subsequent behaviour, she remembered, to check his advances. She had roused him from his room in the night, and though her terror had been real enough, perhaps he had put quite a different interpretation on events, particularly, as she thought with a blush, when she had made it clear that she wanted him to stay with her. And in the bothy? One imperious gesture from her, one chilling word, and she would have returned to the castle unscathed. Indeed, she blushed to recall that he had himself attempted to abandon the seduction. And since their return? Her door had a lock, did it not? That lock had not been used to bar him from her room at any time on the following nights. She had behaved like a light-skirt, she concluded—small wonder if he treated her as such.

He entered her room silently, without knocking, and, throwing off his dressing gown, slid into bed beside her.

"What's this, my lass? Tears?" he said in surprise, kissing her cheeks.

The familiar warmth and tenderness of the man triggered a storm of sobs that would not stop, and he held her close, murmuring softly until she began to grow quiet.

"Now then...that's better. Now tell me why you're taking on so?"

"I was thinking that very soon I must leave for England and leave you behind, Moidart, and...and...it will be hard for me to go away and never see you again..." was the best she could manage to whisper.

He raised himself on one elbow and looked intently down at her. "Would you want to be seeing me again, Elinor?"

She had never been able to dissimulate her feelings for him and, even now when she was coming to suspect his motives, she could not have said other than, "Every day, Moidart, until I die."

"Are you saying, perhaps, that you love me, your ladyship?" he persisted. "And I'm asking you now, before I have made love to you, and not in the outfall when you might say things you wouldn't mean a minute later." His face was alive with an emotion she was not sharing with him. Was it elation, pleasure—triumph, even?

She closed her damp lashes, sighed raggedly, and murmured indistinctly against his neck, "I fear that I do. Yes, I love you Rorie Moidart."

As though he were taking the next step in a set dance, he asked, "And the House of Lindsay? Have you been happy here?"

She looked up quickly at the unexpected question and replied carefully, "I have never been happier in my life. I shall never forget this place where I feel I have lived fully for the first time."

For a long moment, he stared at her, his dark eyes devouring her features and his forefinger slowly tracing the line of her jaw. "Then all will be well with us, Nell Lindsay. Never fear!" And gentle fingers began to loosen the ribbons of her nightgown.

12

The combination of a fine autumn morning and nerves stretched as taut as a fiddle string urged Nell to put on her cleaned and pressed russet walking dress, her bonnet, and boots and leave the hurly-burly of the castle for a brisk walk down by the burn. She was glad also to be able to avoid Moidart, whom she was finding an increasingly puzzling and disturbing presence. He was anxious to know her movements at each moment of the day, and she had the distinct feeling that she was being watched over closely, if not by him directly, then by Coll. She needed time by herself to rehearse her speech to her cousin and to get her thoughts into order. Eluding Lucy and Mrs. Fraser, she set out to walk by the burn and then crossed over to dip into the fringes of the woodland. So enchanting were the light, the stillness, and the woodland noises that she walked farther than she had intended. She realised with a glance up at the sun that she had been gone longer than was wise and that she had long ago strayed out of earshot of a carriage or horse arriving at the castle, heralding her cousin's arrival.

She struck back in the straightest possible line towards the castle and, within a mile of it, where her path crossed the main carriage road, she saw a figure advancing up the road. By his bag and his limping walk, she recognised the old postman from Vennacher. He was waving to attract her attention, and she paused and waited for him.

When he drew level with her, he addressed her in the open way of the Highlands. "Good day to ye your ladyship. Are ye now on your way back to the great house? Ye are? Then it's my lucky day! Would ye consent to take this letter the last bit for me and save my old man's legs?"

Nell smiled and murmured her agreement. He held out the letter and pointed to the seal, involving her in his innocent inquisitiveness, "See here, it's from the Laird's man of law in Glasgow."

Nell turned and started on her way again, looking closely at the letter as she did so. From his lawyer? The contents might very well relate to her own future. It was addressed to Roderick Lindsay, Moidart Castle, by Vennacher. Her eyes slid back along the line of elegant, clerkly script and saw again the words "Moidart Castle." She hurried back on her tracks and seized the old man by his shoulder.

"Postie! This is to go to *Moidart Castle*?" she said. "Where would that be?"

His jaw gaped and he looked at her as though she were mad. "Why, Missie, it's where you've just come from," he said, backing away. "That'd be the House of Lindsay—yon great pile of granite," he added, cocking a splayed thumb at the house. He hobbled off hastily back down the track, casting a puzzled glance back over his shoulder to check that she was walking towards the castle.

Mind awhirl with confusion and suspicion, Nell ran back to the castle and found Lucy stationed by the front door and looking anxiously out for her. "Thank God you've come back, Miss Nell! Was there ever such a stirabout! Moidart's been shouting for you all morning! He flew into a terrible rage when he couldn't find you...thought you'd run away... then he accused me and Coll of not keeping an eye on you! 'This is not a prison, sir!' I says. 'And Coll and I are not her ladyship's keepers! Miss Nell is accustomed to going about wherever she chooses!' I hope I didn't go too far Miss Nell?"

"No, Lucy. Quite the right thing to say. It's a silly fuss about nothing, and you are to pay no heed to these strange Scottish ways. But where is Moidart now?"

"He went off to the stables with Coll, Miss. I heard them saying they were going to get out the carriage and go to Vennacher. Word came that the pastor's horse had gone lame and he and Mrs. Pastor are having to be fetched for the dance. They set off an hour ago. But Miss Nell!" Lucy's eyes sparkled with excitement. "He's here! Your cousin's arrived! Tibbie brought word not ten minutes ago that you are to attend him in the business room the minute you get back. I've been posted here to make certain you got the message."

"Thank you, Lucy, I will go straight there," said Nell with a firmness she did not feel and, pausing only to lay down her bonnet, she hurried in a welter of foreboding and anger along to the business room.

Catching her breath in an attempt to still her pounding heart, she stood for a moment outside the door and then firmly opened the door and stepped in, closing it behind her. Her eyes took in the friendly brown glow of the room; the ranks of leather-bound books; the orderly piles of documents stacked on the table; a copy of Tom Paine's book *The Rights of Man*, recently abandoned on a footstool with a sprig of heather marking the place; and moved to the great, upholstered, high-backed chair by the fireside.

Roderick Lindsay lounged with his back to the door, one arm foppishly extended in its silk embroidered sleeve and lying along the arm of the chair. On his hand, projecting from a frilled white cuff, gleamed the heavy emerald ring she remembered having seen on her great-grandfather's hand in his portrait. Tibbie's words came back to her: "...whiles the Laird will wear it to this day..." This was surely the ring taken from the dead hand of John Lindsay younger on the field of Culloden! With a gulp, she realised that Cousin Lindsay was wearing it in deference to what he saw as an important occasion—a realisation that did nothing to quell her inward quaking. Surely he had heard her enter, yet the figure remained motionless, his long leg, elegant in grey silk knee breeches, white stocking, and buckled shoe stretched out carelessly in front of him.

She approached the chair and said in a voice low with control, "Cousin Roderick?"

Her guardian leapt to his feet, spun round, seized both her hands in his, and leaned forward to kiss her affectionately on both cheeks.

Nell was for the moment turned to stone. When she could find her voice again, she pulled her hands away from his clasp and said, "Moidart! I suspected some mischief or other! What have you done with my cousin? Where is Lindsay? Have you killed him, man?"

Moidart, almost unrecognisable in fashionable morning dress—handsome and confident, his eyes alight with mischief—said, "In a manner of speaking I suppose you could say that I had killed him off, but only temporarily, and now, you see, he is resurrected, and believe me, Elinor, he is enchanted to make the acquaintance of his charming ward."

In a state of shocked disbelief, all Nell could think of to say was, "But...what are you telling me? I don't believe this! You are Moidart, Rorie Moidart—no one calls you Lindsay!"

She sank weakly onto a chair and he knelt in front of her, regaining possession of her hands and saying easily, "Well, that at least is true. And it made it very easy to deceive you. In this country, men of substance are called by the house or the place they live in—why, even their wives call them so. Old Alan McBride, who lives in the great house at Vennacher, is simply *Vennacher* to everyone, including his Lizzie and his daughters. And the short form of Roderick is Rorie, the name everyone knows me by. It was only necessary to make certain that Jennie and Tibbie and Coll knew what I was about...though I had some trouble with Jennie! She did not approve of my deception and was several times on the point of telling you who I was."

"But...I do not understand why...why you are not old? I was expecting to see a man of my father's age..."

"Your grandmother Alice," he explained, "from whom you are to inherit all this, was the eldest child of your great-grandfather, the child of his first wife, as I told you. When his wife died, he married again, and at the age of forty-five he produced my father."

"So there was a gap of twenty years between the sister and the brother—a generation almost," Nell said.

"Yes, and as a result, there are but eight years between us, cousin. I call you cousin," he added with a smile, "though we are but half cousins once removed, because I like the word and I like the idea of our kinship.

It is said that Alice continued to be the old man's favourite and that he had never time for my father, who was a weak and studious boy, one more ready to lift a book than a claymore. And when my father married an Ogilvie, he found himself cut off from his father's estates. They were willed to Alice, good Alice, who had married well and produced a son. I would think Grandfather hoped that this son of an English lord would come home to Scotland and run Moidart, but that never came to pass, and my father was kindly allowed to linger on here, living on borrowed time and using borrowed money, struggling to keep the clan alive!" For a moment, his voice had resumed the bitter tone of earlier days, and she heard again the scathing and dangerous tone that had first made her quail on their ride through the forest on her arrival in the lands of Lindsay.

"So, you see, Elinor, I did not lie or deceive you in that I, and my father before me, have been your stewards, holding these lands but never having them, fostering them for the absentee lord who barely knew of their existence, apart, of course, from the revenue he reaped from them—revenue that should, by rights, have gone back into the land that produced it and not into putting jewels around the throats of hen-headed Englishwomen!"

She was dumb. With a glacial calm, she realised that there was nothing she could do, nothing she could say, to turn the tide of mocking dislike in his tone. He had begun by hating her and all that she, however unwillingly, represented and—could it be?—in spite of all that had passed between them, he was still unknown to her, foreign, inimical. In a moment, her hopes, her future had been undone.

"It cannot have been easy for you growing up on land that had been passed away from you," she whispered with sudden insight.

"No indeed! It would have been struggle enough without the constant reminders from my father that I must not count on anything becoming mine. The work I did, I was doing for an Englishman I had never seen and who cared nothing for us! I was worse off than my own tacksmen! In the end, I grew so sick of waiting for the blow to fall that I embraced a different family tradition and, as you might say, exchanged the plough for the broadsword. Three weary years of march and counter-march through the bare hills of Spain! I loathed soldiering! And my heart—whatever the future might hold—was here in Lindsay lands. I found my heart yearning to be back in my own place.

"The times were troubled, my father was failing, and I was needed here. I sold out and came home. I brought nothing back with me from the wars. Nothing, that is, but a determination to fight if I could to regain my own for the honour of Lindsay and for the people of these glens."

She could not reach him. She could understand him, sympathise, and agree with him, but she felt that all warm contact between them had been broken. "I cannot see why you should so deceive me, Moidart," she said, looking for meaning in his eyes. "Why did you let me go on thinking you were the steward here? Why could you not tell me you were my cousin?"

"Your cousin and your guardian," he said with emphasis. "With the power to make your happiness or break it, at least for five years. How would you have viewed me? As someone hostile who would give an outright no to your schemes? As an unthinking, blind idiot who would give you permission to form an alliance with a worthless booby? Either way, you would have gone posting straight back to London on the next coach and that would have been the last I would have seen of you. Is this not true?" He took her by the arms and made her look up at him.

Dumbly she nodded her head.

"Oh, Elinor!" he said in a voice full of emotion, folding her rigid body closely in his arms, "I could not have risked that! Did you not realise what I was feeling for you from the moment I saw you? I came with Coll through the trees to see if we could help when we heard the shouting on the coach road and stood there transfixed. There before me was a lass bonnier than any I'd ever seen with a cloud of hair the colour of a wheatfield at noon, the face of an angel, and the cussedness of a sergeant-major. I had no idea who you were—I didn't care. I had left home early that day for the hunt and had not received your warning letter—and, indeed, I took you at first for a maid, but whoever you were, I knew you were going to be mine!

"When you told me you were Lady Elinor Somersham, whose very name I had come to loathe and curse, I could not accept it. I refused to acknowledge the relationship of guardian and ward, which would have put us at loggerheads at once and cut short our acquaintance."

"But, cousin, you offered me marriage..." she interrupted in astonishment, remembering the episode that had triggered her flight to Scotland, "You wrote to me—a curt, offensive letter! What did you intend by that? Was that more of your pretence? Were you ever in earnest, or have I wasted my time in coming here?" Anger was beginning to make her eyes sparkle and narrow in a way that had intimidated many a bold fellow, but he looked straight back at her with a guilty grin.

"I regret to tell you, Elinor, that I was not in earnest when I made you my offer. I was so incensed by the notion that you expected me, with so little formality, to sign over everything I possessed to a nincompoop like Collingwood, whom I had the misfortune to encounter in the Peninsula, that I thought I would teach you a lesson. I had my lawyer dash off a very choleric piece of nonsense, and it was only later it occurred to me that the notion of an arranged marriage was not without its possibilities. Even so, I was much amazed by your swiftness in pursuing my cynical suggestion! And, all the more reason, when I met you, for not confessing who I was—I guessed that the writer of that pompous letter would not find much favour with you! I thought I would have a better chance of getting to know you as Moidart."

"You were better placed also to demonstrate to me the injustice of my claim on the estates," she said quietly.

"Aye, that too," he agreed.

"And could you not have done that without...without?"

"Seducing you, I think you mean?" he smiled. "I'll never be certain who did the seducing, your ladyship!"

She blushed with shame and anger at the memory. "I feel as though I have loved a man who does not exist! I loved Moidart! I do not love, I do not know, I do not *want* to know Roderick Lindsay! He is the same scheming, selfish, unprincipled scoundrel as those who line the walls of the ballroom at Carlton House! His motives are the same, but oh, his cunning is deeper!"

For a moment, it seemed his eyes clouded with pain, but he stepped nearer. "Close your eyes!"

Nell stood her ground and glared at him. The scorn in her frosty eyes would have stopped any other man in his tracks, but after an imperceptible tightening of the jaw, he bent his head and kissed her unresponsive lips. "I'm the man I always was, and that's to remind you. Last night you told Moidart that you loved him, and this night you will say the same to Lindsay!"

This night, she decided, looking away quickly to hide from him the thought in her eyes, *my door will be bolted. I have been used enough. This man has plans for me that he has not yet revealed, but which I am beginning to guess at. I do not trust him, but I must be sure to hide my suspicions from him.*

With an effort she collected herself and resumed, "We have many busy hours to fill before then, Moidart," she said matter-of-factly to steer him away from a subject she had no further wish to discuss. "Your guests will be arriving soon, and I am wondering what part, if any part, you would wish me to play in the festivities."

"A central part," he replied, responding with apparent relief to her change of mood. "You will be the focus of all eyes, and you will be by my side. You must be prepared for much curiosity and speculation... after all, there will be many there whose lives depend on your wishes and decisions, not least the Laird," he said with a brief smile. "I do not know whether you have chosen your toilette, Elinor?"

Was he then taking over all aspects of her life? She swallowed a sudden flash of anger and interrupted him. "You had already specified a simple white dress, I remember, Moidart, and I have such a one. You need not concern yourself further."

"Good. Good." He nodded. "And for jewels? What will you do for jewels?"

"I brought none with me on the journey for fear of highwaymen. And to hear your views on jewels around the throats of—what was it you said?—*hen-headed* Englishwomen, I am glad of that!" she said bitterly.

"And, indeed, I should not have liked you to flaunt your wealth, but your pretty neck deserves some decoration and I think I have the answer..."

He picked up a velvet-covered box from the table and handed it to her. She opened the box and gasped with astonishment to see a river of diamonds flashing with icy purity.

"My mother's," he said simply. "Part of her dowry and the last of her jewels. The rest are all sold long ago, but I have managed to hold on to this, her favourite. Everyone will recognise it as hers and will rejoice to see it worn again after all these years. Will you wear it, Elinor?"

"Yes, Moidart, I will wear it," she said. "I will be proud to wear it—to honour your mother's memory. And now, though much remains to be said between us, you must excuse me, cousin, I have little time to prepare for the feast."

Nell had run all the way up to her room and bolted the door behind her before she remembered that she still had Lindsay's letter in the pocket of her walking dress. Her mind was boiling with mixed emotions from her interview with her cousin. She had come away from him convinced that he both hated and loved her, if that were possible. Which feeling would predominate, time would tell—and a very short time, she felt in her bones. Eager for any information that would help her to understand and perhaps even to outguess her lover, her enemy, she went to the window and fingered the letter. The large red seal was, indeed, that of his lawyer, and she knew she must not break it.

And why not? an internal voice tempted her. *Has he not deceived you abominably? You owe him no loyalty. Break the seal!* But she could not bring herself to do that and contented herself with lifting the flap and peeping sideways into the package. She was not surprised to see her own name written on a separate sheet of thick legal paper enclosed within the outer letter. Skilfully, between finger and thumb, she withdrew this from its wrapper and read, "Counterpart of agreement dated...for the Lady Elinor Somersham." This was intended for her! Her mind made up, she took a deep breath and broke the seal.

The lawyer's letter was dated two days before her arrival in Scotland, she noticed. Adam Renfrew had obviously assumed—or been instructed perhaps—that there was no urgency in the matter and spoke in the language of an old friend rather than that of a lawyer. He had pleasure in sending to his friend Lindsay the documents they had discussed and that he had had drawn up according to the formula they had agreed. There was one copy for Lindsay and a counter copy for Lady Elinor Somersham. He wished Lindsay the best of luck and asked him to let him know how the affair turned out.

Wonderingly, Nell examined a copy of the document. Her eyes grew round with astonishment and she blessed the good fortune that had put this letter into her hands before his.

The document was destined to be signed by her and declared that she, from this date (left undated), hereby foreswore all claims in the present and in the future on her Scottish estates. There followed a close and careful description of the extent of these.

Nell sat down, weak-kneed, in her chair. This was what that careful mind had been planning, and, obviously, those plans had been laid well before he had met her. He'd lied. Deceitful, treacherous, conniving and a host of other unflattering epithets sprang to her lips before she calmed herself and acknowledged that, had circumstances been as she had expected, she would have been gratified to find that so much of the ground had already been prepared. Such forethought would have speeded her stay in Scotland. No, the feelings of deception and betrayal she was struggling with all resulted from his keeping his true identity from her. She had loved Moidart and, to her mind, the man no longer existed. He had been entirely supplanted by Lindsay, the glib, scheming man of business...the man she had briefly distracted from his Glaswegian lawyer and his mistress. Moidart had warned her against him on that first evening, she caught herself remembering, and she burst into a hysterical laugh at the confusion behind the thought. A knock on her door and a startled exclamation from Lucy on finding it bolted brought her back to earth abruptly. She quickly hid the papers in a drawer and unlocked the door.

"Time to get ready, Miss Nell! The guests are upon us already, and the band is tuning up! See, I've brought you the Lindsay sash Moidart says you're to wear over your dress."

An hour later, Lucy was satisfied with Nell's appearance. She looked pale but regal in her plain white muslin dress, the dark red tartan sash defining her slender waist and emphasising her shapely bosom. The neck was cut fashionably low for London, and Nell chose not to fill it with a lace fichu but to use it as the frame and her flawless ivory skin as the background for her borrowed necklace. Her cool grey eyes looked back at her in the mirror, every bit a match for the diamonds.

"I've never seen you look so beautiful, Miss Nell," breathed Lucy. "Moidart is not going to be able to take his eyes off you tonight, I do declare!" She blushed and hesitated, obviously regretting her words. But Nell merely smiled and, in an attempt to smooth over the awkwardness, said, "I fear I shall be the target of all eyes, Lucy, and so shall you, both being strangers, so away to your room now and make yourself pretty! We must outshine these Scots tonight!"

When Lucy rejoined her, they moved silently down to the balcony overlooking the hall. From the hall there came a drone of music, and at one end three fiddlers and a flautist sat smiling on a platform erected for them by Coll. From time to time, they essayed a chord. Each was armed with a brimming glass, and they were laughing and joking with the people who now began to assemble.

The older girls and women were dressed in decent black, and as each came through the door, they shed an enveloping shawl, revealing ribbons in their hair. The younger girls were in tartan dresses, their skirts kilted up to the knee, displaying a length of leg that would not have been considered suitable by Mrs. Maxwell at Somersham Hall. The older men were, similarly, in their Sunday best, but the younger men and the boys mostly wore the kilt. Predominantly, these were in the red and green of Lindsay of Moidart, but there were others.

As they watched, Coll joined them, a long taper in his hand. He greeted them and then, leaning far over the balcony rail, he reached out and hooked a chandelier towards him and lit the candles one by one.

"Tell me about the tartans," said Nell, pointing to the unfamiliar patterns below. "I know Lindsay when I see it, but that?"

"Ah, that wee man—he comes from Erracht, and that's Cameron country. He's no lived here so very long. Moidart gave him shelter with his woman and his bairns. And there—see there—that would be Fraser, one of Lovat's men." He looked Nell appraisingly up and down. "I must find you a screen of the Lindsay colours to wear in your hair," he said, crooking a finger at a passing maidservant and issuing an order, "You'll find all the ladies dress so."

At that moment, as if to prove his point, the door opened to admit a rosy-cheeked, white-haired, cheerful figure, diamond studs winking in his shirtfront, clad impeccably from head to foot in black velvet and with his comfortable wife on his arm. A tartan sash was draped over her shoulder, and the colours were repeated in her hair.

"Fergusson of Donuil," said Coll, "and his three bonny lasses." And as the door opened again to admit another family, Coll remarked, "McPherson of Doune and his three bonny lads."

So alike were Fergusson and McPherson as they came forward into the room, beaming and smiling and rubbing their hands, that Nell was tempted to laugh, but Coll continued, "Fergusson and McPherson have been good friends to Moidart, and very pack they are with the Laird."

"The...er...Laird?" Lucy began. "Where is the Laird? I don't see him."

Coll laughed and slapped his leg with considerable camaraderie. "The Laird, are you saying? Have you found your father's snuffy old cousin from Glasgow then? Och, away! It was a black shame to deceive you the way he did, but Moidart will ever have his little game and, see, there he comes now! In the kitchen he was, tasting and approving, and if I know anything about him, trying to change the way things are done! But there, it's his pleasure and it does no harm!"

Nell had hardly listened to this speech, so taken up was she by the appearance of Moidart; he wore a black velvet doublet with its lines of silver buttons, a snow white jabot at his neck, the swirling kilt in the colours of Lindsay and a silver sporran. The shoes on his feet had silver buckles, and there was, in his stocking top, the wink of a jewelled skian-dhu, while a dirk hung at his hip. On his head was a dark blue bonnet with a tartan band supporting a proud blackcock's feather.

His appearance was greeted by a cheer from the men, smiling curtsies from the women and the girls, and open-mouthed hero-worship from the swarms of small children. He passed rapidly round the room, shaking hands here and there with the men, lifting to kiss the work-roughened hands of the wives and shamelessly folding the daughters, each in turn, in an enveloping hug and kissing them on both cheeks, to the applause of the crowd.

From a corner of the room there arose a dismal drone that puzzled Nell for a moment, until she espied Robin Oig standing on a chair tuning the pipes that he held under his arm. As Moidart approached him, he swiftly played a ranting little spring and then struck into the slow measure of a march. Coll cocked his head for a moment and then said with a laugh, "'Lindsay Gu Brath!' It's a fine piece. You might say 'Lindsay for Ever.' And, in a while, we'll all be drinking to that!"

Was there meaning in what he said? Nell pondered, *Lindsay for Ever?*

They began to descend the stairs together and Coll resumed, "He's a very creditable piper, yon wee Robin, for such a young lad."

His words were overheard by an old man leaning at the foot of the stairs. "Creditable, you say, Coll? Why, the boy can pipe like a McCrimmon!"

"What's a McCrimmon?" asked Nell.

"That's a braw compliment, coming from that old fellow, who, if the truth were told, is a very creditable piper himself. The McCrimmon are the hereditary pipers for McLeod of Skye and are accounted the best pipers in the world."

Nell looked across the room to where Moidart was now standing, greeting and laughing with the Fergusson and McPherson families—flirting with the girls and teasing with the men—and soon to be joined by another family, which Nell assumed to be that of Doctor Jameson. Obviously, the company were asking him questions, and, seeking to reply to these, he began to look round the room until his eye caught that of Nell as she stood hesitating towards the foot of the stairs.

He brushed his way through the company and moved towards her, his hands outstretched and, drawing her to him, he said, "I see you have a wee screen of Lindsay in your hair? That'll be Coll, I'm thinking." And, tucking her arm in his, he led her across the floor to make the presentations, shouting as he passed to the small band, "Come on now, boys! Stamp and go! You're not here just to stand about, ye ken!"

Obediently, the band struck up and the Harvest Ball in the House of Lindsay had begun.

13

With no more ado, but with much laughter, the company formed two parallel rows down the length of the hall, clapping in time with the music, a simple skirling and repetitive air, familiar and yet not familiar...and never to be forgotten by Nell. With stamping brogue and clapping hands and now linked in a chain, couples arm in arm passing up and down the line, Nell soon picked up the simple rhythm. At one moment, she was dancing with a rubicund Fergusson of Donuil; at another, with the son of the Moidart shepherd. She even, at one point, encountered Coll and, out of the corner of her eye as she passed up or down the clapping lines, she saw the flushed, excited face of Lucy, the ribbons in her lace cap streaming out behind, her skirt lifted to reveal her dancing feet, her eyes offering a flirtatious challenge to Doctor Jameson.

As the dance drew to its climax and the dancers by a seeming miracle returned one by one to their original places in the line, the two lines swayed together and apart and then together again as the tempo increased, until finally the musicians themselves gave up—exhausted, laughing, and mopping their faces. The dancers repaired one by one to compete, in turn, for one of the black iron ladles hanging in a row above the cauldron of punch. With Nell tucked firmly under his arm,

Moidart led her across. She was greeted by a gap-toothed grin from a face that, by a mercy, she was able to recognise as one of the heroes of Achill Bridge. "Will ye make room now for her ladyship!" he shouted, pushing the crowd aside. "Let her ladyship sup a bit, and she bloated with the exercise!"

The company about burst into laughter at this unflattering description, laughter in which Nell and Moidart joined. "You mustn't mind," he said. "Their English isn't always reliable, and not all of them have any English at all." With only a second of hesitation, Nell sipped from a proffered ladle and at once swallowed spring water, barley, heather, honey, whisky, spices—the distillation of summer, it seemed.

As they turned back into the room, two pipers took their places at the bottom of the stairs, the diminutive figure of Robin Oig between them and a drummer at their elbow, a kettle drum slung about his neck. To attract the attention of the company, he beat out a rapid riff and then deliberately tapped a simple rhythm. This was greeted by a universal cheer, and the company broke up into groups of eight.

"Will you join the reel?" asked Moidart, holding her close by his side, "Or will we watch this one and join in the next?"

"I'm content to watch," said Nell simply, and, accordingly, they took their place on the quarter landing behind the pipers and watched together. Nell looked down on six sets of dancers. "Six eights are forty-eight, she thought distractedly, "That's nearly half the people here."

From above, they looked like six large spinning tops, and Nell's thoughts whirled with the dancers. Rhythmically, as the pattern changed, the great hall became a kaleidoscope of colour and movement. Below her, the pipes skirled and sang, the spectators lining the walls clapped in time to the music, and—unconsciously—Nell's feet began to move with the rhythm. Evidently, the reel was a familiar one, as one by one, the company began to sing the Gaelic words in time. She saw Fergusson of Donuil, rigid as a poker, his hands behind his back, stepping with the young Lady Kintoul. She saw Lucy turning in front of young Jameson. She saw serious children carefully count the steps aloud to themselves, changing hands in the chain and awaiting their turn to move to the centre of their turning circle. And she saw auld Angus, his twisted body at ease in the chimney corner, nodding and dimly smiling, a glass in his hand.

Deeply puzzled though she was, anxious indeed for the immediate past and even more anxious for the immediate future, she was glad of Moidart's warmth and nearness. Victim, although unwillingly, of his blatant attraction, she was finding it difficult to look away from him, and she was acutely aware that her gaze followed him wherever he moved about the room. Unconsciously, her hand reached out and held his sleeve. Sensing her change of mood, he slipped an arm around her waist, and she found him smiling down at her as she briefly glanced upwards. Curse the man! How was it that he could read her moods, her thoughts? He recognised just the right moment to offer reassurance and guidance when the sophisticated Lady Elinor was feeling doubtful. "Like a good sheepdog," she thought bitterly, "I have a notion that he's very gently herding me in the direction he has chosen for me. I wonder what he would do if I bolted in the opposite direction? Would he snap at my heels and fetch me back?" Looking up again at the proud, dark face and the straight, determined brows, she sighed. Yes, he would.

"When this lot are worn out," he was saying, "they'll set to a four-some. No point in asking me why! You know the answer—because they always have! Those that had to watch the eightsome then go into the foursome."

And so, as the eightsome couples drew neatly back to their starting place, Moidart led her by the hand down to the floor, reached his hand out to a placid dame sitting by the fireplace, linked his arm with that of the head shepherd, and said, "Will we show them how it's done, Kirsty?" And so they formed up hand in hand. The old shepherd bowed to Nell with the utmost gravity and, copying his wife, Nell curtsied with the ut-most solemnity to the gentlemen.

Tactfully, Moidart led off with the shepherd's wife to enable Nell to pick up the simple steps, and so they stood up together for two repeats of the tune while the spectators applauded. At the conclusion, Kirsty and Nell curtsied to the gentlemen, who bowed formally in reply.

The pipers, red-faced and seemingly bursting—a triumphant Robin Oig between them—hurried across to the cauldron for punch. "Not too much, Robin," said Nell, automatically, but she was rewarded with a rolling eye and a bibulous smile. From the far end of the room, and contrasting sweetly with the clamour of the pipes, there came a thin and formal arabesque of sound from the fiddlers. Nell became aware of a figure at her elbow.

"It is the custom," said McPherson, bowing and smiling, "to follow the set of foursomes with a minuet before supper. I have not yet taken the floor. I have nursed my energy. I have dared to hope that the Lady Elinor will stand up with me in the minuet."

"Oh, sir," said Nell, "I have hardly danced a minuet since dancing classes when I was a child! I doubt if I can remember..."

"Och, away!" said the old man, taking her firmly by the arm. I've watched ye. Dancing like a leaf in the wind, you were! Come on now, and we'll show them how it was done in the old days, will we not?"

"Whatever happens the rest of my life," thought Nell, "I shall never forget this!" as, with increasing confidence, she stepped her way through the half-forgotten formalities of the courtly dance, much assisted by McPherson's whispered admonitions. "Left foot, girl, left foot! Turn... Right hands...Turn again...Well done! Why, the whole world is watching us!"

As the sets broke up, the few who had stepped their way through the minuet were greeted with rapturous applause by the entire company. Smiling and embarrassed, Nell curtsied this way and that while her cavalier, pink and pleased, bowed at her side.

It was clear that the tradition of the House of Lindsay had reached a new stage because, without a word, the door to the library was opened to reveal decanters, biscuits, and silver dishes winking in the cheerful firelight. Moidart himself stood hospitably at the door, and two by two the gentry left the hall while, with a roar and a rattle and a stamping of feet, the trestle tables were carried in and set up, forming a hollow E. As the library door closed behind her, Nell was aware of scurrying figures setting the tables with all the resources that a great house could command—plates and cutlery and candlesticks, pies and pasties, bowls of vegetables, and roasted haunches of venison.

As she turned to join the company in the library, the young Lord Kintoul, with his wife on his arm, came across to her.

"Lady Elinor," he said, and to Nell, after less than two weeks in the Highlands, his drawling English voice came as a surprise. "Lady Elinor! Charmed to renew your acquaintance, and though I remember you well, I do not flatter myself that you will necessarily remember me, but we met, if you recall, at Lady Radnor's Summer Ball."

Much disconcerted by this intrusion of her London life, Nell stammered as best she could that she remembered the occasion well and was charmed to see him again. Would he not present her to his wife?

Lady Kintoul was, Nell decided unkindly, pop-eyed, chinless, and vacuous, but she was quite undaunted, it seemed, by these disadvantages, for she said at once, "Now do tell me, Lady Elinor—all have been asking—what could possibly bring one such as yourself to this remote corner when the London season is hardly underway? I said to Kintoul—Scotland? No! A thousand times, no! But pleading the pressure of family business, what did the wretch do? Whisk me away when half my dresses had yet to come from the dressmaker, which is why I am wearing this pitiful old rag, quite two seasons old! But do satisfy my curiosity! What could possibly bring you here?"

"Family business," said Nell with a bland smile. "Lindsay of Moidart is my father's cousin, and I am, indeed, his ward. We had things to discuss, decisions to make."

"Satisfactorily, I hope?" said Kintoul.

But before Elinor could reply, Lady Kintoul interposed once more. "Oh, Rorie!" she said. "People have said to me time and again, the greatest catch in western Scotland is black Rorie Moidart, but—poor lamb—not two bawbees (as I believe they're called) to rub together..."

"It isn't bawbees," said Lord Kintoul, "that a man having Moidart's powers of persuasion would be seeking to rub together, I believe. My brother, who is the chargé d'affaires in Egypt, said a damn clever thing the other day (ackers, you understand, are the currency in Egypt); he said, 'Poor old Moidart! More *acres* than *ackers*, what!' And so it will always be unless he clears his land. And unless he does we'll not be seeing many entertainments on this scale, I believe."

Nell felt her temper rising. "I think it's fine that my cousin should care for people before sheep! Why, those who would clear their land of the folk who have lived on it and farmed it for generations are foolishly depriving themselves of the land's most precious commodity! You only have to look at the bare hillsides around us and the burned crofts and then look at the Lindsay lands to see the difference..." Here she stopped in confusion, unable to remember—but having her suspicions—whether Kintoul had cleared his lands. She was relieved when the friendly Doctor Jameson joined them, his wife on his arm, asking polite questions about her journey, how long she would be staying, whether she had ever visited Scotland before.

Nell thankfully sank into innocuous party chatter, interrupted by Kintoul, who inquired politely,

"Excuse me for one moment, Lady Elinor, but I understand from our host that I am to have the honour of taking you in to dine? I look forward to hearing more of your opinions on the management of our estates. Perhaps I shall be able to counter the views of your guardian, to whom you appear to have listened with very close attention."

And very shortly, Moidart himself came across to confirm this, his quick eye noticing the flush on her cheeks.

"But you are the senior lady, Elinor," he said easily, "and Kintoul is our principal guest, so he will be taking you in to dinner."

"I don't like him," said Nell roundly. "I don't like him, and beyond a point I don't trust him!"

After only the most superficial glance around the room, seemingly to ensure that they were unobserved other than by the attendant Doctor Jameson, he leant forward and kissed her cheek, saying, "Worry not, Nell; before the evening's done, I'll astonish them all!"

Before she could question this mysterious remark, the door opened to reveal Coll, who bowed and said, "Supper is served, Moidart."

He extended his arm to Lady Kintoul, and Lord Kintoul extended his arm to Nell, and, two and two, they processed into the great hall, where, once more, their arrival was greeted by clapping in unison. They made their way to the high table. Moidart took his place in the centre, with Nell on his right and Lady Kintoul on his left, followed by others in an order of precedence. On a nod from Moidart, a small man in black at the end of the high table rose to his feet and delivered a long grace in Gaelic, which he followed, to Nell's amusement, with what she supposed was what he thought would be an appropriate compliment to herself: an appropriate grace in English—"Good drink, good meat, good God, let's eat. Slainté!" And the company replied in chorus.

"The Episcopalian curate from Vennacher," said Moidart drily by way of explanation. "The nearest, in these reduced times, that I have to a domestic chaplain."

For a minute or two, and to Nell's relief, Lord Kintoul was occupied with his right-hand side neighbour and Moidart with Lady Kintoul. It gave her a chance to collect her thoughts. Quite captivated by the entertainment, her head still singing with the music, and unable to resist the easy friendliness of the company at large, she couldn't deny that there was somewhere a wellspring of happiness in her heart. Moidart's deceit and a desperate uncertainty as to what he might say or do next—and a certainty that a plan had formed in that complicated mind—left her very uneasy. Somewhere at the back of her mind, the chance remark of Jennie Fraser on first seeing the corn dolly nagged her, and she glanced up at it where it gleamed mysteriously in the shadows over the great fireplace. She wondered. Would the Corn Maiden answer the prayers of these desperate people and bring them prosperity, increasing the flocks on the hills and putting babies in the cradles?

For the first time, a gust of panic swept through Nell, and she was hardly able to return the required commonplace rejoinders to the chattering overtures of Lord Kintoul. She found that she had lost her appetite and merely pushed pieces of roast meat and pastie around on her plate without eating. Moidart flashed her an anxious look of enquiry and an encouraging smile, which she was not able to return. She was glad when, at last, there was a skirl of pipes from the kitchen door and the pipers processed solemnly round the table, leading a blushing Lucy and a beaming Tibbie, as between them they carried the not inconsiderable weight of the cake, now frosted with sugar and decorated with a sprig of rowan. Mrs. Fraser and Coll rose from their places at the foot of each of the lower tables and, with enormous carving knives in hand, proceeded to cut the cake and pass it round, while others cleared the tables. This, it seemed, signalled the end of the meal.

Nell could not remember that she had ever seen so many people eat so much in so short a time. She watched with disbelief as the haunches of venison, reduced to their bare bones, and the crumbs of pies disappeared into the kitchen. Moidart leaned across and whispered to her, "I am expected to make a speech. Forgive me that it should be in Gaelic, but even our anglicised friend on your right, though perhaps not necessarily his wife on my left, will understand what I am saying, and not all will understand the English."

With this, a proud figure in black and silver, sparked with tartan colour, blackcock feathers in his blue bonnet nodding in the candle light, he rapped on the table for silence and began.

His first sentences were obviously formal in nature and traditional in form and were received, it seemed to Nell, as old, familiar friends. His formalities out of the way, he turned to bend a glance so strange at Nell that the rags of her composure left her and, blushing, she could only look down at the table. Moidart resumed his discourse, and at once gasps ran round the entire room. Many jumped to their feet, glasses held aloft in a delighted salute. Everywhere Nell turned when she looked up, she saw smiling faces, and all were looking at her.

Moidart resumed. "And now," he said, "I will say in English for those without the benefit of the old tongue that today is a happy day for the House of Lindsay, for everyone in this room, and above all, for myself. I am honoured and delighted to announce that Lady Elinor Somersham has consented to become my wife. You all know that Lady Elinor is the great granddaughter of John Lindsay of Moidart, and so we can say that this is doubly a homecoming for her. Will you all welcome her home?"

Slipping an arm under her shoulders, he hauled her, crimson, reluctant, and dismayed, to her feet. Her every instinct was to duck under his arm and run from the room. "I can't deal with this!" she thought. "I won't even try. I will deal with it later." And she smiled round the ring of glistening open-mouthed faces shouting approval below her and beside her, hearing almost subconsciously Kintoul's whistle of astonishment and intercepting a meaning glance between him and his wife. She also caught Lucy's eye; she stood a little apart, with her hand to her breast, lips parted and with shining eyes.

She did not have long to withstand the popular applause, for the musicians were tuning again, the trestles were being dismantled, and the benches were being carried back against the wall. Hardly aware of what she was doing, she allowed Moidart to lead her into a round dance that was forming, hearing only his whisper, "I said we'd astonish them, did I not?"

"I don't know about them," Nell whispered grimly back, "but you have certainly astonished me!"

"Can you say so?" said Moidart with seemingly genuine surprise, but the noise of the music drowned out any further conversation.

The round dance completed, Coll made his way to a trophy of arms hanging on the wall and pulled four crossed claymores from it. Waving the people back from the centre of the room, he set these down crossed on the floor, and the pipers moved forward. To the applause of the company, two young men stood to the weapons, and their feet in their buckled shoes began to twinkle among the steel to the cadence of the pipes. This was evidently in some measure the high spot of the evening and became the subject of rigid attention on the part of a room clearly full of highly critical experts. Amongst these was Moidart himself, who, taking his seat on a stool in front of the dancers, stared from one to the other with close attention, his foot tapping and his head nodding in time.

Only too delighted no longer to be the focus of attention, Nell backed into the crowd and began to thread her way carefully towards the stairs. She delayed for a while in her progress from the room to accept the smiling good wishes of the eldest Fergusson girl and left her side promising that, as her new neighbour, she would certainly call on her as soon as might be. More warm invitations and plans were offered to her as she slipped away up the stairs to the safety of her room. She bolted the door and made her way by the firelight across the darkened room, threw open the shutters, and leant out into the night, desperately seeking air to cool her burning cheeks. As she did so, a shaft of light broke below her as someone opened a door.

Into the courtyard stepped Mr. McPherson and Lord Kintoul.

The speech of both was somewhat blurred, and both were laughing confidentially together as, unbuttoning themselves as they walked, they went to stand against the courtyard wall. Their voices rose clearly to her.

"I'm telling ye, Kintoul," said McPherson, "it's five pounds you now owe me!"

"Five pounds?" said Kintoul. "Five pounds? Where do you get that from?"

"Now, my boy! I'm not letting you off! I'll repeat the terms of the wager if you've forgotten—it was on this very spot and on this very day a year ago when first we heard the terms of Hartismere's will. I said this to you: 'Young Rorie will never stand for that! I'll wager you he'll find a way to overturn this preposterous will.' And you said to me, 'I'll wager that even Moidart will not outsmart the London lawyers,' and, 'Proud Lindsay rides for a fall at last!' And I said to you, 'Here's five pounds that says he will do nothing of the sort.' 'Go away, man!' you said to me. 'Here's my hand—I've no objection to picking up five pounds by the roadside.' Deny it if you can, you dog!"

Supporting each other, they both stood laughing for a while until Kintoul said, "Very well, then. Five pounds Scots."

McPherson snorted and said, "You're no getting away with that! Five pounds sterling, and you know it!"

"You're a hard man!" said Kintoul, but Nell heard a chink of coin. "I have to admit it," Kintoul went on, "although Lindsay's had his own way long enough and I wouldn't have been sorry to see him dinged down— I've got to admire the man for the way he's done it! And the speed! I remember it took me a good twelvemonth to bring Laetitia to the boil! And one day perhaps he'll tell me what you have to do to secure the hand of one of the richest heiresses in the two kingdoms—and one of the choosiest, as all declare! 'Pon my soul, McPherson, I could give you a list as long as my arm of Nell Somersham's rejected suitors—and all richer and better connected than our friend."

"What you have to do, you say? Will I tell you what you have to do?" said McPherson, lowering his voice in sly confidence. Nell listened intently, riveted to the conversation below. "If I'm to believe what my shepherd lads tell me—what you have to do is to choose a rainy afternoon to lure the lass into an empty bothy on the hill and spend four hours with her! Now, maybe they were discussing the price of sheep and maybe they were playing knucklebones, but if you were to ask me I'd say—the dog!—he was making sure of her! And show me the maid who could deny the attractions of young Rorie—and he determined to have his way—in a four-hour siege on her virtue! I knew he'd stick at nothing!" He laughed heartily.

"Good Lord! 'Pon my soul! Nell Somersham! Hah! Undone like any farm girl in a hillside sheep pen? Can you be certain, man?" The astonishment in Kintoul's voice was unmistakable. It gave way to a mischievous satisfaction as he added, "Well, well! That'll strip her ladyship of some of her London airs and graces, I'm thinking." Chuckling together, the two men reentered the house below her.

A great weariness crushed Nell's limbs, and she left the window and went to sink onto her bed. Stunned by what she had just overheard, but in a strange way not surprised, she began to go over the day's startling events and to consider her position. With a dry sob, she recognised herself for a gullible idiot. Incredibly, the worldly wise, experienced Elinor Somersham; survivor of a hundred proposals of marriage; intelligent, alert, and aware, as she had always considered herself, had fallen without a murmur into a trap so cleverly laid that she had imagined herself to be the seducer! With a blush of shame she remembered that her original plan had been to take Moidart as her lover and lure him back to Suffolk when she returned! What a naive idiot she had been!

For how long, she wondered uselessly, had he been planning this marriage? She thought of the legal documents tucked safely away in her drawer. At that time, he had obviously merely intended to suggest a mutually beneficial arrangement to secure his estates. But having met her, having taken her, unwitting, into his web of intrigue, a better idea had obviously occurred to him. By marrying her he became at a stroke the possessor not only of the Lindsay lands for good and all, but of her whole fortune—a fortune that he would lose no time in putting to use to rescue the Clan and the estates from the poverty into which they were sinking year by year. Wait! Wait! Was this not an estimable aim and one in which she could easily have shared? Could she possibly have any objections?

Yes! Yes, she could! A swift rush of anger swept over her as she registered again the methods he had used to secure her. She felt very like one of the golden grouse on his table—caught, plucked, trussed, and barded, ready to be consumed. He had made no attempt to keep their illicit relationship a secret and had even smiled at her discomfiture when it had at last occurred to her that others might be aware of what had been going on between them. And the announcement tonight! He had not gone through the preliminary of asking her to marry him, never intending to risk a refusal. And the surveillance under which she suspected she had been held over the last few days? She had assumed with the smugness of a girl in love that he could not bear to have her out of his sight. But now...his constant attendance took on a more sinister interpretation. He knew her for a bolter, a headstrong girl who had already shown by her appearance on his doorstep that she thought nothing of dashing a thousand miles on a whim. He needed to be sure of her and must—even now, she thought with a shudder—be wondering where she was, searching the crowd for her...checking with Coll or Lucy perhaps.

What was it that Lucy had said to him? Brave Lucy, intuitive Lucy, had realised that something was not right in his behaviour and had told him roundly that this was not a prison and she not Nell's keeper! But perhaps she had been mistaken? Perhaps that was exactly what he intended? The cage was golden and comfortable and full of laughter and companionship but nonetheless a cage. Gritting her teeth with rage, she concluded that Moidart was no better than Jemmie Fanshawe in his dedicated pursuit of her money—worse even, because at least Jemmie Fanshawe had not thought it necessary to seduce her and ruin her reputation!

She sat up, sniffed, rubbed her eyes, and consigned her grief and the love she had mistakenly felt for the man to a lower layer of feeling. She could deal with it later, let it out to tear her spirit and her heart to pieces, but not now. She was facing a resolute, clever, and charming man for whom she recognised that she still felt a considerable attraction and probably always would, and she knew she would have to work skilfully to evade his grip. But evade him she was determined to do and—buoyed up by her surge of anger—she began to plan with all the resources of her cool brain. Her mind scurried about here and there, down blind alleys, returning, until she suddenly saw her way forward.

A brusque rapping at her door made her start with foreboding. It was surely not Lucy's discreet tap..."Elinor! Open the door! My love, are you all right?"

14

Moidart! With pounding heart, Nell decided to put her deception into place at once. She knew exactly what she had to do; her courage was rising and her determination growing to use his own weapons of smiling deception against him.

Calling weakly as she ran, she dashed to the fire and held her face dangerously close to the glowing embers for as long as she could bear it, and then she opened the door to him. As he entered, she collapsed, murmuring indistinctly against his chest.

"My darling Nell! What is the matter? Oh, my God!" he exclaimed, kissing her forehead. "But you're burning with fever! Will I fetch Doctor Jameson up?"

The sound of the distress and alarm in his voice and the familiar warmth of his arms about her were very nearly her undoing, but she rallied and managed a brave smile, saying, "No, Moidart! I want no one but you by me, and after all, 'tis you who are to blame for my feeling thus..."

"I?" he said in astonishment.

"You! Oh, darling, can you be so unaware?" she murmured huskily. She looked up at him teasingly under lowered lashes. "Did you not notice that I could eat nothing at the feast tonight? I came up to my room because I am feeling so faint and strange and sick...Will you please, my love, dampen for me a washing cloth as you did the other night and press it to my brow?"

Wondering, he did as she asked, thinking deeply, and then he said hesitantly, "Nell, my dearest, could it be that...? Would you know already that...? I am not well versed in such female matters..."

She allowed a shaky but proud smile to light her face for a moment before replying shyly, "I do believe, if my old governess had it right, that one may sometimes know the very next day." She hadn't the slightest idea if this were true but knew it had the ring of truth. "So it seems that the Corn Maiden has begun to work her magic already! I believe the sickness to be a passing phase," she said, inventing fluently, "and quickly passing when it occurs so early, but...I was thinking...my dearest Moidart, that perhaps this evening I should be alone...I do not think I shall be good company for you, and I feel so wretched..." She gulped queasily and touched her mouth with the back of her hand.

The joy and triumph that flamed in his eyes was almost overwhelming as he lifted her and spun her around in a tight embrace. "In a happy day," he said, "this is the happiest news! A child! To have a child in the House of Lindsay again! My lovely lass! But, Nell, we must be married at once! I was thinking that perhaps a Christmas wedding would please you, but now...we must be married next week! For your pride's sake, you understand, my darling...I care not and no one else hereabouts will give a thought to a six-month child, but tomorrow at first light I will ride to Glasgow and procure a special license..."

"Oh, Moidart! How long shall you be away?" The distress in her voice amazed her. She clutched his hand. "I have grown so used to your company; I do not know if I can spare you even for such a matter. Could you not send Coll?"

She instantly regretted her subterfuge, thinking she had certainly gone too far, but luckily, he replied, "I fear not, my love. There will be documents to sign, and I should like to buy you a wedding gift while I'm in the city. I have never given you a gift...it will not be grand but will be given with all my heart. I shall be back as soon as I can!"

"Well...I have many things to do here at the castle...um...*home* as I now must call it," she said with a shy smile, "and I shall start tomorrow to pass the long hours while you are away by going to call on my new neighbours. I was pressed by several of your—our—guests to make a call as soon as I could, and I thought I would go first to Vennacher where I may see the Misses Fergusson and the pastor and his wife. If I am feeling better, that is—I should not quite like the pastor to guess my condition! Would you have Coll harness up the carriage for me and I will take Lucy with me...or Tibbie?"

"Of course, my love. I was pleased to see you in conversation with Lottie Fergusson. You will find that she will be a good friend, and I am glad also to hear that you are not contemplating riding there in your condition—I had not thought you so careful!" He held her a little away from him and looked at her searchingly.

"I have all the reason in the world to be careful now, Moidart!" she said with sincerity, daring to meet his dark eyes with her own clear, open grey gaze and knowing for the first time since he had entered the room that he would read only truth in her face.

After a long tender kiss, he left her. She heard him pause outside the door and held back her hand from instantly pulling the bolt across. She decided to leave her door unlocked even when the time came to go to bed, even though all her instincts were screaming at her to make it safe. Lucy had arrived flushed and excited from the continuing dance to attend to her mistress but had been dismissed by Nell, who was in night-dress and already tucked up for the night.

For long hours more, it seemed, Nell remained wakeful, her busy brain planning and checking. The sounds of jollity down below grew fainter but continued on until late into the night. She guessed that for as long as there were people drinking and dancing, Moidart would be with them. When, finally, the last shout of laughter faded, she began to be afraid. Would he honour her plea for solitude? Surely by now he would himself be so exhausted he would simply be grateful to fall into his own bed before his early start tomorrow? She thrust her face deep into the pillows and tried to go to sleep herself, as there was nothing more she could usefully do that night.

Her heart bumped as she heard her door open, and she made her breathing sound perfectly regular, even whimpering slightly and then breathing deeply again as she was conscious of him standing listening by her bedside in the darkness. The lightest of hands reached out and stroked her head, and the gentlest of kisses brushed against her cheek before he left the room.

Nell was awake again at first light and silently slid out of bed to make her preparations. She stayed alert until she heard the sound of a solitary horse starting out from the courtyard below, and then she found her clothes and shook and folded them, gathering together her few possessions. With a painful stab in her heart, she found the diamond necklace she had worn at the dance and put it back into its velvet box. A cheerful whistling from the courtyard drew her to the window, and she looked out to see Angus and Robin Oig going purposefully about their business, clanking off with pails towards the stables and laughing together. There was one more thing she had to do.

Opening the drawer of her dressing table, she took out the document drawn up by Moidart's lawyer and looked at it again carefully. Her lips moved slightly as she read out the formal yet simple phrases to make sure that nothing had escaped her attention. Yes, that was right, Lady Elinor Somersham would hereby declare that she agreed to forfeit now and in perpetuity any right to the title on the Lindsay estates. She took up a pen from the writing desk, signed the document, and added the date. She would ask Lucy to witness her signature when the girl arrived with her breakfast. The signed document, along with the necklace, she would place in his business room. She agonized for a moment as to whether she should write down for him the reasons for her departure, but her heart was so numb that the words would not come. On an impulse, she added a line at the bottom of the document—"This I do for Robin Oig." She was certain Moidart would understand.

When Lucy arrived, looking a little pale, she was amazed to find her mistress dressed in her walking dress and boots and poised for flight. Elinor felt sure that the girl had become fond of Coll in the few days they had been thrown together, so it was with many misgivings that she explained to Lucy what she wanted her to do.

"You mean, just like on the way here, Miss Nell? Pack secretly, sneak off and...and...never come back here again...is that right?" She looked so stricken that Nell went to her and hugged her and tried to explain.

"Well, I had been wondering, Miss Nell...in fact, you could say I had my suspicions, especially when I found out who he was and how he'd been tricking you, but Coll, well, Coll said it was all right and the best thing that could happen for both of you and the clan. I believed him... he's a good man, is Coll. He's not deceitful." Her eyes filled with tears and her lips trembled.

"Lucy," said Nell gravely, "do you want to stay on here? I think I understand how you are feeling about leaving Coll. I would not wish to snatch you from him. Listen—I could probably take Tibbie with me—she says she has always wanted to see London...She could come with me as far as Park Lane and return whenever she wished. In the spring, perhaps."

"No, Miss Nell. No," she replied slowly. "I wouldn't want to be staying on here without you. No, this isn't my place."

Having come to her decision, Lucy worked away with heavy heart but light hands on the now familiar routine associated with bolting. She went to the stables and checked that the carriage was about to be made ready for her mistress and arranged for the portmanteau to be carried down and hidden away in the carriage while she distracted Coll.

By ten o'clock, Nell and Lucy were sitting in the carriage chatting easily to each other and waiting for one of the stable lads to be called to drive them over to Vennacher to call on Lottie Fergusson. Nell even smilingly accepted a commission from Mrs. Fraser to deliver ten jars of apple jelly to Mrs. Fergusson and, waving a goodbye, they started out.

Half an hour later, they rattled into the village street of Vennacher, and Nell called to the puzzled groom to pull over at the Golden Lion and wait in the inn yard. Before his startled eyes, Lucy hauled the

portmanteau out of the back of the carriage, and Nell told him firmly
that he was to return to the House of Lindsay.

As he pulled out of the inn yard with his empty carriage, the groom
had to move over abruptly to avoid the mail coach calling in to pick up
passengers for Glasgow on its way from Callander and, with a sinking
heart, he began to rehearse what he would say to the Laird when he got
back the following day.

Their journey to Glasgow was slow and uncomfortable, and Nell feared
at any time they might be overtaken by a horseman from Moidart and
borne back to the castle. She had calculated that if they could post on at
once from Glasgow they could vanish into the busy traffic of the coach
roads now covered by Mr. MacAdam's new surface, which enabled the
carriages to bowl along uninterrupted at almost twelve miles an hour. If
Moidart took two days over his trip to Glasgow, he would be well behind
them and, she thought, would not even attempt a pursuit.

Sinking back against the hard leather seat of the coach, Nell closed
her eyes to avoid the curious gaze of the other four inside passengers and
tried to blot out the events of the past days, wrapping herself in a cocoon
of insensibility to all the things she had said and done with Moidart, all
the hopes she had filled her head with over the short time she had been
at his side. But her reaching out for oblivion was unsuccessful, and her
lowered eyelids simply made his image clearer.

She loved him and could see no way now of unloving him, although
she was in no doubt as to his having attempted to use her for his own
ends. And could she blame him for having tried to acquire her at all cost
and by any means to solve his problems? Rationally, she knew that the
answer was no. The impoverished Lord Kintoul had married his wife
for her large fortune, it was generally known. The lady herself made no
secret of it, and yet they seemed perfectly happy together. Many Scottish
noblemen were taking rich wives, even American women, it was ru-
moured, to get them out of financial straits in return for a title and a
family history. There would have been no shame attached to the match,
she knew, and the world, with the possible exception of her stepmother,

would have been happy for her. So why had it been impossible for her to stay and share his life? "Fairy tales!" her stepmother had snapped at her when she had clumsily tried to explain to her the need she had to feel loved for herself alone, and perhaps she had been right. Nell tried to swallow the lump in her throat, and tears slid silently down her cheeks under her closed lids. If only he had been the steward of her cousin as he had said he was, she could have forged a life of sorts for them, but as her guardian—with all to gain from a quick match with his rich ward—there was no hope.

Had he ever loved her? She wondered sadly how one could tell. She knew so little of men. Her mind ranged back to their afternoon in the bothy, and she flushed hotly at the memory of her shame. His lovemaking had been convincing enough, but perhaps that was how it was for all men? Perhaps that was how it always was for Moidart, the chill thought came to her. What had Lady Kintoul said about him—"the best catch in the Highlands"? She was obviously far from being the first to admire Rorie Moidart. She had watched him at the ball fondling and kissing the girls. The Laird's privilege? And the girls? They had dimpled, giggled, flirted, sighed, and looked at him with long backward glances and then danced off with another cavalier.

And so, she told herself sternly but too late, should she have done.

One kiss. That was all it had taken to buckle her knees! What a fool he must have taken her for! What a pliable, gullible fool! And, once having stripped her of her virginity, why had he then continued to make love to her so assiduously? Had that been necessary? The cold voice inside her head answered her again. It was rare for one lovemaking to end in pregnancy. He was "making sure of her," as old McPherson had said to Kintoul in the courtyard. She would never forget his burning look of triumph when she had feigned sickness the last evening. All that he had been working for was his, he must have thought. The cold voice spoke again, more chilling than before, and said, "And what if he has been successful? That is something you cannot possibly yet know..."

She sighed and shivered slightly.

Lucy opened her carrying bag and took out a plaid, stretching it over Nell's knees, and kicked up a thicker pile of straw around her feet. "Coll gave me the plaid. I didn't just take it, Miss Nell," she whispered in her ear.

One of the passengers opposite, a friendly looking old Scotsman, had been looking for an opportunity to start a conversation since they had boarded the coach and now seized his chance. "Ah, ye'll be a Lindsay woman, I'm thinking, going by the tartan," he said cheerfully and was horrified a second later when, in response to his overture, large tears began to roll down her cheeks, and she said with choking voice, "Almost...I was almost a Lindsay woman."

15

Nell closed her book with a snap and banged it down onto the table. "Stepmama! How many times must I tell you that I will not go to a ball or, indeed, to any of these tedious soirées you keep dangling in front of me?"

"I do declare, Nell, you have been in a fret ever since you returned from Scotland," replied Lady Hartismere tartly. "For six weeks I have been suffering from your rages, your bad temper, your bullying!" She dabbed at her dry eyes with the corner of a lacy handkerchief. "And this extraordinary, reclusive behaviour! Why, you have been behaving like a hermit! It is most unnatural in a girl of your age." She sniffed and allowed a look of feigned concern to twist her features for a moment. "All will remark on the change in you, and don't suppose other than that people will wonder—you may depend on that—and speculate, as I do myself, as to what transpired in Scotland. Heaven knows—and for sure I do not—why a 'business meeting' with your guardian should leave you looking like a dishcloth! I know not how to answer for you when I am constrained to refuse each and every invitation that comes your way."

A new relationship had developed between the two women since Nell's flamboyant show of independence. There had been fences to mend, ruffled feathers to be smoothed, but, most compellingly, appearances before the world had to be repaired and maintained. To their mutual surprise, the two women found themselves working towards the same goal. Undisguised hatred had given way to enforced mutual support and, in these changed times, Nell felt free to reply frostily, "Do not attempt to deceive me, Stepmama! You only seek my company to lend you countenance. There is no point in my attending these balls! I become a target for every unattached man in London, and if I did find one I could bear to take as a husband, I would not receive my guardian's permission or yours to marry, so why should I continue with the pretence?"

Her stepmother gave her a sly look and replied, "Whatever your views, dear Nell, I am afraid that tomorrow night you *must* attend." Triumphantly, she passed a gold-edged invitation card across the table and smiled with satisfaction. "I had told you of this, but you chose not to remember. It is from the Prince Regent and, accordingly, it is not to be regarded as an invitation but as a command. We will leave for Carlton House at eight tomorrow. Please be ready."

Seeing Nell's mutinous expression, she added, weighing her words carefully, "Besides...there will be someone there who wishes to renew acquaintance with you, my dear—though I doubt that you will want to see him. No, not Jemmie!" she said waspishly, catching Nell's thought. "Oh, no. I speak of your guardian—your so detested Scottish guardian." She smiled with satisfaction at the effect her news had on Nell. Her head jerked up to search her stepmother's face for the truth of what she was saying and, reading nothing there but gloating satisfaction, she bit her lip and said nothing.

Not fully satisfied by Nell's reaction, Lady Hartismere pressed on, "I have, indeed, met him on several occasions recently. He has been in London for a month, and I am quite surprised that he has not taken the trouble to call on us...are not you, Nell?"

As Nell remained in stony-faced silence, she prattled on, "I can understand, of course—I am not so insensitive—why you should have taken him in such horror as he thwarted your matrimonial ambitions...Such a long journey, my dear, and all for nothing," she sighed with affected sympathy, "though I do myself feel for the man in this regard. What did you *expect* him to say? Could you seriously have thought that he would sign away half Scotland just like that—just on your request, because Elinor Somersham wished it? Poor fool! If you were not such a selfish, headstrong girl who dashes about the place creating difficulties for all with whom she has dealings, I would find it in me to pity you! But Nell—sly puss!—you deceived me as to your guardian!"

Nell looked up startled and, pleased to have provoked at last the reaction she was waiting for, Lady Hartismere continued, "You gave me no indication of your cousin Lindsay's youth and personal attraction. I had imagined him, from your description, to be decrepit, mean, and unalluring, but you misled me, Miss!"

Seeing Nell's cheeks flame, she pressed on with purring satisfaction, "Certainly the ladies of London Society do not endorse your opinion of Roderick Lindsay! Oh, no! I have seen him at several routs and soirées, surrounded—quite surrounded—by rich young beauties. It appears that now he has, thanks to your extraordinary and to my mind inexplicable generosity, regained his lands, he is firmly in the marriage market. It is well known, of course, that he has pockets to let, but the attractions of a title and several thousand acres—though Scottish—have made him the prey of every young girl with a rich father who wishes to buy his daughter a respectable situation. I believe the lead horse, if I may so express it, to be a certain Miss Amelia Sinclair, daughter of an American, though of Scottish descent. The on dit is that she has fallen head over heels in love with your cousin and will accept no other, and her indulgent papa—the world, it seems, is full of indulgent papas these days—is only too willing to give her a marriage settlement of enormous proportions." She sniffed with disapproval, "For a Glasgow family whose origins are in trade, it is probably money well spent," she mused.

"I have heard quite enough about the marriage market!" Nell said with all the restraint she could muster. "Pray do not go on, Stepmama!"

"But such wonderful gossip you are missing, Nell! I have barely begun! Surely you would want to hear about his other conquests? Kitty Wetherby or Sarah Felsham, Lady Kintoul's cousin? Now that is a match I know Laetitia Kintoul very much favours—then she would have her

cousin close by her in Scotland, for I believe the Kintouls to be neighbours of Lindsay's...Indeed, I understand from Laetitia, who is newly
returned from that wild place, that they were so fortunate as to catch a
glimpse of *you* at a rustic Highland rout..."

Nell nodded imperceptibly. So this was where the cat and mouse
game was leading! The moment she had been dreading when news of
her disgrace was carried south had come. Calculating that her stepmother was quivering with suspicion and in possession of details sufficient to torment her for the rest of the day, Nell decided to speak out.
"Say no more! I know where you are leading. The truth of the matter is
that Lindsay never proposed marriage to me, and I would have refused
him had he done so. If you hear anything to the contrary, you have my
authority to deny it. I'm sure it is not in Laetitia Kintoul's interest to
spread rumours, and you will not need to strain credulity in giving them
the lie on my behalf, Stepmama." And Nell hurried from the room.

Back in the haven of her own room, Nell flung herself on her bed and
sobbed into her pillow, biting and tearing it in her pain and anger. How
dared he flaunt himself in this way? Challenging her on her own stage,
her own territory? And he had been offering himself on the London
market for a month? Despicable! How lucky that she had refused all invitations since her return! How could she ever face him again, and in
public? She knew there was no way of evading the Royal Command of
the Prince Regent's Ball, and etiquette would insist that she at least greet
him. How could she bring herself to look into his treacherous brown
eyes and murmur, "Cousin Roderick, I hope you are well?" "Cousin
Roderick, I wish you in Hell!" would be her more natural response.

When her rage and shock subsided, the agonies began again. The
memories of the days she had spent with him pierced her heart with such
exquisite spasms of pain that she had got into the way of endeavouring to
suppress them by any means at her disposal. She rode and walked a great
deal, played her piano constantly, even painted.

For six weeks she had suffered from her self-imposed loss and was
becoming alarmed that the pain of severance from him grew no less. She

had bullied her stepmother into seeking out her old governess, needing, in her isolation, to have someone by her who could distract her with meaningful and witty conversation. Thérèse had returned happily to take up a post of companion to Nell, and a great part of their days was spent in conversing in French, visiting the libraries and setting out the gardens in the Park Lane house. Her stepmother was relieved of Nell's company by this arrangement and happy that her charge was innocently employed.

It had been a great relief also to Nell to confide her distress to Thérèse and seek from her the assistance she knew she was likely to need in the coming years. Thérèse had been horrified to find her pupil so changed and daily exclaimed at Nell's loss of looks. Her glow was gone, the bright challenge of her eyes dimmed and replaced by a guarded watchfulness. She had lost weight, and her body was a mere shadow of its former sensuous invitation. Her normally healthy girl's appetite had waned to nothing, and she would absent-mindedly eat only reluctantly and when urged to. Thérèse, who knew the reason for her sorrow, was powerless to do anything but lend her calm and understanding support and her prayers that time would heal the dreadful hurt the girl had done herself.

Drying her hot tears and calming herself, Nell attempted a rational examination of her stepmother's news. She must start to use her head and the powers of reason she had always prided herself on. The moment she had let her heart and emotions run away with her, they had destroyed her, so she realized that she had to deny that impulsive, careless side of her nature for evermore. As she was able to think more calmly, it was evident that this would be his course of action, and she should have realised that, inevitably, he would set about acquiring a wife—a rich wife. With the example of his neighbour Kintoul before him, it was the obvious thing to do. And for the sake of the land and people of Moidart, she could only wish him well. He would put any fortune that came his way to good use for the improvement of their lives. Of course he would. And he now was free to have the heirs he so keenly desired.

This thought sent such a shaft of agony through her body that she collapsed again with racking sobs, recognising that she would never be healed of the hopeless love she still felt for Moidart.

"Which dress shall I get out, Miss Nell?" Lucy asked for the third time. "It's nearly time to leave, madam, and you're still sitting about in your underpinnings..."

"What? Oh, I'm sorry Lucy. I don't know. Choose something... anything..."

"Well, it can't be just anything to go to the Prince Regent's ball!" said Lucy distractedly. "What about this pearl grey silk? You've never worn it before. You always said it was too dull, but I think it's very pretty, the way it gleams. And it's very unusual. You'll look like a moonbeam amongst all those sugared almonds!"

"If you say so, Lucy," Nell sighed, and she put up her arms to receive the shimmering slip of fabric, which hung rather loosely on her slim body. "And the pearls?" she suggested, beginning faintly to take an interest in the preparations.

"And the court feathers, Miss Nell!" reminded Lucy. "At Carlton House, court feathers are *de rigueur*!"

"The Countess of Hartismere and Lady Elinor Somersham," proclaimed the scarlet-coated major domo as Nell and her stepmother swept together up the wide steps of Carlton House and towards the colourful group that surrounded the Prince Regent.

The Carlton House ballroom, in spite of its soaring height and vast size, was suffocating. The myriad wax candles in the twenty-foot-deep chandelier that hung from the domed ceiling in a cascade of ice along with the branched candles in their mirrored wall sconces created a heat that struck like a furnace, while the vast sheaves of arum lilies combined with the predominating scent of frangipane and lily of the valley cloyed the senses and made it difficult to breathe. "I shouldn't have come," thought Nell wildly, and, "Surely I'm not going to be so missish as to faint?"

For a moment, the garish Oriental colours with which the Prince Regent's flamboyant taste had clothed the austere classical detail of the room swam before her in the drowning throb of strings playing from the gallery. She shook herself firmly and looked about her. She saw silks and satins, nodding feathers, bare shoulders, a sparkle of diamonds, and bold eyes. She also saw military coats, predominantly scarlet but here and there the forest green of the newly formed rifle regiments and the prestigious yellow and blue Windsor uniform. Though muslins and silks, daintily sprigged in white, ice-blue, and pale yellow, dominated among the younger women—which meant that Nell found herself, in silver grey, in the van of fashion—the older women still favoured stronger colours; crimson and emerald green and even gold velvets and satins were much in evidence. The Prince's known preference for older women (according to unkind gossip, they did not challenge his masculinity) could be seen by the concentration of bright colour around him. So he stood, it seemed, in a bed of tulips.

In the centre of this group, the Prince was striking a heroic pose, his hand holding a pair of white gloves on his hip. He was wearing a bottle-green broadcloth coat cut with such skill as almost to suggest a waist. Sharp collar points framed his pink, smiling, boyish face, and a black stock enclosed (and partly concealed) his spreading dewlap. A cabochon emerald winked from his shirt front.

Nell, who had dreaded and would have avoided this encounter if such a thing had been possible, was at once heartened by the frank and unselfconscious affability with which he looked about him and a little overwhelmed when, on catching sight of her, he came forward to greet her with hands outstretched as she floated up from her formal curtsy.

"Ha! Dammee!" he said. "Lady Elinor Somersham, I declare! Egad! I've been waiting to see you again!" His eye beaming with affectionate malice, he wagged a reproving finger at her.

"Again, Your Highness?" questioned Nell hesitantly.

"Can you have forgotten?" he asked with an explosion of mirth. "Meant so little to you, did it?" And then, catching the attention of the company around him, he cried, "Lor! What would be said of any subject of my father's who, yelling, I declare, like a fiend from hell, rode down the heir to the throne? Eh, what? What would be the judgement? High treason no less! Committed to the Tower, would you not agree?"

Much embarrassed, Nell found his bubbling good humour so infectious that she joined in the general laughter as he gathered the attention of his already intrigued audience and embarked on an explanation.

"Yes indeed! Now—did not some wise fellow once say that Princes learn no art truly but the art of horsemanship?"

"Ben Johnson, sir," an unctuous young courtier dared to supply. "I believe the poet you have in mind is Ben Johnson."

He was skewered by an icy blue eye regarding him through a quizzing glass. The audience gasped at the ill-considered interruption.

"Once again, Mallison, you stun us all into silence with your knowledge..." The Prince sighed and began again. "Horsemanship! An art at which this Prince is, as all allow, an adept." Murmurs of assent encouraged him to continue. "But I met my match one fine morning in September. Out riding in the park, I narrowly escaped being overset by a raging chestnut stallion, loosely in the control of a charming young Amazon—an Amazon breaking all the rules of good conduct and almost breaking her sovereign's neck! You should know that this innocent seeming young lady was within a whisker of becoming a regicide! What do you have to say for yourself, Miss?"

The blue eye now twinkled with good humour, and Nell dared to reply. "I'm sure Ben Johnson—or Mallison," she said with an inclusive nod and a warm smile for the embarrassed young man, "would explain that 'The brave beast is no flatterer. A horse will throw a Prince as soon as his groom.' I assure your Highness that my mount and I were equally ignorant of your identity."

Enjoying the reply, the Prince threw a triumphant glance at his distraught courtier. "Touché, Mallison! Here's a lady whose wit cracks as sharply as her whip, they tell me. But she knows when to keep a discreet silence. Indeed—your ladyship evaded a just reprisal by wisely bolting to Scotland, I understand, to put yourself under your guardian's protection. I have not yet heard your explanation nor yet exacted suitable redress!"

Haltingly, Nell began to give a more level account of their near collision, but he went on teasingly, "It is useless to protest—I will have a penalty! Can't commit subjects of the King without trial these days, but a lesser penalty, dammit, and I'll not take no for an answer—you'll stand up with me for the next quadrille! Eh, what! And we'll cry quits! What do you say?"

Nell bobbed an assenting curtsy, saying as boldly as she dared, "Your wish is my command."

The Prince rolled an ogling eye towards her saying, "Better perhaps if my command were your wish—saucy minx!" And he looked round the company to assess the dutiful laughter in which all but one readily joined. At the back of the group and beyond the circle of light, Nell had been aware of an elegant figure whom the Prince now beckoned forward. "Now, my boy," he said, "I don't need, I believe, to present you to this wild creature, since Kintoul tells me she's your ward. (And a devilish agreeable guardianship I judge!) But let me present," he said, turning away from Nell and addressing his entourage, "Roderick Lindsay of Moidart, whom Arthur sent home to me with the Talavera despatches and not the despatches alone by God! No—with the Eagle of the French Seventy-First Regiment of Foot! Finest thing you ever heard of! Don't believe I could have done better meself! At the head of not more than half a squadron—Lindsay here carried a French battery and routed the relieving column of infantry, taking their Eagle into the bargain!"

"Arthur?" thought Nell for a moment in puzzlement, and then she realised that the prince was referring to Arthur, Lord Wellesley whose triumphant advance into Spain in pursuit of the defeated French had won the admiration of the nation. To be sent home with the despatches after the Battle of Talavera would indeed have been a signal honour and a reward for conspicuous courage. She remembered Moidart's dismissive remarks about the boredom of march and countermarch in the bare hills of Spain and turned astonished eyes on him.

Nell had steeled herself to seeing him again, but in these circumstances, her composure was worn threadbare. She looked away again, avoiding his eye, and listened intently to the Prince's monologue on the bravery in battle of his Scottish troops and of Lindsay in particular, and she flinched as the Prince finished, "...runs in the family, it would appear! And the Froggies must count themselves fortunate that they did not have to face Lady Elinor galloping at them!" Laughing heartily at his own sally, the Prince turned aside and wandered off, his eye caught by another acquaintance.

Good manners demanded that she greet her guardian, though instinct was urging her to hurry away. Nell forced herself to meet his eye at last and found that he was smiling formally at her and appeared to be totally at ease. He was wearing a skilfully tailored black coat, buff breeches, and white shirt, his snowy cravat arranged in a complicated fall and secured with a diamond pin, the very picture of London elegance. She wondered dumbly how she could ever have thought that this man would look out of place anywhere.

He was surrounded, she became aware, by a laughing and intrigued crowd, which included several young and pretty girls who were regarding her with speculation and envy. A girl who was on such terms of teasing affability with the Prince Regent was someone who could command their awed respect and interest, and they stared at her assessingly, trying to reconcile the Prince's story of hoydenish élan with the demure deportment of this slip of a girl before them. An exquisite figure in a wisp of pale grey silk with tiny waist and high girlish bosom, she had lowered her clouded grey eyes shyly on hearing the Prince's story and had seemed to wish him to come to an end of it. Her fair hair shone, and her ivory complexion was as faultless as the pearls around her elegant neck, but there was a sadness and a distance about her that made their friendly overtures die in their throats, and they too fell into embarrassed silence, looking to Lindsay to fill in the awkward gaps with polite formulae.

He took easy charge of the formalities, presenting four or five of the girls and their escorts to her and introducing her as his ward. A chestnut-haired beauty with large brown eyes was showing particular attention to her, and Nell was not surprised to hear the name Amelia Sinclair. She replied to Nell's greeting with a cold elegance and instinctively moved closer to Lindsay, placing her gloved hand on his arm. In spite of the unwanted chill the slight movement brought to her heart, Nell looked back with unforced approval at his choice. Miss Sinclair was undoubtedly a handsome creature, tall, full-bosomed, cream of complexion, aglow with life and self-confidence. The necklace of diamonds and amethysts at her throat told Nell all she needed to know about the girl's fortune, and the decisive cut of her chin and the tilt of her head reassured Nell that this girl might even be a match for her scheming guardian. "Good," she thought. "Here, I think, is one girl over whom he will not ride roughshod! I wish her well of him!"

At that moment the orchestra struck up and the crowd broke into pairs and moved off to the dance floor. Amelia, much to her chagrin, Nell guessed, was claimed by a handsome, red-coated soldier and was towed off to join the dancers with many a reproachful backward glance at Lindsay.

Left alone with her guardian, Nell avoided his eye and could think of nothing at all to say. This was exactly the scene she had most been dreading, and she was finding it difficult even to stay on her feet. He started forward with a soft exclamation and passed an arm around her waist. "Elinor, you are not well, I think. Are you able to stand? Come with me, I will find you a seat. The heat in this room is quite overpowering. I do not wonder that you are swooning."

Still supporting her with his strong arm, he snatched a glass of lemonade from a passing footman and half carried her from the crowded room, away from the noise and the glare, away from the heat, into the cool dimness of the Prince Regent's vast gothic conservatory. Pointed arches opened on secluded alcoves and slender clustered cast-iron columns sailed upwards to burst, at a great height above them, into iron fan vaulting. A thoughtful hand had set windows open and, by the light of the few dim lamps and from the low voices, the subdued laughter, and the delicate rustlings on every side, Nell realised that they were not the only couple seeking seclusion on the small, softly upholstered benches within the artful screening of trailing greenery. She sank down and gratefully sipped the lemonade, regaining some of her poise but still agitated by his close, familiar presence.

"Thank you, Moidart. It is indeed overheated in that room. It is a surprising event, your appearance here, is it not? I had thought you never left Scotland."

He too seemed to be finding an awkwardness in the situation now that they were face to face and alone. "I had not, indeed, thought to give you greeting before I had yet said goodbye, Elinor," he said in a voice like a whip crack.

Her mind flashed back, as so often, to the last time she had spoken to him before her flight and to her deceitful ruse to send him away from her without, as he now pointed out, saying goodbye. There was only the space of a dance in which to talk to him, not time enough for explanations and recriminations. She ignored his jibe and said formally, "I had not thought to see you leave your lands unattended."

"After the harvest, I am not so busy. I have left the estate in Coll's hands until the spring when I shall return."

"I see. And you are, I understand—if the gossips who claim to know your intentions have it right—preparing for a harvest of a different kind? You are spending the rest of the season seeking to secure your future?"

"Yes, you understand correctly. That is exactly what I have in mind. I have passed several candidates in review and have made my choice. I am putting wheels in motion."

His brief, unadorned, barefaced admission roused her flagging spirit, and she looked at him with scorn. "What then? It is true that proud Moidart trades his title for money? And what of your boast that you would never marry for convenience? Did you not say that would *not be your way of it*?" She taunted him with his own words.

"Marry? If it comes to marriage, let us say I have learned a lesson from you, Elinor," he said fiercely, "a lesson in the heartless pursuit of a selfish goal. I have learned from you how to play with affections, to torment and tease and throw away your toy when you have had enough! Though, to be fair to you, you did tell me with touching openness that Lady Elinor always got what she wanted; still, you failed to warn me that she could be just as ruthless and single-minded when it came to disposing of outworn playthings!" His voice was chilling her to the bone, and she shrank, wide-eyed, away from him, unable to believe what she was hearing.

Remorselessly he pressed on, his dark eyes scorching her with his intensity. "Have you ever considered what I felt when I returned from Glasgow with the license for our wedding in my hand? The love you said you had for me—for what did it count? And the child—my child—you led me to believe you were carrying was gone—was never there! A phantom, a cruel trick! That, above all, was abominable!"

Nell turned even paler and put her hands over her ears in her distress. He leaned over and pulled her hands away, retaining them in his grasp. "No, madam! You will hear me! I have not finished, for I have also to thank you," he went on with not the slightest trace of gratitude in his cold voice, "for the so-generous gift of the Lindsay estates that I found waiting for me on my return. Over generous, I would have thought, as payment to your steward for services received but no longer required? I prefer to think that, at the last, it was a sense of justice that swayed you in your decision. But, madam, a bargain is a bargain and I should like you to enjoy your half of it."

He took an envelope from his pocket and put it in her hand. "I did not want to entrust such a document to the mail," he said, "fearing that your stepmother might chance on it and secrete it."

She looked at him wonderingly.

"I had my lawyer draw it up. It is my written consent to your marriage with Henry Collingwood," he explained, "in return for my lands. I understand that his regiment has felt able to forego his services for a few more weeks and that the man is still in London and eagerly awaiting my blessing on his union with you. Poor fool!"

At that moment, the dance music in the ballroom flourished to a close and the dancers surged off the floor. Nell's stunned silence was interrupted by the appearance beside them of a man in Windsor Uniform. He was in the last stages of petrified agitation.

"Good God!" he began without preamble. "Good God, Lady Elinor! What can you be about? You are to stand up in the quadrille with His Highness, and already the musicians are tuning. Make haste and follow me, I beg! I don't know when I was more shocked! Dallying here! In the face of a command! His Highness is never—never—kept waiting. Such behaviour!"

Lindsay rose slowly to his feet and extended his arm to Nell. "That'll do, Rossiter!" he said coldly. "You have delivered your message; you do not need to embroider. I will escort Lady Elinor to her tryst with—er—shall I say?—the First Gentleman of Europe."

Her ears drumming with his cynical words, Nell rose unsteadily, took his proffered arm, and allowed herself to be supported back into the ballroom and across the room while the dancers divided to make way. All, that is, save Amelia Sinclair, who stepped forward eagerly to greet Lindsay and remind him that the next dance on her card was his. She looked in suspicion from one to the other, aware of the highly charged atmosphere between them. Lindsay gave her an ironic smile and said for all to hear, "My ward has just achieved a long-held ambition! She has finally persuaded me to grant my consent to her marriage. My dear, I hope you will find the married state all that you hope it will be and that your husband will prove to be loving, amenable, and above all—absent. Your servant, Lady Elinor."

He bowed and, taking Amelia's hand, led her onto the floor.

Nell remembered the envelope in her hand. Hastily tucking it into the side pocket of her dress, she was able to curtsy before the Prince and, with breaking heart and eyes gleaming with unshed tears, proceeded to dance with every appearance of graceful enthusiasm and chatter with gaiety and wit. She flirted and laughed and charmed, finding in her partner a very willing if ignorant accomplice.

"'Pon my soul, Lady Elinor," he said, his eye moist and his face glowing with exertion, "we make a fine pair! Do you not see? All look on us with admiration! Would that we could dance on together..."

The visiting figure of the quadrille parted them for a moment, but he resumed, "Egad! People envy Princes, and, yes," he waved his hand about the room, "there is much to envy, but the simple delights of other men are not for me." His moist hand tightened on Nell's waist. "I know—dammee—your kind heart would pity if ye knew how devilish lonely it can be amongst all this glitter. But I haven't been lonely these few precious last minutes..." His large, China blue eyes favoured her with a speaking glance.

The speech had been pat; the glance well rehearsed; it came to Nell that it had been delivered many times before, and with this realisation came to Nell a temptation—and an irresistible temptation in spite of the stress of the evening—to laugh. The Prince stopped dead and so suddenly that another couple, crimson with embarrassment, cannoned into them. Pop-eyed with indignation, he looked at her laughing face and understood. As he looked, his shoulders began to shake, a broad grin spread across his face and he burst into a bellow of laughter. "God, Nell!" he said, mopping his face with a silk handkerchief. "Sly Puss! You'd say that little face was scarce out of the schoolroom, but—God dammee—I'd swear you could outwit, outride, and outface me at every turn!" He laughed again, while the room stared in discomfort and puzzlement. "Why! We treat like old friends already, after five minutes. A little time—but a little time more—and who knows what we might not achieve!" and they rejoined the quadrille.

As she turned and spun, she continually caught the dark gaze of Lindsay upon her, but each time she glanced away.

At the end of the dance, she curtsied thankfully and withdrew, working her way through the press of dancers until she reached the door. As she was on the point of escaping over the threshold, a swaggering figure in Hussar uniform entered. Henry Collingwood stood still in surprise and then smiled and spoke eagerly to Nell. To his evident amazement, she gave a small cry of frustration, stamped her foot, burst into tears, and pushed past him to flee from the room.

As she did so, she was aware to her mortification that Lindsay had witnessed this encounter, and her last impression of that strange evening was of him standing transfixed by what he had seen. The bold dark face was at a loss—a mask of astonishment.

It was a vision of him that was to remain with her.

16

Moidart rode purposefully across the bridge and, hitching his horse, banged with his riding crop on the heavy front door of Somersham Hall. He stood back a pace and contemplated the house of which he had heard so much loving detail from Elinor. She had not exaggerated its beauty, he thought. The milky sunshine of late autumn illuminated the elegant line of pedimented palladian sash windows and reflected in the still waters of the moat. The central doorway was surmounted by a towering classical pediment with its crowded statuary; terminal pavilions—each with a delicate carved floral wreath—were embellished with classical urns; while on every side, lawns—smooth even in November—stretched away to be lost amongst the massive, encircling trees.

In the distance, a domed pavilion topped a neat, artificial mound. Comfortable sheep grazed the distance, and from somewhere unseen but near at hand came the tinkle of a fountain. The air was of peace, tranquillity, and centuries of ordered prosperity. Unbidden, there came to his mind a vision of Moidart Castle, stark and severe, defensive on its rocky island, and surrounded by its purple hills with its courtyard gardens within battlemented walls and with siege and foray within living memory.

He thought too of the trim villages through which he had passed, the timber-framed solidity and rustic luxury of the Somersham Arms, where he had paused to ask for directions, and the well-mannered, well-fed country people who had greeted him as he rode.

Angrily, he compared the scene before him with Moidart, its poverty and its perils—compared the blackcock and the curlew with the peacocks and the fat doves. As if to underline his thought, a tumbling cloud of fantail pigeons wheeled through the sky and settled on the parapet of the bridge, cooing incuriously to see the stranger.

The door swung open and he was faced by the bland, expressionless face of the butler. He strode into the hall and announced, "Mr. Roderick Lindsay to see Lady Elinor Somersham."

"I am sorry, sir, but Lady Elinor is not at home." Poulson blocked Lindsay's advance politely but firmly.

Glowering, Lindsay took off his mud-splashed cloak and handed it to him, saying impatiently, "Get someone to see to my horse. Lady Elinor *is* at home. I am informed by her stepmother that she left London a week ago and intends to spend the rest of the season here. I am her guardian, and I insist on seeing her! Where is she, man?"

Poulson was not impressed or intimidated and merely replied calmly, "I repeat, sir, that Lady Elinor is not at home to anybody."

A figure moved on the landing above, and a face peered over to investigate the disturbance. Lindsay looked up and shouted, "Lucy! Lucy, tell your mistress I must see her!" But Lucy turned on her heel, aghast, and hurried off down the corridor.

In a few strides, he evaded the spluttering butler and took the stairs three at a time. He found himself in a wide gallery, the fading light from its line of sash windows illuminating a line of portraits. Here he paused, uncertain of his direction, but a whisk of white cap ribbons revealed the hurrying figure of Lucy as she slipped through a distant door. In seconds, he had overtaken her. She rounded on him with outstretched arms, barring his way, alarmed but determined.

"No, Mr. Moidart, sir! You may not see Miss Nell!" she stammered. "She is engaged with...she is busy...Oh, sir, will you not leave at once? She will not see you!"

He growled at her, "Lucy, out of my way! I will see my baggage of a ward, whoever she is with! Is it her steward she is dallying with? Or a footman? Or the Prince Regent himself? Nothing would surprise me! Get out of my way, girl!" He lifted her up like a marionette and put her down firmly on one side, looking about him.

There were just two doors remaining, and he opened the first one to reveal a bedchamber. From the pretty, colourful appointments, the shining furniture, the bed covered with a gaily patterned country quilt, and the faintest trace of familiar perfume in the air, he guessed that this was Nell's room. It was unoccupied. Half in relief and half in disappointment, he went back into the corridor and paused by the second door. Hearing a murmur of voices and laughter within, he paused for a moment and then gently pushed the door open. He stood in the doorway taking in the small, bright room with surprise.

A fire crackled in the grate and pale afternoon sunshine flooded the room. It was sparsely furnished with a low table along one wall and a small pine bed along the other. The walls were decorated with pictures of animals, mainly horses, and an alphabet he remembered from his own childhood—'A is an Archer that shot at a frog, B is a Bullfrog that sat on a log...' A row of dolls sitting along a shelf watched him with beady eyes. In a corner of the room, two armies of toy soldiers faced each other across a battlefield roughly painted by the hand of a child. The elaborate cradle bearing the Hartismere crest, in pride of place in the centre of the room, marked it out as the old nursery.

His first confused impression was that the small room seemed to be full of women. Directly opposite him and teetering on the top of a set of library steps was a stout, middle-aged lady dressed in black bombazine. Scissors and a pair of spectacles dangled on her vast bosom and she was offering up to the window a length of gaily patterned fabric. Directing operations from below was another lady in black, slim with iron grey hair and, he noted as she swung round to stare at him with peremptory and handsome black eyes, undoubtedly foreign. The third was, at first glance, a maidservant, sitting on the floor in front of the fire with her back to him. She had kicked off her slippers and with her stockinged feet stretched out in front of her, toes in the air, was busy with her task of plaiting up the tail of a rocking horse with a red ribbon. She was wearing a simple loose yellow house dress, and her cloud of corn-coloured hair hung untidily about her shoulders. Sensing the tension of the other two ladies, she stopped what she was doing and looked over her shoulder.

His voice was a harsh exclamation. "Elinor!" For a moment, his heart went out to her, seeing her so absorbed and unprepared and childlike in her simple occupation. The elegant, fey figure in grey silk, flirting with consummate ease with the Prince Regent—where was she? Could this girl playing with her rocking horse possibly be the person who had raised so many eyebrows and turned so many heads the other evening?

Nell rose to her feet, hiding her confusion and saying breathlessly, with a poor show of composure, "Cousin Roderick! How very unexpected! I do not believe we heard you announced...Thérèse, Mrs. Dalrymple, I fear our work is interrupted. My guardian, Mr. Lindsay, I take it, has urgent and unforeseen family matters to discuss with me. Would you please leave us now? We will continue tomorrow."

Thérèse de Bercy, on hearing his name, stepped forward at once with a sharp exclamation, putting the full force of her dark and scornful regard between him and Nell. She seemed about to speak, but Nell took her hand and, exchanging an intense look with her companion, gave her reassurance enough to leave the room, though not without a final and warning backward glance at the unwanted visitor. The seamstress viewing the scene in astonishment from her precarious perch took Lindsay's proffered hand and gingerly dismounted. She gathered up her equipment, folded her fabrics, bobbed an agitated curtsy, and left the room.

Lindsay seemed taken aback by the comfortable domestic scene he had disturbed; he remained standing, silent and awkward, with his back to the fire, staring at Nell. She swept him with frosty eyes and said, "I have no idea why you should choose to intrude on my privacy here, Lindsay. Your presence is most unwelcome, and I wish that you would leave."

As he neither spoke nor moved but simply continued to glower at her, she went on angrily, her curiosity getting the better of her, "Why are you here? At least you can tell me that before you go."

"I called on you in London and Lady Hartismere told me you had left with your companion for the country and were not intending to return this season."

"That is so. But what was your motive in calling on me? You had been in London for six weeks and had not thought it necessary to call on me..." She turned away from him to hide the sting of hurt in her eyes, wishing she had not so betrayed her feelings, praying for the strength to stay calm and unconcerned.

"I am your guardian after all, Elinor. Not a very effective or concerned guardian, perhaps, but I thought it my duty to hear from my ward herself why she had disdained my written permission to marry Henry Collingwood. After delivering it to you at Carlton House, I waited for a week, but no banns had been called, no special license applied for. And the lucky groom returns to Spain next week...Why, I even accosted Collingwood myself and affected to congratulate him on his forthcoming marriage! He told me, Elinor, in some surprise, that his plans in that direction had come to nought. Indeed, he was very inclined to lay the blame at my door. A very awkward exchange ensued, I can tell you! Am I to understand that you have rejected my offer, madam? That you no longer are seeking your freedom?"

Nell coloured and looked at her feet. He went on in a more kindly tone, "Is there perhaps someone else you would wish me to approve of? Some other union to which I may give my blessing? You may speak out, for I am conscious that I owe you much and would like, in spite of all, to see you happily settled...or at least, settled in a way of your choosing."

Nell sighed and replied with obvious difficulty, "Cousin, I thank you for your consideration and for your belated remembrance of your duty, but no—there is no action I wish you to take on my behalf. I have no schemes to marry. Indeed, marriage, for me, will always now be out of the question." Her voice trailed away, and she hurriedly turned her back on him again. Would the man never leave? Surely he would have the decency to go before she was overwhelmed by her emotions and burst into tears?

At the ball a week ago, she had been painfully aware, through his scorching accusations, that she was still in love with him. The calm and resignation she had worked for weeks to acquire since her departure from Scotland had been shot to pieces in minutes by his appearance at the dance. The last thing she had been prepared for had been to see him the elegant man about London, soigné, handsome, even fêted for his bravery by the Prince and the target of much female admiration and, though quite a different figure from the rough poacher she had fallen in love with, she had had to admit that the Roderick Lindsay she had met that night would have turned her head had she been seeing him for the first time. What a cruel irony that here was the man she had unconsciously been seeking through all those tedious balls and soirées and had in the end lost hope of ever finding. Doubly cruel that she should have fallen in love twice, and each time her choice the same impossible one. His angry words to her at Carlton House had been bitter and accusing, and she wondered at the effrontery that enabled him to attack her—and she still suffering from the effects of his heartless scheming.

Every glance had been a dagger in her heart, and it had been more than she could bear to see him in the proprietorial arms of Amelia Sinclair. So why was he now come here into her private place, to disturb her calm retreat from the world? Could this sudden concern for her welfare be genuine? He was talking in the annoyingly sententious tones of a guardian, but it seemed to her that his eyes were giving her quite a different message. This was too much! He had hurt her beyond reason, more than he could possibly know, and now it seemed she must defend herself from a further onslaught on her emotions.

He moved over to her and put his hands on her shaking shoulders, gently turning her towards him. No! This was unfair! Bad temper and accusations she could withstand, but tenderness would melt her resolve at once.

"Come, Elinor, surely there is some direction in which happiness lies? You have given me mine with the utmost generosity, and I would see you happy. I have a guardian's power, with no more effort than to sign my name to any document you choose, to set you free to find your happiness. If you will only tell me how."

She remained silent and rigid, fighting down tears.

He shrugged, unable to penetrate her silence.

"The world seems peopled with men you have refused to take as husband—Fanshawe and a hundred others, Collingwood and myself—all rejected. Tell me, Elinor, why did you not accept Collingwood when you could have had him?"

Wearily, she replied, "Because I did not love him, and, poor, obliging fool that he is, I found I could not deceive him."

"This is not the sprightly, scheming Elinor Somersham I pulled out of the mud ten weeks ago!"

"You are right. I am greatly changed. You do not know how changed."

"And why did you not accept *me* when you could have had me?" The question was asked with such intensity that she knew she would have to reply, though she dreaded being shaken out of the security of her monosyllabic answers.

"I thought you had formed your own theories as to that, sir. At the ball you set them out very clearly for me..."

"At the ball I was angry still at your treatment of me and eager to punish you for running away, for refusing to commit yourself to me and mine. I blamed you for indulging wantonly in a piece of romantic dalliance that satisfied a passing whim. My opinion of a woman who could behave with all the convincing appearance of a passionate attachment to a man, only to run away from him when he offered her his hand is low indeed. I despised you for tricking me and going back to your glittering empty life in London, for saying you loved me when you were simply playing with me. But when I saw you dash away from poor Collingwood in tears, I...I began to wonder whether I had reasoned aright."

"So you came all the way up here to Suffolk to find out? This is very meticulous of you, cousin! Your effort deserves a reward, and I shall tell you the plain truth," said Nell with a flash of scorn. Anger at the injustice of his accusations pushed her at last to drop her protective silence and offer some explanation of her thoughts and actions. Confronted with this demanding man, she could no longer keep a cover on her bubbling sense of outrage. "I left you because I would not be entrapped into marriage with a man who did not love me. It was clear to me that from the moment you knew who I was you were determined to lay siege to me with the object of appropriating my fortune for your own purposes, and you began the moment you hauled me onto your horse. You encouraged me fall in love with you by pretending to be other than you were, and then you set about destroying my reputation and...and attempting callously and knowingly, I do believe, to get me with child in order to—how did McPherson express it? 'To make sure of the girl, the dog!'"

"McPherson?" he asked in amazement.

"Yes, your neighbour McPherson. I overheard him in the courtyard conversing man to man with Kintoul. They were very admiring of the way in which you had single-mindedly set about gaining control of your estates, if not by law than by other devious means, and," her voice choked on the words, "the money to sustain them by seducing me into marriage."

Into his stunned silence, she rushed on. "Such was McPherson's faith in your scheming and so notable your prowess in dalliance that he had a full year before wagered five pounds on a favourable outcome for you! Five English pounds," she added uselessly. "A year ago you knew nothing of me except that I had what you so dearly wanted. You determined to get it from me one way or another, and if the legal path proved impossible, then you would get it by marrying me. I could have been ugly, unalluring, and disagreeable like Laetitia Kintoul, and it would have made no difference to your schemes! But you were lucky, Moidart, were you not? It must have been so easy for you! Your prey was impressionable enough to be swept off her feet by a handsome Scottish rogue! Your prey sprang willingly into your trap and did not even recognise it for the trap it was! How pleased with your schemes you were, Moidart! You must have thought you had captured the Corn Maiden herself—she who would ensure bounty and increase for your clan and a full cradle in your own house before the next harvest! I even conjured her up myself!

How you must have laughed to see me plaiting up with my own fingers the symbolic sacrifice..." She broke off with a sob.

His grasp on her shoulders had tightened, and the pressure of his fingers was hurting. "Elinor! Is this true? Oh, look at me, girl!" She knew that he was, with difficulty, restraining himself from shaking her. "Are you saying that you loved me when you ran away? That perhaps you still do?"

She raised a tear-stained face, looked searchingly into his eyes, and could tell him nothing less than the truth. "Yes, I did love you, and I begin to acknowledge that perhaps I always shall, but I despise you and fear you for so tricking me and attempting to ensnare me. For it is true that you did so, is it not? McPherson was not mistaken, was he? Was he?" Her wide grey eyes, awash with unshed tears, were searching his face, drawing the truth out of him, hoping that, at the last, he would deny her accusation, sweep her into his arms, and kiss her into insensibility.

Looking steadily back at her he said quietly, "Yes, it is true, Elinor. Your suspicions were well founded. I have deceived you enough. I will not make myself more loathsome in your eyes by continuing to deny it."

He sighed and dropped his hands from her shoulders before continuing in a dull tone, "It was the letter you wrote to me asking my permission to marry Collingwood that put the scheme into my head. I had met the fellow in the Peninsula, thought badly of him, and was incensed by the idea that a chit of a girl could so carelessly attempt to pass my birthright and the lives of my clan on by marriage to such an oaf...That Moidart of Moidart should count his new English lord's sheep, sow his corn, mend his roofs, polish the boots of the incompetent jackanapes was unthinkable. I wrote back to you proposing a marriage of convenience, being quite certain that one liaison would be as good as another to such a heartless schemer as yourself. I hated the whole idea of Lady Elinor Somersham and would not have hesitated to do her down. I had not expected that you would take my proposal seriously and was quite astonished to find that you had delivered yourself into my grasp. I would have married you for certain, yes, and if you had been unattractive I would not have cared, indeed it would have made it easier for me to have sent you off back to England with my name in exchange for my lands."

Although she had known this to be true, it was still a shocking thing for Nell to hear it from his lips. She turned pale but listened intently as he went on in the same measured tone, "I set out to entrap you. I confess it. But Elinor, it was not long before I realised that I was, myself, ensnared. I was not lying to you when I told you why I let you go on thinking of me as Moidart. By the time I pulled you off the road and onto my horse, I knew there was a strange feeling linking us, a feeling I wanted to explore and encourage to grow, and I was determined that you should know me without the barrier of guardianship between us. I deceived you, yes—because I was head over ears in love with you from that first evening, and I was sure that if you knew me as Lindsay you would rightly regard me as your enemy and would be off back to London in a trice. My deceit was to keep you close to me until you had learned to love me." He paused for a moment. "I struggled hard not to force you, Elinor...I had thought that you came to me willingly."

"I did," she whispered. "No, we were equals in loving, Moidart."

They were silent for a moment, the thoughts of both flying back unbidden to the days and nights they had spent together in companionship and love.

"I did not set out deliberately to get you with child, Elinor," he said slowly. "It would be unjust to ascribe such a depth of cunning to me. I loved you, I wanted you, I was sure you wanted me, and I thought no further than that. But in this, too, I was guilty of deceiving you—I knew that all would be well with us, that our loving each other was innocent, was good, and would lead to the security of a legal tie, but you, Elinor, I left you without the comfort of that knowledge, and for that carelessness I cannot forgive myself!" He looked away, unable to meet her eye. "I was selfishly enjoying the sensation of knowing that you loved me, had given yourself to me without consideration of rank and fortune. I was secure in the knowledge that you had given me all because you loved me and for no other reason."

Nell guiltily censored the thought that this had been her motive too—to be loved for herself—but she remained hurt, agitated, and unconvinced.

He went on, slowly. "And over the days, the physical attraction I felt for you was swelled by a deep admiration for your other qualities—I thought you were a fitting wife for Moidart, Nell Somersham! It did not take me long to see that there was a fine woman under the layer of spoilt sophistication. The girl I watched gleefully cracking the head of a McGregor at Achill, the girl who could argue about the price of wool and plait up a corn dolly..." his voice sank to a low intensity, "the girl who welcomed me with passionate directness on the hill was surely a Lindsay. I had thought that you had understood this, had seen the life I could offer you and were ready to embrace it as you embraced me. It was unimaginable to me that you could not prefer it to a life of shallow, meaningless amusement in London." He sighed and gave her a bitter look. "Unimaginable until I watched you at the Prince's Ball dancing like a moth in the moonlight, as lovely and as ephemeral. But Elinor, I asked you if you loved me and if you loved the House of Lindsay. Surely you remember what you replied?"

"I remember it well, but my reply was given to Moidart, whom I loved and would have spent the rest of my days with at whatever cost—not to sleek, complicated, scheming Lindsay, who had not the courage even to ask for my hand, lest I should refuse it!"

He flinched and hung his head. "I am ashamed so to have pushed you along, but I feared you would prance skittishly away at the last moment and, for the first time in my life, I took the coward's way and avoided the risk of your refusal." He smiled and shook his head. "The hero of Talavera, Elinor! You see to what you can reduce him! I could more easily have faced the blast of the French cannon than listened to your denying me. But, that last night we were together..." Nell quivered at the memory, but he went on, "You said you wanted to spend every day of the rest of your life with Moidart. I took that as your acceptance. I am still Moidart...I always was. I am still the man who met you on the road and who knew that he loved you before he set you down from his horse." He looked down at her with the compelling dark gaze she had seen in imagination every hour since she had left him and gently brushed a tear from her cheek with his thumb.

He took a deep breath and said softly, "Elinor Somersham, Roderick Lindsay, Laird of Moidart, is asking you if you will marry him because he believes you love him and he knows he loves you and cannot live his life without you. If there are impediments to the match—as, for example, your ridiculously large fortune—he recommends that you make it over to your stepmother or Henry Collingwood or your butler or any other deserving party..."

"But Lindsay needs a fortune..." she began.

"And Lindsay could have had any of three fortunes the equal and better of yours had that been of importance to him," he reminded her gently. He slipped an arm around her shoulders, unwilling to kiss her, for both knew they would be lost to reason if he did.

Nell's eyes, which had been lifeless and unfocussed with grief and staring abstractedly into an uncertain future, had begun to brighten and fasten on his with awakening hope. She looked up at him searchingly. Could it be that her judgement had been so at fault? Her wretched fortune, the subtleties of her father's will had conspired to make her suspicious and mistrustful, and she had ignored the evidence of her own heart. She studied his face intently, reading there nothing but love and concern. She could scarcely believe that her situation, which had only minutes ago seemed without remedy, was so transformed. The hopes she had stifled for the past weeks were suddenly blossoming all about her, the yearnings she had fought down were springing up as strong as ever. He was here with her now, was he not? He was saying that he loved her, and his eyes were clear and direct and, at last, telling her no lie.

Suddenly, the effort of keeping up her pretence before the world—her barriers, her fragile concealment—was too much, and her forces crumbled. Her knees gave way, her head drooped, and she fell in a swoon against his chest.

In alarm and murmuring her name, he gathered her up and carried her to the little bed, sinking down and holding her close on his knee, cradling her face in one large hand, uncertain what to do. When she opened her eyes and smiled at him, he said, "You are not well, Elinor. I thought you greatly changed when I saw you at the ball. Is it...can it be unhappiness that has so affected you? Have you been missing me? I dare to ask this because—God knows—I have missed you! I must admit that was the first thought that gave me hope that perhaps you were not so indifferent to me. Shall I summon your maid? Shall I fetch Lucy?"

She shook her head and, sighing, snuggled her head against his chest. "No, Moidart. I am not ill. I have been so fatigued with cares, but the cure is here in your strong arms...and in the course of time..." She fell silent, unsure how to go on.

He was abruptly struck by a thought, which appeared to paralyse him. He looked around the small, bright room, at the rocking horse, the cradle, the fresh paint, and the general air of refurbishment. Tilting her face gently towards him and looking into the clear depths of her eyes, he asked, "You were not deceiving me when you? My darling girl! Do you now say that you are indeed carrying our child?" He searched her face with the anxious hope of one who had been cruelly disappointed and was determined not to be deceived again.

She returned his gaze with such glowing reassurance that he could no longer be in doubt. "Then it is true! But...but how can this be? You are grown so thin..." His gentle hand caressed her shoulders wonderingly.

"It is but two months," she whispered. "My condition will not be evident for some weeks yet. And it is as you suspect—I have been heartsick and eating nothing unless urged. Thérèse knows, Lucy knows, but no one else."

"Lucy! I do not wonder that she greeted me as though I were the Devil himself! But, my darling, you would have said nothing of this to me? How would you have managed your life? It does not bear thinking of!" He strained her to him in his distress. "How could you consider for a moment such a painful concealment? And suppose I had married Miss Sinclair only to find that you had borne our child!" A shudder racked his body, and his voice was thick with emotion. "I cannot bear to contemplate this! Oh, Elinor! Thank God I came in time! We will be married this day! I still have the license I acquired in Glasgow." He searched in his pocket and produced a crumpled paper. "We can ask Poulson or your companion to sign it in witness."

"Oh, Poulson!" exclaimed Nell, looking up distractedly, "Thérèse and Lucy! They must be anxious!" And with something of her old zest, she jumped to her feet and went to the door. "Lucy!" she called to the girl who was hovering within reach. "All is well! Do not be concerned. You may go downstairs. Please tell Poulson and Thérèse that my guardian and I have urgent business to discuss and we wish to be undisturbed. Mr. Lindsay will be dining, and a room is to be prepared for him."

She closed the door and, in the same decisive mood, turned to him again, holding out her hands. "Come with me, Moidart!" and she opened the door to her own bedroom and led him through.

"Nell, what are you doing?" he asked hesitantly. He glanced around the simple room and then back at her laughing face. For a moment, she luxuriated in a long, caressing look at the elegant dark man, a stranger and yet not strange, whom she was holding by the hand, daring now to meet his eyes and linger on his mouth, which was smiling a question.

Her eyes sparkled with mischievous invitation as she put her arms around his neck and announced with mock solemnity, "Welcome to *my* bothy! The accommodation is not so romantic for the Laird of Moidart, perhaps, but the welcome is no less warm for that! I have given all possible proof of my love to Moidart, but I have never made love to Lindsay. If I am determined to secure the hero of Talavera, perhaps I should make sure of the man! Four hours I understand is what it takes, if McPherson's shepherd is to be believed!"

Joy flooded his features and he held her close, rubbing his cheek on her hair, stroking her back gently, and whispering, "Elinor, four lifetimes would be too short! You guess rightly that I am quite desperate to hold you in my arms and love you again, but...but, you are not well...you should not..."

"Can you not understand? I am unwell from lack of you. Please do not draw away from me now, or I shall surely fade away!"

He smiled down at her with loving indulgence and murmured, "Lady Elinor always gets her own way, I believe, but if all her demands are as delightful as this, I shall be a shockingly compliant husband!"

She opened her eyes later that afternoon to find that the room was in darkness but for the glow of embers in the fireplace, and her mind flew back to a similar but wilder scene in a remote Scottish croft. She smiled again with satisfaction to see his clothes interlaced with hers in a hasty pile by her bed and stirred sleepily in his arms. Warm lips dropped a kiss on her shoulder and gentle hands tucked the quilt more securely around her. She turned to him with a contented sigh and snuggled under his arm. "Moidart?"

"My love?"

"Now that you have acquired your rich wife, there is nothing further to detain you in London, I take it?"

He playfully bit her shoulder and growled, "Silly girl! It was not for a wife I came to London! I came to find a man—a very particular man, an architect and engineer, the very best designer of mills in the country, I hear, and to conclude with him my business regarding the opening of the Lindsay Tweed Mill!" He laughed to hear her gasp of astonishment and went on, "I found I could not ignore your advice, Nell. It seemed as though it were a trust you had left for me to honour for the sake of our people—the people you had made your own. And as soon as you gave me back my land, I was inspired to move in the matter at once. I sold my mother's necklace and raised enough money to pay for the first stages at least. The plans are almost drawn up, and the work will start in the spring."

"So those are the wheels you will—literally—be putting in motion!" With delight, she stroked his firm chin and traced his eyebrow with her finger. How she had misjudged him! This was not a man to dangle himself before rich women, and yet..."But why did you attend so many receptions in London? You say you were not seeking attention from the likes of Amelia Sinclair, but I can tell you, Moidart, that you were receiving a good deal of attention and surrounded by interested, eager faces..."

"There was only one face I wanted to see, and she would not come. Evening after evening, Nell, I suffered the exquisite boredom of the London social round, expecting to hear you announced, but you did not appear."

"Why did you not call on me in Park Lane?"

"Would you have been at home to Roderick Lindsay?" he asked simply.

"No," she said and smiled, "No, it took a Royal Command from the Prince Regent to force me out of my self-imposed seclusion!"

They laughed together at the memory of the Prince's unwitting role in their reunion. "Poor Prinny, what would he say if he realised he had been playing Cupid? He certainly has the figure for the role," snorted Lindsay disrespectfully. He was silent for a moment and then continued, "Unlike our other unlikely benevolent deity!"

"Who can you mean?" asked Nell in puzzlement.

"You have never guessed the identity of our guardian angel?" he asked. "Why, none less than the Earl of Hartismere, your father."

He chuckled at her expression of blank astonishment. "You were unaware that, six months before his death, he travelled to Moidart? He came for the first time and the last to inspect his Scottish properties. I liked the man and had thought he liked me—we shot many a grouse together and drank many a dram. We met warily, as enemies, but we parted good friends—or so I thought. I had high hopes—no, I was certain—that he intended to right a wrong and return my lands to me in his will. He knew he had little time to live. But it was not to be. What he *did* leave me was the irksome guardianship of his wretched, spoilt little daughter!"

Through her amazement, Nell was beginning to laugh and to cry. For the last time, and with complete understanding, she whispered, "Oh, Papa! What on earth were you about?"

Moidart held her close, whispering gently, until her sniffing and gulping stopped. "Dearest, your father—are you thinking? I have wondered..."

"I am certain! My father was a hard-headed man when it came to business and soft-hearted when he dealt with me—indeed, he was much criticised for spoiling me and letting me have my own way in everything. I think his gesture in making you my guardian, Moidart, was his last piece of spoiling. He knew I was too contrary ever to accept as a husband anyone put before me as that, even by himself. He knew me well! It's my belief that he calculated that in order to circumvent the conditions of his will, I would be driven to meet my guardian, to have dealings—even negotiations—with him, and in the course of this, fall in love with him! He must have liked you very much, Moidart."

"Thereby satisfying his conscience on the fate of the Scottish estates but, above all, caring and planning for his daughter. I think you are right. Hmm...Elinor..." he said with a radiant smile of dawning comprehension, "do you realise what this means? No? I fear it is *I* who have been manoeuvred and entrapped into marriage by a scheming Englishman and his seductive daughter! Do you think I should bolt at once?"

She laughed up at him through a dazzle of tears and damp lashes. "Well, if you do decide on bolting, you are holding an expert in your arms, and I will advise you on how it is done on condition that I may bolt with you. Moidart, if you have finished your business here in England— the weather is fair and the roads are open—I wonder if you would take me back to Scotland? To our home?"

"Will you be strong enough to undertake the journey, Nell?" he asked in surprise but with an eagerness she could not mistake.

"Will *you* be strong enough, rather, Moidart, for I intend to spend the journey lolling in your arms! You had spoken to me—do you remember?—of a Christmas wedding at the castle. I shall be happy indeed to sign our special license this evening, but I shall be happier yet to celebrate our marriage at home with our own people."

"Our own people," she said again, savouring the phrase, liking its sound. "When I was exiled in London, I thought all the time of Somersham. I thought of the people, the animals, and this little room, and I longed to be here."

"It's your place, Elinor," he said gently.

"But when I came back here a week ago, I saw only one thing—the House of Lindsay—Lindsay of the Loch and the Hills and the running water. The thought that I would never return was anguish to me. And if I closed my eyes, I saw only you."

"But this is your place," he said again.

"Lady Elinor Somersham I was born, but Elinor Lindsay I shall be. Of course Somersham will never go away, and of course I shall keep faith with the people here. But..." she hesitated and, taking his face in her hands, said seriously, "more than anything I've ever wanted, I want our child to be born in the House of Lindsay. Besides," she added, "there are others to think of..."

"Others?"

"Yes. I wouldn't want Lucy to peak and pine and fade away."

"Lucy?"

"Oh, Moidart! Have you no eyes or ears? What about Coll? It is hard to picture that rough Highlander fading into a decline, but is he perhaps of the kind to die of a broken heart?"

"Well, upon my soul!" said Moidart, gathering her to him with a shout of laughter, "I am glad I gave instructions for your Corn Maiden to remain in place over the hearth! One day you must tell me exactly what spells you wove into it! And Nell—make certain your nimble fingers do not lose the art! I have a feeling we shall be needing a fresh one each year for many a year!"

End

Made in the USA
Middletown, DE
06 August 2017